Separation Games

The Games Duet
Book Two

Praise for Marriage Games

"Marriage Games is one of the most powerful novels I have ever read. CD Reiss gets into the soul of her hero and heroine and never lets go. A strong, clear picture of the psychological and emotional challenges of a D/s relationship, especially in a marriage. Why it works and why it might not. Can't wait for the next one." *Desiree Holt, USA Today bestselling author*

"Commanding and complex, Adam Steinbeck is the Dom of my dreams. CD Reiss delivers the most compelling kink." *Skye Warren ~ NY Times bestselling author of The Pawn*

"Through glimpses of past and present, the world of Adam Steinbeck and Diana McNeill-Barnes are revealed in such clarity that readers can't help but visualize the whole picture painted by CD Reiss' pen. Fans of the author will definitely fall in love with this new twist on this Dominant/submissive relationship between Adam and Diana." *~ RT Book Reviews*

"I devoured this book; and it devoured me! Spellbinding, swoony, emotional, and mind-blowingly addictive." *Katy Evans ~ NY Times bestselling author of Real*

"Marriage Games by CD Reiss absolutely blew me away. The characters intrigued me, the story grabbed me, the sizzle thrilled me, and the writing style enticed me. Trust me, this is one book you don't want to miss!" *J Kenner ~ NY Times bestselling author of The Stark Trilogy*

"Marriage Games was enthralling! Seriously a fascinating game of cat and mouse. I couldn't turn the pages fast enough." *Aleatha Romig ~ NY Times bestselling author of Infidelity*

"CD Reiss writes the best erotica I have ever read." *Meredith Wild ~ #1 NY Times bestselling author of the Hacker series.*

"Marriage Games is a gorgeously intense story! The BDSM was white hot, and Adam is my favorite kind of dominant...he lives and breathes absolute control." *Annabel Joseph ~ NY Times bestselling author*

"Marriage Games left me breathless. CD Reiss is beyond brilliant and this is an absolute must read." *Sawyer Bennett ~ NY Times Bestselling Author of Sugar Baby*

"Bold characters, hot sex, brilliant writing—CD Reiss has done it again!" *Jennifer Probst ~ NY Times Bestselling Author*

Separation Games

CD REISS

ISBN: 978-1-682305-98-0

Chapter 1

DAY FIFTEEN

Today is the first day of the rest of my life, and I have no idea how to live it.

Today is the day I make a plan, implement it, and see it through to the end.

Today is the day I prepare to win.

I will take no prisoners but myself. I'll defeat no enemy but my fear.

This is worth it. He is worth it.

Hold your breath.

Hold it for 1, 209, 600 seconds.

Then.

Breathe.

Because he will be yours.

Chapter 2

DAY SEVENTEEN

What can you learn about a man from his office?

I hadn't even had the sense to ask that question when I met Adam, and I should have. His R+D office was stark and clean. It had no history. It gave away nothing. You didn't sense a thing about its owner but the level of his taste.

That was simply the way he ran his business. But standing in his office, with the afternoon sun bending through the glass tabletops, I knew he had run his personal life the same way.

I'd walked past Eva on the way in. She'd warn him I was here. I was ready for that.

The office building across 53rd Street seemed close enough to touch, and the street below seemed far enough away to kill on impact.

My phone said he was a block away. He hadn't shut off the phone tracker after Montauk, and neither had I after he'd found me at the Cellar. Despite everything, we tracked each other. Proof that no matter what the level of our hearts' betrayal, our souls knew where we belonged.

Two days, and I didn't know how I was going to get him back. I'd managed, somehow, to get through the trip home from Montauk. I'd managed to let myself into the loft, walk past my four bags just inside the door, put my keys on the counter. I'd managed to move a chair to the window and sit there looking at the water towers, rooftop gardens, and fire escapes.

Staring was not a plan. It wasn't how a woman in charge ran her life. It wasn't how a person finished a thing. But that was what I had done, and I forgave myself for it. I'd left my husband with a note on the counter. I'd spent months gathering the courage, composing the note, being sure in my head and heart that it was the right thing.

I didn't have months to get him back.

He'd agreed to an easy divorce if I gave him thirty days. Sixteen were gone. It had taken me that long to love him again. The real me loved the real him. It had taken that long for him to fall out of love with me.

Fourteen more days, and I didn't have a plan.

That morning, I'd found stockings and garter in the bottom of my drawer. The bra had a crystal heart between the breasts, and the panties had one to match. I tossed them onto the bed. I shaved myself smooth and put the lingerie on. I stood in front of the mirror and watched myself fall to my knees. I put my ass up, lower back down, forehead to the floor, knees apart. I stayed that way, thinking about nothing but his body until my thighs ached.

Holding that position with that thought cleared my mind enough to do something. Even if it was the wrong thing, it was something.

His phone stopped moving in front of the building. He'd taken a cab.

Deep breath.

He had a small table by the couch. The top was made of cracked tempered glass. There used to be a picture of me on that table.

The dot on the map moved again. He'd arrived in the city at the crack of dawn, according to the tracking on his phone. I didn't know what he'd done during the past two days in Montauk. I tried not to think my worst thoughts.

I'd considered positioning myself on my hands and knees when he arrived, sitting with my legs crossed, spread-eagled on the desk, standing like a lady, hiding in the closet. I figured it would come to me when I needed it.

My strategy was set. My tactics were planned. I left room for inspiration in the minutiae.

Even when I knew he was coming down the hall, I hadn't decided.

I heard his voice outside the door. Eva's reply. Business. Did she tell him I was here?

When the door swung open, I was standing by his desk, wringing my hands as if they were made of dough.

He wore a grey suit I hadn't seen before. His shoulders seemed straighter than ever, and his green tie was knotted in perfect symmetry. He looked taller. He walked like royalty. As if he were unstoppable, as if breaking through obstacles was a waste of time. There were no obstacles. Not for him. Not for a Master.

I must have been a madwoman to walk away from him.

He stopped two steps in, seeing me. Eva was right behind him, wearing an emerald-green suit and shoes.

"By the way," she said, winking at me behind his back, "Diana's here."

I dropped my hands to my sides because my heart submitted, and I leaned all my weight onto one hip because my mind was petulant. "Good morning."

He looked me up and down. "Good morning."

"I'll catch you when you're done," Eva said, backing out of the office.

"No," Adam commanded. "Stay. This won't be long."

He came to his desk. Nine steps. Big steps. I didn't move. Eva cocked her head slightly. Our gazes met, and she widened her eyes a little, letting me know she didn't want to run interference.

Adam put his briefcase on the desk and snapped it open. "How was your ride home?"

"Lonely."

"Sorry, I—"

I cut off his meaningless, pat answer. "You should have been there fucking me."

His hands stopped. He tapped his briefcase twice, thinking. His lashes were closed curtains over his emotions.

I continued while I had the upper hand. "Eva being here isn't going to stop me from doing what I came to do."

I put my hands on my jacket buttons, pushing the top one through the hole. He looked up just in time to see that I wasn't wearing anything but a bra under it.

"You kids," Eva said. "This is great fun, but I have a job."

The door whooshed open and clicked shut as she left.

Adam's presence took up my entire world. I leaned on the desk next to him. My skirt rode up enough for the garter to peek out. I wanted him to tell me to do something, anything. Get off the desk. Button your jacket. Walk three steps. Spread your legs. Open your mouth.

"Too bad," I said, hands behind me. My jacket strained against the last button. "I would have done whatever you asked in front of her."

He took a few folders out of his briefcase and slapped them on the desk. "That's the problem, Diana."

"What? That I'll do whatever you want?"

"Yes." He closed the briefcase.

"We have two more weeks. I'm sticking to the agreement."

"The agreement's done. You win." He slid the folders toward me. I didn't even look at them.

"There were only contingencies if I quit. There's no contingency if you quit." I put my hands together behind me and spread my feet. I was uncomfortable as hell, leaning back on the desk with my legs apart.

"You get everything," he said, eyes coursing around the arc of my body. His dick was hard.

"I don't want everything. I want you."

"Diana. I can't... I can't do this."

His body said otherwise. He leaned toward me slightly. His breath had gotten shallow and slow.

"Yes, you can. You can do whatever you want to me. Things you never thought I'd do. You can hurt me. Hurt me so bad, and I'll beg you for more." I throbbed with those words. I wanted to come for him.

He put his hand on my thigh, sliding it inside and upward. I groaned. His touch was magic. I had to hold back from losing my shit right there.

"I didn't want this for you. I didn't want to turn you into this."

"Into what?"

"This." He ran his hand where my panties would be and found nothing but soaking wet pussy. "Look what I've done already. You'd do whatever I asked in front of Eva. In the office. Wearing nothing. I don't want you to be this."

"This what?"

"*This!*" He pinched my clit, and I grunted in surprise and pain. "This," he whispered in my ear while his hard cock pressed on my thigh.

"Your whore?"

He grabbed my hair with his other hand and yanked my head back. No one had ever done that to me, and I loved it. Loved the pain. The domination. The way he growled at me.

"Don't you ever, ever—"

"Your. Whore."

With a sharp breath, he took his hands off me, holding them up as if he had to prove they were empty. "Stand up straight."

He commanded it, so I did it.

"I can't do this." He cut the air with his determination. "Listen to me when I tell you I can spend the next two weeks fucking you blind and beating you raw. At the end of it, I'm walking away and you're going to be worse off. I promise the longer this goes on, the less I'm going to care how much I hurt you. Drop it now, while it's not that bad."

I straightened my skirt. "It's not that bad?"

"Before you get in deeper and there's no way out. Please."

His plea was a command. I'd take a certain kind of order from him. I'd humiliate myself if he asked the right way, but I couldn't stop loving him just because he demanded it.

I buttoned my jacket. He took my pause as agreement.

"You'll see it's better this way," he said, tapping the folders. "I've had my lawyer draft a revised divorce settlement. You should look at it."

"Should I send you back the ashes when I'm done burning it?"

"Diana—"

"Don't Diana me. Don't tell me how I feel. Don't protect me. I didn't ask you to. All I'm asking you to do is finish what you started. Train me. Don't leave me half done."

"I can't."

"Why not?"

"Because if I continue, whatever feelings you have are going to get blown out of all proportion. It's the nature of the game. I'm protecting you."

"From what?"

"From me," he barked.

I tensed from the sudden change in volume.

He pressed his lips into a line and held up his hands as if warding me off. "I don't care if you like it or not, but you'll thank me in the end."

"I'll thank you now." I stood straight and picked up my bag. "I'm going to be in the office. Our office. And you know where I live. You can sign the divorce papers, but I won't file them until our agreement expires."

I turned my back on him and walked to the door. As every step pulled me farther, the tether between us got thin enough to break.

"You can hang onto them then," he said from behind me.

I stopped but faced the door. I couldn't look at him. He pitied me, and it was impossible to truly love what you pitied.

"Take your time," he continued. "You get everything, don't worry about that."

Everything.

Sure. Everything that could be transferred by a piece of paper.

I didn't tell him how woefully inadequate "everything" was, because he wouldn't understand it. I just walked through the door without looking back, down the hall, nodding at Eva in her emerald-green suit and earrings, to the elevator. I kept my chin up, but a cloud of sadness and despair hung over me, ready to descend as soon as I got onto the street.

I pressed the elevator button, and the red light in the center glowed as it was supposed to. It wasn't broken. Press it and the light went on.

Like Adam.

When I'd offered him my body, he lit up like a Christmas tree, exactly as I thought he would. He'd touched me. He'd put his fingers on me. His hands took what his mouth said he didn't want.

Me.

The little red light went out, and the elevator doors rumbled open. They closed with me alone inside, and I went down, giving birth to an idea that was nearly fully formed by the time the doors opened again.

This was doable. I just had to finish what I started.

Chapter 3

DAY EIGHTEEN

Dad had put his desk in my office, leaving my space untouched. He hadn't been the more organized of the McNeill-Barnes husband-and-wife team, and obviously that hadn't changed. My inbox was piled high with things that could wait but shouldn't.

We sat on my office couches, and he briefed me from a handwritten notebook on his lap. He wasn't using the oxygen tank, which initially gave me confidence. After a few words, I realized my confidence was his goal.

"Nadine put little Ray over there." Dad pointed at a bright blue blanket with boxes of Legos stacked to the side.

"Why?"

"Just Tuesday and Thursday mornings."

"It's fine. But why?"

"I couldn't just let her call in sick. And he's a good boy."

"Dad. Is. She. All. Right?"

He stopped to take a breath. Talking too much was a strain and I was sorry to make him do it. Not that I could stop him.

"You can write it down if you don't want to talk," I added, but he took a big suck on his oxygen and waved away my concern.

"Gary's making it hard. The divorce. Fighting her on everything. Weaponizing Ray. He hired their sitter in his office two days a week."

"So, that should be fine."

"Not as a sitter. As a marketing intern. So she can't sit for Ray on Nadine's weeks. When she had a hearing scheduled about it, he postponed. So she brings Ray here until she finds someone else."

"Is he all right in the corner? Ray?"

"He just builds with those damn bricks for three hours. It's like a drug. Then her sister comes."

"Okay. Moving on."

"Zack Abramson's back." Dad crossed him off the list of things he had to tell me. "Can't hire him because he left before the freeze. Could use him to move stuff off your desk."

"Agreed. I'll call him."

"And that Kayti girl? She can't keep her mind on a single thing at a time."

"That's her superpower."

He closed his book. Brushed his silver hair into place. Dad hadn't lost his hair as he aged. He was still handsome and well put together, but he'd never shown an interest in a woman after my mother died.

"You're back early," he said. "It wasn't because of the business, I know that. Unless Miss Superpower started with the alarm bells."

"There were no alarms."

"Are you back because the trip failed? Or because it was successful?"

"It's not that simple."

"Are you all right? How is it all with him?"

I closed my notebook. I didn't want to lie to him, but I didn't want to declare the battle won or lost until the war was over. And it was a war. I didn't kid myself about that. I was fighting for the very things I'd thrown away.

"I don't want you asking too many questions because you're not breathing well. So I'm going to just tell you everything I can, all right?"

He nodded and held his hand out as if giving me the floor.

Now I had to figure out what to say and what to leave out. I was his daughter. News that Adam didn't love me anymore, or that he did but just a little, wasn't going to cut it.

"We went. We talked more than we ever have. I learned about him. Things I didn't know. We both changed. There's still stuff that we have to work out. I want to prepare you for the fact that even though I've come around, we might still split up. I love him. I can't tell you how much I do, but it might not matter."

"What can I do to help?"

"Nothing. It's between us. Just... thank you. Thank you for taking care of things around here while we went away."

"You're welcome."

"You can stop coming in if you want."

"Nah. I can come in."

"Dad, I don't want you to tire yourself out. You retired for a reason."

He shrugged, tapped the tabletop with his fingertip, wheezed a little. "Maybe I'll stick around the rest of the week. You need me until you get your feet under you."

Another man protecting me. I was grateful and resentful at the same time.

Chapter 4

DAY EIGHTEEN

I watched my phone for Adam's movements, obsessing like a tenth grader with a crush on the captain of the football team. I shooed away a constant, humming anxiety that manifested as a twisted stomach. My insides felt like a wet washcloth that had been twisted tight and left in the sun.

He wanted me. His body wanted me and his heart called for me, but his mind had decided to cut me loose. Without him coming to the office, I wasn't sure how to get in front of him so his mind could get out of the way.

Kayti had her bag slung on her shoulder when she poked her head into my office. "Zack's on his way up."

"Leave the door open. Have a good night."

She left me alone. The tracker found his phone in the Meatpacking District.

He was at the Cellar.

My first emotion was anger, then a sense of urgency, then despair, then all the bad things I could think and feel ran together like a ten-car pileup on the

FDR. Anger/lust/panic/jealousy/desolation—boom boom boom.

"Hey, there." Zack tipped his head into my office before sliding his whole body in.

I couldn't talk to another human being. All I could do was look at that green dot on a map. I flipped the phone glass-side down.

"Come in."

We gave each other the double-euro kiss. His blond scruff scratched my cheek.

"It's good to see you." It wasn't good or bad, but it was terribly inconvenient, because I wanted to go to the Cellar and curl my body at Adam's feet so no one else could.

Zack and I sat on the couch. He was as handsome and rugged as always, but he looked tired and drawn out, as if he too had been wrung out and left in the sun to dry.

"I'm sorry to hear about your mother," I said.

"It happened so fast. I was there four hours, and boom. It was like she just needed to see me before she died."

"I'm glad you went then."

"Me too. But with the funeral done and my sister in charge of the arrangements, I had to come back. I was going crazy in Dayton. Nice people. Wonderful people, actually. If I could take everybody there and move them to New York, it would be heaven."

I smiled. The fast-paced intensity of the city attracted the most driven people in the world. They weren't always easy to live with. "I can imagine."

I was filling space. I wanted to go to the Cellar or, at the very least, look at my phone again to see if he'd run to some sub's apartment for a fuck.

Zack must have read my mind.

"I heard about you and Adam."

Of course he had. My big blabbing mouth meant I was going to have to say we were getting divorced, or not.

"It's in process."

"Figured as much when you needed to use my apartment but you wouldn't say why."

I'd seen his empty apartment as an opportunity and used it to bulldoze away my fear. I saw it as a sign that I needed to stop delaying the inevitable.

Zack moved on the couch until he faced me completely, draping his hand on the back. "You were miserable. You played the part though." His finger touched my shoulder, stroking it through my blouse. "Played it really well."

I shifted to face him, which showed I was paying attention and got my shoulder away from his finger at the same time. "I wasn't playing. I was trying to hold it together."

"I know. But I could tell. You didn't look at him unless you were talking about work. He had you trapped, didn't he?"

He did, but not enough, obviously. Not enough for me to see why I should be.

Zack's voice was deep and husky with warm admiration. "You were very brave to let him go."

That was the exact story I'd told myself before I left the note. "I was a coward. I told you more about how I felt by asking to move in than I told him."

"He's not the easiest guy in the world to talk to."

Zack made eyes at me. *Eyes* meaning if I wanted to fuck on the couch, I could fuck on the couch. And I did want to fuck on the couch, but I didn't want to fuck him.

I stood and brushed my skirt down. "There's a freeze on new hires, so I can't bring you back. But we're falling behind, and it would be great to have a freelancer we didn't have to train, if you're interested."

He stood in front of me, too close, but the coffee table kept me from stepping back easily. Also, I wasn't going to back away. It wasn't my job to be the only one with an ounce of sense. He should take a hint.

"I'm interested. And when you finally take that ring off, I'm interested in that too."

"I'll make a note."

...

The loft was a block away from work, but I got in a cab as soon as I knew Zack was gone.

"Gansevoort," I said.

"Got it." And he was off.

I checked the phone. Adam was still there. I had to see him again. The urgency was a physical thing sitting in my gut as if I'd swallowed it whole. I couldn't digest it.

Zack's come-on had pushed me deeper into wanting Adam's touch. The ease with which he'd propositioned me made my position with the man I really wanted feel even more tenuous. Every hour I let pass was an hour closer to the end of our contract.

The cab dropped me on the corner. I walked quickly to the plain building that was the Cellar. A man in a leather jacket stood in front of the black door.

"Hi," I said, trying to act as if I belonged there.

"Hello." His voice was a deep baritone.

"I'd like to go in?"

The door opened behind him, and a couple came out. I recognized Charlie, but not the woman he was with.

"Do you have a member number?" asked the baritone.

Charlie gave me a second look as he led the woman to the curb, then he turned away.

"No, I just—"

"Can't do it."

"A minute. Just a minute."

Was I begging? I didn't want to beg, but I wanted to see my husband. Maybe I'd beg him. Maybe I'd just get on my knees.

"Sorry, ma'am. It's members only tonight."

I turned to Charlie. Did he remember me from our wedding? Did he know where Adam was? Could he get me in? I could beg him too.

But even as I thought he might help, he got in the cab after the woman and closed the door.

"How do you become a member?" I asked the baritone bouncer.

"You need recommendations from three active members," he answered.

"Thank you," I said. "Thank you very much."

I wasn't stalking Adam, but maybe I was. I walked around the corner, wrapping my coat tightly around me. The neighborhood was packed with people going out after work. Laughing, smiling, noses red in the cold, damp night.

Zack thought I was available, and he was a counterpoint to all the women who saw Adam the same way. They'd flock to him. He wouldn't be single another hour. And what was he doing in there? Was he going to leave with someone?

Not on my watch. No way. Whatever he was going to do with whomever he was going to do it with, he was going to have to hide it, because I would stab myself repeatedly with whatever he did. Oh yes, my pain cried out to multiply a hundred times over. If he left that club with someone, I would watch it happen and he would know the level of his betrayal.

I was around the corner when I looked at the phone again. The green dot had moved to the street. I ran, crashing into a lady carrying a little dog, nearly tripping on a garbage pail, navigating patches of ice like a ninja. I ran back around the corner until I could see baritone at the front door and a cab pulling away.

I got my phone out again. It was him.

Don't text him.

He was in that cab, and I had no way of knowing if he was alone or with a sub who would do whatever he wanted without the baggage, without the love, without a care in the world.

Do. Not. Text.

In the middle of the sidewalk, I watched that cab wait at a light two blocks away, turn north on Tenth Ave., east on 23rd, north on Park Ave., and east again into Murray Hill. Home. He went home alone or otherwise.

—I want to be a member of the Cellar—

I walked south on Hudson, toward home. I had to work off the energy. My body needed something to do besides panic about the fact that he wasn't texting me back.

I stared at my phone. No dots either. He'd gotten the message but wasn't answering.

Because he's fucking someone else.

Maybe, maybe not. But why would he go to the Cellar unless it was to find someone to fuck? Maybe he'd gone to talk to Charlie. Maybe he'd just wanted to be among his people. Maybe he'd tried to find someone and failed.

I got all the way home and heard nothing.

He had to be too busy with a sub. A woman with no problem doing what she was told. A woman who could offer her ass without delay. A pure, true, trained submissive who succeeded where I failed.

He couldn't love a sub, but that wouldn't stop him from fucking them.

I took a deep breath when I hit SoHo and emailed Kayti.

Kayti—

First thing in the morning. Pull up the wedding reception invitation list. Not City Hall. The Lafayette Hotel reception. I need phone numbers and addresses.

He could refuse to touch me, but he couldn't stop me from pursuing my submissive nature. Even after these two weeks were finished and he drifted even further away, I still had a chance to pursue him. Everything about the idea was crazy, but I didn't feel sane.

His text came in just before I went to bed.

—You will never be a member of the Cellar—

It took a ton of effort not to answer his text, because I saw hope inside it. He cared. Even if his dick was wet with another woman, he cared whether or not I was a member.

I didn't sleep well, but that sentiment gave me a couple hours of rest.

Chapter 5

DAY EIGHTEEN

The journey of a thousand miles starts with a single step.
I learned not to expect anything. Or if not that, I learned that what I expected could be wrong, a fantasy, a fear, a bunch of meaningless tropes slapped on a mundane reality.

The old Garment Center red brick building still had brass-fitted mail chutes in the hallways. I stopped by one and pushed the flap. It had been sealed shut. When exactly had the post office stopped using them? Why? And the old glass mail chutes? When had they stopped working?

You're stalling.

In the eighties, 23 bags of stuck mail had been retrieved in the chute. Years worth of unpaid bills and business correspondence. Contracts and notices. Thoughts, feelings, typewritten and scrawled. Stamped and stuffed, and in the mass of fluttering business detritus, a woman received a letter from her dead husband. Yet another got a letter her dead husband sent to his girlfriend years before. The emotions were still there on the paper, even if the muscle holding it was long gone.

Was anything stuck in there now? An old love letter, begging for a reconciliation? The declaration of a long-denied love? What was caught in the seams between the floors? In the digital age, messages were lost in the ether. In the analog, a letter could get sealed in a chute forever.

The door at the end of the hallway opened, and a woman in her forties strode out, holding the knob until the door clicked. She didn't look at me as she passed, her heels clopping on the marble, but she'd forced me to look outside my distractions at the brass plate on the door.

INTERNATIONAL OBJECTS

I didn't know if a more bland name existed, especially in contrast to what was actually sold there. A wedding invitation had gone there, and I followed the trail by deduction.

The brass knob was warm where the woman had touched it, and I added my own warmth, turning it and entering.

After the first step, you still have to walk the thousand miles.

. . .

The reception area had been completely bland. Almost insultingly empty. The conference room, however, was completely different. Rich with tapestries and soft cushions, dark woods and a window onto neighboring factory rooftops, it invited the truth.

Which was why Charlie met me in here in his dark denim sports jacket and khaki slacks. I wondered what Adam had meant when he said Charlie had his dick shot off.

"I can't help you," he said, leaning on his cane. Neither of us was sitting.

"Of course you can. You *won't* help me."

"So we agree. It was very nice to see you again. I'll have someone show you out."

Yeah.

Right.

"It means your mind can be changed."

"Ms. McNeill-B—"

"I can convince you."

"I am not going to train you."

"Why not?"

"Are you mad, woman?"

"If you mean angry, no. Not yet. I'm assuming you mean crazy, which yes, I am crazy. Just a little. Adam started to train me and didn't finish. Now I'm supposed to just find my way around? Half done like a runny egg? I don't accept that, and if he's not going to finish, someone has to."

He regarded me for a long time. His eyes were a dark, cloudy grey. They gave away nothing. "He told me you were vanilla. Not a submissive bone in your body."

"He missed a bone, obviously."

"More than that." He held out his hand. "Sit. Please. You're making me tired."

Was he going to sit? Was his order just for me, and why?

"If you can't even take a simple request, Mrs.—"

"Diana." I pulled back a leather chair. It rattled on the casters.

When I sat down, he sat across from me. A little pod of office supplies sat on the end of the table. I folded my hands in front of me and leaned forward. I didn't notice the aggressive posture until I wondered if I should be more submissive. Hands in lap? Eyes down? Knees together or apart?

None of the above. I kept my elbows on the table and my ribs pressed to the edge as if I was going to leap across it. I couldn't second-guess myself all the time, and I thought being myself was safer than trying to be the kind of submissive I wasn't.

"What do you expect to get out of training?" Charlie asked as if he'd asked it a hundred times before.

"Is there a right answer?"

He matched my posture. Hands clasped. Elbows on the table. "There are only wrong answers."

"Wrong answers like 'better sex' or 'a boyfriend'?"

"Those are definitely wrong."

"Why?"

"They're not true, for a start."

"And they're facile and immature."

"Yes. And they can be achieved another way. If you want better sex, find a more compatible partner. If you want a boyfriend, there's always Tinder. So if you want to do this, you do it because there's no other way to achieve what you're trying to achieve."

"Which is?"

"You tell me. What do you want out of sub training?"

"Adam."

I answered quickly because it was true, and because there was no other way. I was ready to argue my reasons all morning if he'd let me. At the same time, I figured he'd call any answer I gave wrong and dismiss me. Then I'd chase Adam without him or his help. I didn't know how long the chase would last, but I knew it couldn't go on too long before I quit in despair. I was a sprinter, not a long distance runner, so I told myself I had two weeks to do whatever I could.

"I hate to be the one to tell you this." He leaned back. "Fact is, he should be the one telling you and I should kick you out of here right now without another word. But I'm a nice guy."

I pressed my lips together so snarky words wouldn't come out. I practically had to cover my mouth.

"You're wasting your time," he said. "The only woman he ever fell for wasn't a sub."

"That woman was me."

"It was."

"He loves me. I know it. You know it. He's fighting hard to make the biggest mistake of his life, and you're going to let him. How are you going to live with yourself when he's sixty and fucking random submissives he can't love? Do you want that? Or do you not care?"

"This is none of my business, you know." He pushed his chair out and put his hand on his cane. "I'm not getting involved."

I snapped up a pen and pinched a scrap of paper from a pad. "Here's my number if you change your mind."

"I'm not going to call you."

"I'll see you at the club then." I stood.

"You have a membership?" He seemed genuinely concerned.

"No. But I need three members to vouch for me. It can't be that hard."

"Really?" He took his hand off the cane, lacing his hands across his lap. "How easy is it?"

"Tryout night's next week. I can convince someone I'm capable of getting on my knees. There are Doms in the paper looking for—"

"Hold on there, sheila."

"What?"

"You don't know those blokes, and you have no way of checking them. This is a dangerous business."

I shrugged.

"You're going to let some bloke you don't know, never met, no friends in common... let him tie you up? I'm not even talking about fucking. No good Dominant's just going to fuck you without clear consent, but there are bad ones out there. Bad, bad men."

"I can handle it. But thanks."

I couldn't handle it. I was terrified of everything about it. I didn't want to submit to another man, ever. Didn't want to be touched or ordered around by anyone but Adam. Charlie was tolerable because his relationship to my husband meant that no matter what he taught me, he wouldn't touch me.

So I had to go to plan C. I didn't have a plan C, but I was sure I could come up with something. I was halfway through the bland, no-nonsense reception area when Charlie's voice echoed off the walls.

"I can get you someone." He leaned on his cane, a three-legged man against the stark white hall.

"A stranger?" I asked.

"What am I then? I said four words to you at your wedding and you've seen me twice since."

"Adam trusts you, so I do."

He sighed deeply. "I'm going to get no end of trouble for this." He reached into his breast pocket and retrieved a slim card case. "But better this than you running around half-cocked."

With just his thumb, he slid out a card partway, then he held the case out to me. I crossed the distance between us in three steps and grabbed the white triangle, pulling out the rest of the card until the entire rectangle was revealed. On it, just a word in silvery grey.

INSOLENT

I turned it to the back and found a number neatly written in thin black felt tip.

Text: (212) 867-5309

"Give the bloke a fair go."

"You're referring me?"

"You're a brat," he said without insult. "I don't train brats. Don't have the patience anymore."

"Well, thank you. I appreciate the time you took to meet with me."

"Be careful."

"I will," I lied. There was no way to be careful about what I wanted to do. I couldn't do it.

Chapter 6

DAY TWENTY

My father and I had a very open, loving relationship, but he was still my father. He wouldn't want to hear the details of my sexual exploits with Adam any more than I'd want to tell them. Life and relationships were uncomfortable, awkward, and messy in general. Telling your father how it felt to be paddled while people watched from the snowy yard wouldn't bring us closer. It would make him worry.

"I thought the vacation would sort you two out," he said, flipping teabags into white cups. The cups had come from my mother's family, and they were priceless. The whistling teapot was from my dad's father, and it was just old.

"It didn't."

I counted pills and dropped them into his plastic container. *Click click click.* I checked against the calendar and marked off the week I'd allocated.

I kept a log of his meds and prescriptions with refill dates and dosage changes. I was terrible at this sort of thing. I could barely keep a grocery list in one place. But for some reason, I was obsessive about keeping his pills in order.

"And it's him? Not you?"

"I don't know. I mean..." I sighed and snapped the container shut. "I love him, but I think this made him rethink what he needs."

Dad brought our tea to the table. I made an effort to let him do it himself, though I wanted to jump up and take the tray from him.

"He's a good man. He'll make the right decision."

"Maybe." I squeezed my teabag and dropped the dry lump onto the saucer.

"Or." Dad shrugged as if he didn't want to suggest the thing he was thinking and hoped I'd meet him halfway.

"Or?"

"They can take a man's... you know... stuff..." He scratched his head. "Your mother didn't get cancer until later, so maybe it's not worth it."

"Take a man's sperm?"

"Yes. And, you know. Blah blah."

"Artificial insemination?"

"Sure. Yeah. And the other one. In the test tube. You go to a clinic and they have it frozen. You pick from a catalog. Or... what I'm saying is, I know you were worried."

"I'm still worried." I blew the surface of my tea into crescent-shaped ripples. "Maybe I just don't get to have children."

"You're giving up?" He hacked out two coughs. "Come on."

"It's a race. You lose some races. And if I can't see what I'm racing against? If I have no idea if the cancer is coming tomorrow or never? And what if I make these terms with him? Just a baby, right? He might say yes, but that's letting him off the hook. I want all of him. I'm not splitting the difference. It's all or nothing. I'll give up on this race with Mom's genes, but I won't give up on the dream with Adam."

"This is the man you left." Dad raised an eyebrow, and I detected a little smugness. He'd never wanted me to leave my husband.

"I did it because I wanted time to have a family with someone else. Which was wrongheaded. I'm not making decisions based on how Mom died anymore. If my time's running out and I lose this race, so be it. It's my life to waste, and I'm going to waste it racing with him."

"You seem like you've made up your mind."

I placed my cup in the saucer as if it was the last bingo chip on the winning card. "This is going to the finish line. You mark my words."

He took my hand across the table. His skin was cold and dry. "I'll be here for you. Win or lose."

Dad must have been where I got the strength to stand up to my husband's rejection. His eyes were as sharp and blue as ever, and I could believe in the strong but icy grip of his hand that he'd be there to help me see it through to the end. Adam. A baby. The inevitable fight with renegade cells. He'd taught me how to fight.

"There's always another race," I said.

"I'll be there for those too." He put his cool hand on my cheek and patted it.

He'd never leave me. Never stop. And I'd never stop chasing Adam.

Starting tonight.

I threw back my tea in one gulp. "Okay, you're all set." I stacked the containers and picked up my cup and saucer. "I have to go."

"It's nine at night. Where are you going this late? On a weekday?"

"Ready, set, go, Dad." Newly inspired, I put the cup and saucer in the dishwasher. "We don't get to decide when the gun goes off."

"What?"

I kissed his cheek. "See you in the office."

Chapter 7

DAY TWENTY

Monthly tryout night at the Cellar. Anyone could walk in. Last time, I'd been clothed in anger and disappointment and driven by a curiosity about what my husband had been seeing when he saw sex.

The second time I went to tryout night, I didn't have that armor or that drive. I was curious about myself. I was curious about my trajectory. I wanted to feel what it was like to be single in that world. I wasn't accepting defeat with Adam, but I was getting a feel for being single and I didn't want to wait another month to go to the Meatpacking District to find my place.

This time, I heard every command, smelled the lubricant, tasted sex in the back of my throat as I got off the elevator onto the sixth floor. I withheld judgment on everything and everyone. Having been to Montauk, most of the activity in the room seemed tamer than I remembered. The clothing was outrageous on some and dowdy on others. Sitting at the bar, I noticed the ratio of observers to participants disproportionately favored the observers, who were usually huddled couples holding their drinks with two hands and sipping through stir sticks.

I sat with my knees pressed together and my hands resting on them. I'd worn a blouse and slacks for modesty. As a new submissive without a Master, I felt vulnerable. Beyond being there, I didn't even know what I wanted out of my trip downtown.

The young Dom I'd seen paddling his sub in the observation room was on the other side of the bar, talking to a man and a woman in black. The young Dom wore a crisp white button-front and grey tie. They could have been talking about real estate.

Our eyes met, and he stopped, tilting his head. I flushed with prickly heat and looked away, hiding behind my ginger ale. I held the glass in two hands, sipping from the rim. Avoiding him. My fingers were cold and wet from condensation, but I didn't let the glass go. His gaze held the promise of dirty feet buckling under the weight of his paddle. The sound of it hitting skin. The knowledge that someone was witnessing my domination and degradation. I wanted all of it, but not with him.

What do you see?

At two o'clock, a woman was cuffed to a big X. She was getting her bare ass whipped by two men. At ten o'clock, another woman was sucking off two men, alternating hand and mouth every few seconds. At one and four, collars and leashes, and at every minute in between were observers trying not to stare when staring was the point.

What are you feeling?

Lonely. Curious. Aroused in a non-specific-free-floating sort of way.

"What attracts you?"

The voice wasn't in my head, but next to me. Bass-deep and accented in thick Ts and dropped hisses. He'd spoken to me the first time I'd come. Adam had called him Viktor.

I didn't respond right away. All of it attracted me, and none of it.

"I don't bite," he said. "Bark a little, maybe."

I smiled and tilted my glass. The ice had melted into smooth-shaped stones. I glanced at the young Dom. As if he knew I was looking, he turned, and seeing me, he nodded.

"I'm not sure what attracts me," I said, looking squarely at Viktor.

"None of it?"

"None specifically, but in a general way... all of it."

He tipped his drink at the woman on the X. "What do you like? The cuffs or the pain?"

I stayed silent, considering my options.

"This is only curiosity. I'm not in business to give you either. Just to talk."

"I think," I said, watching the woman's behind flush pink, then red. The transformation was gorgeous. Like petals blossoming. "Both together. She needs the cuffs to stay still for the pain. To feel safe."

I shook the ice. My wrung-out lime flopped like a dead fish on top.

"Your drink. You'd like another?"

"Ginger ale."

The bartender was a woman with a long braid that twisted strands of blond, black, and red hair. She wore a corset and platform wedge sneakers. "This asshole bothering you?"

"No. He said he wouldn't bite."

"He barks." She raised a penciled eyebrow.

"I've been warned."

"Ginger ale?" She picked up my glass.

"On me," Viktor said.

"On the house," the bartender parried, filling my glass with fresh ice. "You're Adam's wife?"

"Hey," Viktor said, "put the lid on it."

Some kind of silent message passed between Viktor and the bartender. A conversation the woman with the soda gun won. She slid the glass to me.

"You're being watched," she said. "Protectively. But you're not anonymous here."

"Is this the only club in the city?" I asked, annoyed.

"Ten years ago, three clubs had to merge or the scene would die. Next nearest club is in Newark. Blame gentrification. Call your congressman."

"Could also call your husband," Viktor interjected.

"Someone did that already, I'm sure." The bartender gave me an apologetic face and went to the other side of the bar to help a couple who looked as though they'd taken the train right from their law firm jobs.

"At least you know I'm not trying to pick you up," Viktor said. "And I liked your answer very much."

"So you're watching me?"

"Making sure you don't get into some trouble. We look out for each other and each other's subs."

"I'm not his sub."

"This is between you and him. Ah, and here he is!" Viktor held out his hand and Adam appeared from behind me.

He was wearing a T-shirt and jeans with a coat. He looked as if he'd run the whole way from the gym.

Great.

He and Viktor shook hands. Adam thanked him. I flipped the red stirrer out of my drink and sipped from the rim. I was feeling furious and butch.

"It was nice to talk to you," Viktor said then pointed at Adam. "You take care of this one."

I hid my face behind the glass. My sneer was inappropriate. Viktor meant no harm.

When Viktor was out of earshot, Adam said, "Huntress."

"Fuck off," I said from behind the glass.

He put his hand on the bar and leaned on it, putting his body close to mine. "You know how I feel about you being here?"

"Tell me more about how you *feel.*"

The braided bartender smiled when she got to us and folded herself over the bar to kiss him on the cheek.

"The Glenallen," he said. "No ice."

The girl on the big X was taken down. She had a blindfold on, and she was smiling. Her Dom carried her away. I didn't know what to make of it. I hadn't decided how I felt about seeing other people do what I didn't know if I wanted. With Adam, it was all fine. I could figure it out. Without him, I was afraid to experiment, and I was afraid not to.

"I have a right to be here," I said. "I don't need the whole tribe breathing down my neck."

"This isn't you."

"Are you serious? You just spent two weeks showing me that it is. Then you left me hanging."

"I mean it's not you to stalk me."

I almost poured my soda down his pants. "Were you always such a narcissist? I'm here for *me.* I'm trying to figure out who I am, what I like, and what I want."

"You've always known what you wanted. This was never it."

His chest rested against my shoulder, and his breath warmed my ear.

"I want something else. I think. I don't know if I'm submissive or what type and I can't decide from home. If you're going to make me decide without you, I'm going to do what I have to. This place is the first stop for anyone working through this." I faced him nose to nose. "Maybe you're the one who's stalking me."

He put the whiskey to my lips and tipped it. I drank. It made my lips cold and my throat hot.

"Can I show you something?" he asked.

"Isn't that what I've been asking?"

He helped me off the stool and guided me to the back hallway that was for members only, even on tryout nights. The hallway where I'd met Serena. He walked quickly, keeping me on his arm, nodding to a few people but not getting distracted. Leaning on the brass handle, he pushed through a frosted-glass door to a narrower hallway with doors on one side.

He took me down it until he hit an open door. A young man who looked as if he hadn't seen a lick of sun in years furiously tapped a device in the dark room. When he looked up, the light from the device revealed a movie projector.

"Hey," he said. "Looking for something?"

"Number nineteen," Adam said.

"On it." He kicked the door closed.

Adam pulled me to the next door to the left. It opened into a small theater with about two dozen red velvet seats with lights at the bases.

"There was this guy in Marine Park who collected vintage pornography. When he died, one of the clubs uptown took it and preserved it. When all the clubs merged, they reels moved here."

"We're going to watch porn together?"

He guided me down an aisle. "Yes."

"How adventurous of us." I smiled at him, flirting.

He smiled back a little, but was reserved in his enthusiasm. We sat in the center.

"Now I'm sorry I wore pants," I said.

The lights dimmed to black. I took his hand, and he paused before dropping our entwined fingers in his lap.

"I'm trying to illustrate something. I want to talk. So I'm glad you wore pants."

The bullseye countdown appeared. Adam leaned his head back, closed his eyes, and exhaled. They went back to the screen as if all necessary strength had been gathered.

She's blindfolded, arms tied above her. He's lashing her.

"These are from the late sixties," he said as the picture flickered. There was no sound. "The stuff here is very real. There's no retouching. It's 16mm, so there's none of the porny quality of video."

He's wrapping her tits in black tape.

"I see," I said.

He was right. The frame was raw. The beauty of her submission wasn't on the film. I didn't feel as though I was watching something. I felt as though I was witnessing something.

He's clamping her nipples until they're elongated meat.

"This is called tit torture," he said matter-of-factly. "Every step of this was worked out beforehand. You're not seeing the dozen things he's *not* doing." He twisted in his seat to face me. He was backlit, so I couldn't see his expression. "Give me an adjective. What do you think of it?"

"Is this your thing?"

"Answer me first."

I loved him. I wanted him. I'd get on my knees and submit to him.

"It's gruesome."

"It's not my thing." He sat back and faced the screen. The light flickered on his face. "There's so much more though."

He's putting the business end of a hairbrush in her anus.

I've never seen skin that shade of purple.

What is she eating?

In all of them, the submissive may have cried or screamed, but she always came back for more. She kissed the Dominant's hand or looked at him admiringly. Her lips did a dance of gratitude.

Thank you.

Ten minutes in, I couldn't hold my questions anymore. "Why are you showing me this? You don't want to wrap me in duct tape."

"Someone might. I want you to know what it looks like first."

"Adam Steinbeck!" I stood and put my fists on my hips. "You fucking shit!"

He crossed his legs, shrugging as if it wasn't his fault. He just worked here. "What?"

"You're trying to scare me."

"I'm trying to inform you."

"To hell with this. I'm going out there right now and getting someone to fuck me with a wooden spoon."

I stomped down the aisle. He grabbed my arm. I spun around to face him. Behind him, a woman was getting choked, and every time she breathed, the ecstasy on her face was unmistakable.

"Let go of me," I growled.

"Look at it. You weren't meant for this."

But he was? But Serena was? Was I too good? Too weak? Too strong? None of that mattered.

"You love me. Say it, Adam."

"I'm keeping the love I have left."

"Why can't you love a submissive?"

"I don't know."

"You can't love weakness?" I asked.

"I said I don't know."

"You're unworthy of a woman who would kneel for you?"

"What do you want out of me?"

He was hurting me. I jerked my arm away, and he let go.

"I want you to leave me for a reason. A real reason. I left you because I was unhappy. I thought we were incompatible. You're leaving me because you asked me to submit to you and I love it. You're leaving me because you love me a little but not enough. What is all that? It's not a reason."

"I'm protecting you!"

"You're protecting *you*."

No snappy retort. No defense. Behind him, the clips continued.

She's naked. Blindfolded. Hands tied behind her back and a high collar that forces her chin up. She's stumbling across the room, following his touch.

"That looks like fun," I said.

When he looked around to see what I was talking about, I slipped away.

"Diana!"

In addition to being easy to keep on, pants were good for running. Which I did at a respectful jog across the hall and into the club. Not too fast. I wanted him to catch me, but I wanted him to chase first.

I ran into Viktor, who kept me from falling on my face. Adam came behind at a slow trot, unfazed. I smoothed my hair and thanked Viktor the Russian for catching me. Adam took my arm without breaking his pace and led me to the elevator.

"I don't want to go," I said.

The doors closed, and we went down. When they opened, Charlie was standing there with his cane.

"Hello, there."

"Hi!" I said, expecting a conversation, but Adam led me out, down a hall and to the street.

He put his finger up to me. "Hear me. I am not training you. Period. And you are not to come back here. Ever. I don't care if it's the only club in the city. It's not open to you."

"You can't expect me to go back to the way I was."

"I loved you the way you were."

"Wake up, Mr. Steinbeck. Your heart's not talking to your head. You still love me."

Like a chariot from heaven, a cab pulled up. I didn't wait for him to deny the truth. I opened the door myself and told the driver to go.

I was in the long game now.

Chapter 8

If I was going to play a game of cat and mouse with Adam, then I had to make sure I was the only mouse worth chasing. He had to see only me through a field of hundreds of beautiful, submissive women who could satisfy his every need.

When I listed my limitations in my journal, I didn't use the words to become depressed or hurt myself. I didn't fall into despair. I made a calculation that he would have made. Without doing that first, I'd fail. So I didn't get my self-worth wrapped up in the reckonings.

I was inexperienced. Unsure. I carried a ton of baggage with his name on it. He might never trust me again. He might always think I was apt to leave him at any moment. I represented an emotional risk.. On paper, I was the least likely candidate for his affections.

Coming back to me would be crazy. The morning after the tryout at the Cellar, I had a come-to-Jesus moment. I knew him well enough to know he'd told himself leaving me was about protecting me. I was sure he believed that, but I didn't. Without truly understanding what I was saying, I'd told him he was protecting himself. He was legitimately protecting himself from a terrible mistake.

Adam Steinbeck was the jealous type. He still considered me his possession and responsibility, that much was obvious. Best-case scenario, he was telling the truth and wanted to protect me. Worst-case scenario, he wanted me to stay away from the Cellar so he could do/fuck what/whomever he wanted without my eyes on him. Even if that was the case, it proved there a bond between us that hadn't broken yet.

I felt in my bones that the bond would start to fray at the end of the thirty days we'd promised each other. Any legal action would be legitimized. I'd have nothing to hold over him, and we'd split.

Also, I wanted to finish.

Also, he was mine.

Also, every day that passed without me taking action was a day he drifted further away.

I had to take a risk. I had to do something he didn't expect. His reaction would save us or end us. What I was going to do could give him ammunition to justify taking another woman to bed before I could bring him closer to me.

But every day that passed brought us closer to the day he'd find someone else.

Every day, we'd be closer to irreconcilable.

Every day that passed brought us closer to the day he'd stop trying to protect me from someone who could hurt or humiliate me.

My thoughts felt calculating, but my heart was getting closer to panic.

The longer I looked at the card marked INSOLENT as it hung from the refrigerator magnet, the more I knew the panic would get both better and worse if I texted that number.

Success or failure, I had to find out who I was. I still had to understand what my submissiveness meant. How deep it went. How it could complement or destroy my life.

> **—Hello. My name is Diana. Charlie gave me your number.—**

—Hello Diana. You must be a brat—

—Apparently. This
makes me hard to
train, right?—

—"Hard to train" is in the eyes of the trainer—

He didn't seem very bossy or Dominant. There was nothing sexual about anything he'd said so far. Was I supposed to be attracted to him? I wanted to want him, but it was hard through text and, to be fair, impossible as long as Adam Steinbeck lived and breathed.

—How's your
vision?—

Maybe making a joke wasn't a good idea. I waited a full minute for a response. Note to self: if the Dom doesn't have a sense of humor or his standard of humor is too high, walk away. I actually got out my journal, started a new page, and wrote that down.

1)   Sense of humor
2)   Low bar for laughter

Seemed as good a time as any to make a checklist of the perfect Dom.

1)   Tall
2)   Gentle and hard at the same time
3)   Sexy voice
4)   Patient with me on the submissive stuff
5)   Takes no for an answer
6)   Named Adam Steinbeck

Right. Well, I could push hard for #8 while knowing I might not get it. Or

I could just pretend that every future man I ever dated could hold a candle to him. The world was going to run out of candles.

My phone rang. I didn't recognize the number, and I would have sent it to voicemail if Insolent's card wasn't right next to it. The numbers matched.

He was calling me. Why?

Should I answer?

Odds his name was Adam? Slim.

Odds he was the man for me? Also slim.

List of what I had to lose? Again. Slim.

I tapped the green button and put the phone to my ear. "Hello?"

"Let's talk."

Not Adam's voice. Bottom line. He wasn't Adam. All I heard was an English accent and the one man he wasn't.

"I can't promise anything."

"It's early for promises. Don't you think?"

"Yes."

Too early, and too late.

Chapter 9

DAY TWENTY-TWO

Ten minutes on the phone the day before, and I felt as if I'd done most of the talking. I'd been focused on what I didn't want to tell him. Adam's name, for one. My feelings weren't his business, and neither were my intentions. I'd highlighted my inexperience and curiosity. I couldn't tell him what I'd discovered I liked in bed. It felt like cheating on Adam, so I danced around it. He must have seen right through me. Who wouldn't? I was a stumbling idiot.

He said he wanted to go very slow.

God, what was I doing?

This was the stupidest idea ever.

I had to focus. Shed the shame and get the job done. This was my life now.

Facts about Master Insolent

1) English
2) Six-one
3) Fifty-two YO

4) Dark hair/eyes
5) Master's degree—London School of Economics
6) Humor: 6/10
7) Bad humor tolerance: 8/10
8) Dom for 22 years
9) Currently single
10) Goals: break a brat

I didn't want to break. At least, that was my initial reaction. Adam had broken me. He'd shown me my limits of pain, pleasure, and humiliation. He'd dragged me out of myself, folded me into his will, and put me back together.

How could I let someone else do that? I'd lived for years without getting broken. Why did I need it now?

I took the train to Dad's place, rocking with the movement of the subway, submitting to its size and speed. I held a pole in my gloved hand, steadying myself against it, working with the inertia to stay steady.

Could I ever go back to vanilla sex? If Adam got the final word and I was in the cold without him, I was going to have to decide between being single the rest of my life, leading a vanilla life, or taking on another Master. Could I welcome another man into my bed for a lifetime of nice sex? Good sex even?

No. I couldn't. I'd changed. I was a different woman.

Could I ever let another man beat and humiliate me for pleasure?

No. I couldn't imagine it. There was only Adam.

Staying single forever seemed like the only option. Staying single or getting him back.

And yet...I couldn't make that determination. Not yet.

The train stopped, and I was pushed against the pole. The doors swept open, and a cold blast of air hit me. I stepped onto the platform.

Adam was Adam. I'd worked side-by-side with him for four years. He always got what he wanted. His decisions ended discussions. He decided which result he wanted, made a plan to achieve the result, adapted in process, and won the game every time. If he decided to live without me, I could either accept his decision or stand in the way and get run over. Move with the flow and stay upright, or resist and fall under the train.

I changed my mind with every breath, going from hope to despair and back to hope again. Heart and mind battled, changed allegiances, declared victory, surrendered, and ambushed each other. By the time I got to Dad's apartment, I was exhausted.

Chapter 10

Dad dealt the cards, skitting them across the kitchen table.

"You want to bid on a trump, peanut?"

"Just flip it."

He turned the top card. Ten of diamonds.

I fanned my cards, plucked out the tricks, and laid them down, melding a nine of diamonds just to get rid of it.

"Do you want to talk about it?" he asked, laying out his own little fans. He leaned his elbow on his oxygen tank. His mask was looped over the valve by the elastic band.

"No."

"Came back early," he said, sliding a card off the top of the stack.

I could tell from the set of his shoulders that he didn't have another move. I took a card.

"I know." I put the queen of spades next to the king for a meld.

"You don't want to talk about it."

"Not yet."

"What happened?"

"I'm not sure. Can we not talk about it? Pick a card."

He took a card, slid it into his fan, moved stuff around. "Okay. You don't want to talk about it. I understand."

"Thank you."

He threw a royal in diamonds. He was killing me already.

"Then I'm going to bring something else up."

"Good." I took a card from the stack. It was completely useless.

"I want to stay in the office." Dad's card wasn't useless apparently. He laid out a fan of four aces. Damn. "Help out. Learn maybe."

"Learn? Dad, please."

He took a card from the stack and laid it on the table with the rest of his hand. I tossed him my cards to count up with his points. I tapped out my score in three seconds while he separated his counters from his nines.

My phone buzzed. I flipped the glass up while Dad counted.

—If you're interested in continuing this conversation, I'd like to meet—

It was Insolent. I decided to ignore it. Take an hour or two. Think about it. I didn't have to decide anything right away, right? I didn't have to jump in bed with the guy today, tomorrow, or ever.

Then it dinged again.

—I have a safe, public place in mind—

"Hundred forty plus ten for the last trick is a hundred fifty," Dad said.

I put the phone back and noted his score.

"I mean it," he continued. "I feel useful again. Not some old codger puttering around the house. Or dragging my tank to the park to feed the pigeons."

He scooped up the cards for a shuffle. He did seem more lively than usual. His eyes were still red from the constant effort to breathe and he was thinner than I liked, but his voice had real intention and force.

"Do you miss cigarettes?" I asked.

"Every damned day." He shuffled nimbly. "Almost as much as I miss your mother. But they were killing me. Life isn't worth much if you're dead." He dealt the cards, flipping a queen of hearts from the stack. "Hearts trump."

"I remember you smoking in the office."

We shifted our cards around.

"That was before you were born," he said.

"I caught you out on the balcony more than once."

"You were little. Now I can't smoke at all in my own building. It helps actually. You go first."

I had a trick of kings. Laying three down was a guarantee of thirty points, but I didn't put it down. "You still want to smoke? After everything it's done to you?"

"The blood wants what the blood wants."

"Ain't that the truth."

What did my blood want? Did it want Adam, or did it want submission?

To my own detriment, I laid the king of hearts next to the queen of hearts, keeping the other kings close to the vest for later, or never. Or tomorrow.

I picked up my phone while Dad made his moves.

—That sounds all right—

Let the queen have her king. The kitchen table could be their tiny kingdom while outside, they broke each other apart.

Chapter 11

DAY TWENTY-THREE

In the daytime, as the night, the Cellar wasn't more than a sealed and locked black doorway in the Meatpacking District. I went around to Horatio, as instructed in the latest text, until I hit a brick arch at the entrance to a narrow, clean alley. A brass plate was bolted to the bricks.

THE GREENS
Members and Guests only

The solid metal gate was open, and I walked past it, heels bucking and slipping on the uneven pavement. The effect of the alley was of something older than me. Older than New York. A place as old as desire.

Insolent knew about Adam. I felt fine manipulating my husband, since it was for his own damn good, but I didn't want to drag someone I didn't know into my personal dramas. Insolent seemed game for the game, but I didn't know how committed he was to winning.

Be at the Greens at 1:20 p.m.
Wear a skirt
White underpants. No garter. Nothing fancy
Take a cab
Do not put a napkin or bag in your lap.
Place your phone on the table, glass up.
Wear a string of pearls.
Sit with your back to the door.

A heavy metal door stood at the end of the alley. On my right, the red brick of the building, and on my left, windows looked onto a winter garden with patches of snow and twisted brown rosebushes. Since there was no roof, the alley was as icy as February. The bitter air stung my bare legs, and my face and hands were red from the cold.

A handsome man in an open wool coat and a shirt unbuttoned at the collar stepped out of the black door.

"Are you the guest of Master Insolent?" he asked.

Kick off the heels.

Run away run away run away.

"Yes."

"Come this way."

He led me through the door into a restaurant enclosed in glass. Cool winter sun drenched the white tablecloths, and the low hum of conversation filled the room. It looked almost normal.

The handsome man didn't grab a menu or ask me where I wanted to sit. He took my coat, gave it to someone who whisked it away, and led me to a four-top table in the center of the room. He pulled out a chair for me. I hooked my bag on the back of it and sat.

No water. No menu. Just me in a room full of Cellar members.

I didn't want to be there. Flat out. I didn't want to do what this stranger told me. It wasn't arousing or fun. I wanted Adam. I wanted Adam to tell me to go to some strange glass-encased restaurant that was hidden behind a building. I wanted to know he would be sitting in the seat across from me, not some guy I'd texted. Some guy I'd never seen before.

Was Insolent here? I glanced from face to face. The customers looked like anyone else, with a twist. Business suits. Dresses. Normal voices. A closer look revealed a few collars, a young man with a T-shirt tight enough to reveal nipple clamps. I could tell who was Dominant by their relaxed posture. The submissives had their hands flat on the table, or were sitting on them. Eyes down. A woman in a carefully tailored pants suit patiently fed her tablemate his melon.

A small white plate was placed in front of me. A card stood in the center in an inverted V.

So it begins.

My phone buzzed. I could see the preview without touching the glass.

> **—Open the card
> and read it to your-
> self—**

As if I needed to be told. Right down to not reading it out loud to a room full of people. Jesus Christ. I was submissive, not stupid.

Annoyance probably wasn't a good way to start. Actually, it was the exact opposite of what I should feel. I was supposed to feel excitement. Trepidation at the very least. This whole experiment was a fail. I was going to leave. This idea sucked.

That being the case, it wouldn't hurt to look at the card. I was curious. I could read it then go.

Pick up your skirt.
Take down your underpants.
Remove them.

Wrap them around your wrist.
Put the crotch out for everyone to see.

I hadn't been doing this long, but I understood the purpose of the command. I was supposed to get turned on by the exposure. I was supposed to feel a thrill at pleasing him. I was being trained to react like a submissive with a happy master. I was supposed to be aroused.

Right?

Nothing about this was arousing. It was either too soon or I wasn't submissive.

I fished a pen out of my bag and wrote on the back of the card.

I'm sorry.
This isn't working for me.

I placed it back on the plate the way I'd found it. I was sorry in my heart that this had failed, but I needed Adam to make my submission work.

As if my thoughts attuned me to the tones in the room, I heard his voice. Far away, nearly lost in the ambient noise in the room, his presence tightened my ribs around my lungs. I turned, scanned the room. I had to turn my head almost all the way around to see him with Charlie and Stefan. Their table was against the back wall, and Adam sat in profile, leaning one elbow on the tabletop as he made a point I couldn't hear. The remnants of lunch and coffee were scattered before him, and even at a table with two Dominants, he was the master of the space.

The sight of him opened the floodgates of arousal that another man hadn't been able to tap into. Stefan spoke, and Charlie looked up, making eye contact with me. I froze, wide-eyed, and whipped my head around.

The card sat on the plate.

What are you going to do?

I turned around again and shook my head slightly at Charlie. I didn't want Adam to know.

Yes, you do.

No, I didn't. But I did. Just not today. Or ever. Or now. What kind of plan was this anyway? I was playing a game I didn't have the intestinal fortitude to win.

Before I turned back to the plate, Adam held up his hand for a waiter, shifting ever so slightly to get his attention. He was going to see me.

Unless I could turn in time.

But he was so beautiful, and the grace of his hand held me.

And as he made the check sign, he saw me.

Shit.

Fight or flight?

His eyes were blue in a world drained of color, and his jaw tightened into angles of fury.

What did he see?

Heels.

Bare legs.

A single card on a plate.

Charlie put his hand on Adam's arm. A calming gesture. It wasn't going to work.

Fight or flight?

Stefan followed their attention right to me, and he leaned back in his chair and crossed his arms. I faced forward.

Fight. It's fight.

I pushed the plate away. The card tipped and dropped, hiding my writing. I could see the Dom's instructions inside.

Pick up your skirt.
Take down your underpants.

Remove them.
Wrap them around your wrist.
Put the crotch out for everyone to see.

I curled my fingers around the hem of my skirt. Looking straight ahead, I pulled it up.

Adam was watching. I felt it. The arousal I'd been missing flooded me. I was tight as a drum when I lifted my bottom to get at my underpants. I wiggled, sliding them down my thighs.

He barked something, and the volume in the room went down a notch.

Too much. It was too much. I had to look. Charlie clutched Adam's arm tightly. My husband was halfway out of his seat. I couldn't hear what they were saying, but I didn't need to. Like a good sub, I faced forward again.

Fight, Diana.

Down my thighs, looser now, past my knees, down my calves, the white cotton underwear dropped, cuffing my ankles together. I reached down, hooked my finger in the fabric, and took my right foot out of its shoe.

"What the hell are you doing?"

His voice. Like a hundred hands on my skin. He'd had the same voice the entire time I knew him, but my reaction to it had changed in Montauk. He could fuck me with that voice.

In the corner of my vision, his hand leaned on the table, fingers flexed against the white cloth, angled in tension. Sky-blue cuff peeking from a navy jacket. Black cufflink with an anchor in silver.

I'd bought him those cufflinks for our first anniversary.

He was my anchor. He was the one who kept me from going adrift.

I'd bought him those fucking cufflinks to express what he meant to me, and he was fucking wearing them to a fucking club and—

Fight.

I got my right foot out of my underwear and wedged it back into the shoe. "I'm letting someone else finish what you started."

I took the underpants from my left ankle. I didn't look at him. All my resistance would have drained from me.

"Who?" he growled.

"What's the difference?" I sat up straight with a handful of underwear.

"Huntress." His tone softened enough for my heart to hear him, but not enough for my head to disregard the warning in his voice.

I didn't like it. Not one bit. I made eye contact with him, making sure not to waver. "Don't call me that unless you want to know what I'm hunting."

He didn't break away from my gaze when he snapped up the card and opened it. From below, I could see my note on the back, but he couldn't.

I coiled the underwear around my wrist. The crotch had been bone dry until I heard Adam's voice across the room. I tucked the edges in tight as Adam tossed the card onto the plate.

"Diana?" Charlie's voice came from the side opposite Adam. He yanked out the empty chair next to me and sat in it. "I'm taking you home."

I expected Adam to interject, but he didn't.

"I'm fine," I said steadily, making sure they all understood that I meant it.

Charlie nodded and got up. "You know where to find me."

"I do. Thank you."

Charlie stopped in front of Adam for a beat, just long enough for them to speak without words. He sent a warning to my husband by doing no more than standing there, leaning one side of his body on a cane. Even though the warning was soundless, Adam nodded as if he heard it.

Charlie trudged off. I barely saw him meet Stefan by the exit.

Adam cocked the chair beside me sideways and threw himself into it, crossing his ankle over his knee and leaning one arm on the table. "So."

"Buttons. Sew buttons. You were supposed to be in a meeting. You have to go."

"Why?"

"Someone's coming."

"Yeah. I was curious about that. Those are really nice heels by the way. No stockings. It's thirty-five degrees. The streets are still icy, and here you are. Frostbite and a broken ankle waiting to happen."

"You can't get frostbite at thirty-five degrees."

"What are you hunting, Diana?"

"What?"

"You said you were hunting something. Someone, maybe? Tell me."

You.

"Someone to help me finish what you started."

I'm hunting you.

He kept his face on mine. He was implacable. Still as deep water.

I continued. "I know that's not what you wanted or intended, but it doesn't matter what you want. You dug up a part of me I need to know. And I'm sorry you have to watch it happen, but this is the only reputable club in the city. So you're going to have to move to the one in Newark or deal with seeing me sometimes."

"I won't sign off on you being a member. As long as there's breath in my body. That's not going to change."

"Your illusion of control is charming."

He attacked, pushing himself forward as if he was capable of biting off my head. "I don't have any illusions. Not since the morning I found a note on the counter. Remember it?"

"I do," I said low in my throat. Probably the least submissive voice on the sound spectrum. "I remember that day. And the weeks after it when you took me away to degrade me so you wouldn't love me anymore. Then you cut me loose just when I knew I loved you. Way to take control. sir."

I said *sir* as if it were the most cutting insult I could muster, and it was. He didn't flinch. Not exactly. His upper lip tightened and his hand stopped fidgeting with the surface of the table. Yeah, I'd gotten to him.

I expected him to answer quickly with some equally cutting tone, but he didn't. He looked at his watch.

"What time is he coming?" he asked, flicking his hand at the empty chair across from me.

"Ten minutes ago."

Adam nodded. "Waiting's a thing. How long you'll stand for it, how still you are, how you react." He laid his palm on my wrist. "How long you'll sit here with your underpants bracelet."

"Fuck you," I whispered.

"Damp," he said, using his thumb to stretch the cotton crotch thin. "When did they get that way?"

"When I heard your voice." I shut down tears. I didn't want his heart to soften. I didn't want pity. I'd been strong for this entire conversation, and I wouldn't ruin it with tears.

"What if I trained you? Just until the end of the contract."

"Too late."

"Why?"

My phone buzzed and lit up.

—Patient girl. There's a car outside—

Adam must have seen it. He saw everything. He was an information-seeking missile. But you wouldn't know he'd read it from the way he continued the conversation.

"I know exactly what you need. Let me do it. It's a safest way."

Yes would have been the easiest word in the dictionary. He was offering what I wanted. Him.

"I have to go." I picked up my phone and my bag. "And no. You're not safe. Nothing about you is safe."

I walked out with my head high. He was behind me. I felt his presence and heard his footsteps echo mine in the stone alley.

A black limo waited by the curb. A man in a black coat and a felt hat stood by the closed door with his hands folded in front of him. From his posture and manner, it was obvious he wasn't the Dom. He was the driver.

"I'm the only safe one," Adam said from behind me. "And you owe me two weeks."

I spun on him. "You nullified that agreement."

"Kind of. Yes. No. Yes, I did. But you wanted to finish."

I crossed my arms. "What are the terms?"

"The loft is a safe shared space. We play there. You'll have to rethink your redlines. But I'm going to push them hard."

"And sex?"

"No sex."

It wasn't optimum, but I considered it for a second. I could have said maybe, or even yes, but before I could decide one way or the other, he spoke up.

"And no club. I don't want you in the Cellar."

I remembered what he'd said when he found Stefan's note. He didn't want me to be part of that world. The piece of love he held for me would be destroyed by that.

He might believe that nonsense. I didn't.

"Thank you for your kind offer," I said. "But fuck you."

I turned to the limo, and he grabbed my arm.

"Do not get in that car."

"I'm fed up with the mixed messages. Fed. Up."

"Then we can talk about it."

Had he always been this much of an asshole? Even when I left him, I didn't imagine he could be this manipulative and blind to his own motivations.

Yet I loved this asshole on the sidewalk more than I loved the nice guy I'd shared a bed with.

"Tomorrow," I said.

"Now. Don't make me tell you again not to get in that car."

"Let go of me." I spoke with such gravity, I felt the words lower in my throat.

He clenched his jaw but let my arm go. "This is a mistake."

His comment wasn't worth an answer. When I stepped toward the car, the driver opened the door, and I got in without looking back. The door shut with finality, and I faced forward. I didn't want to see him. I didn't want to know what he did or if he came to the window to tell me how much of a mistake I was making.

When the driver pulled away, I hit the intercom.

"Hello," I said.

"Hello, ma'am."

"Would you take me home, please? Crosby and Prince?"

"Sure thing."

I shut the intercom and rubbed my eyes. My panties were still around my wrist. I yanked them off and stuffed them in my bag. I couldn't have felt less sexy. I only felt a deep, twisting pain.

Chapter 12

DAY TWENTY-FOUR

I hadn't let myself consider what would have happened if I'd done it differently. If I'd sat him down and explained that I was unhappy. If we'd gone to counseling. Opened up communication. Maybe I would have broken through to him.

More likely he would have retreated further, burying his inner Dominant under another few layers of shit, and tried to be the perfect man for me. At least, the man I thought I wanted. No matter how I twisted it in my mind, my only options were this miserable empty bed in a cavernous empty loft with uncertainty in my future and past.

Stick to the plan.

I could live like this for another two weeks. That was my cliff. Once I was midair I had to either fly or hit the ground in a mess of blood and bone.

Only his love could stop my trajectory. I was submitting to him in ways he didn't know and I didn't even understand.

Kayti caught me at the receptionist's desk, green eyes wide with the sheer import of what she was about to say. "He's in your office."

"Who?" As if I didn't know. As if I should have been the least surprised.

"Adam," she whispered.

"Thank you," I said. "Hold my calls."

"Should I cancel your ten-thirty?"

It was nine thirty. One hour. "No. I can make that."

The ten-thirty meeting was a perfect excuse to keep my clothes on my body and my knees off the floor.

I strode into my office, letting the door click behind me. Adam stood with his back to the window, hands in his pockets, all dressed up in like a god in a suit.

"What?" I said. "Didn't hear me yesterday?"

"How was it? Your session with what's-his-name?"

"Why?"

"I want to know. I'm your first Dom. It's my job to make sure you're taken care of."

"I don't know if I believe that."

"You don't have to. I see it as my job. That's the end of it."

I crossed my arms and leaned on my desk. I needed more than posture to protect me from him, but my arms and a desk were all I had. "Do you want the gory details?"

He went to the side of the desk chair, two feet closer to me and out of the glare of the morning sun. Close enough for me to see that he hadn't slept. Close enough to smell his cologne and hear the undertone of worry in his voice.

"I want it any way you're willing to tell it," he said.

My throat went dry. He hadn't said anything unexpected or piercing, but I realized my plans were detouring. If we hadn't been honest with each other before the split because of the things we hadn't said, a tidy obfuscation now wouldn't be the right answer.

"I didn't go," I said. "I went home. Not that it's any of your business."

I hadn't realized how tense he was, but his body relaxed noticeably and his smile was one of release.

Which annoyed me. I'd given him what he wanted and he hadn't earned it. Not even a little.

"Get out," I said. "Just go."

"Diana, listen, I—"

"Are you going to tell me you love me?"

"No."

"Then get the fuck out!" I slammed a book on the desk and took inventory of anything on it that I could throw, ready to go full tantrum. "Get—"

Like a wind, he crossed the distance between us. One hand behind my head, the other over my mouth. "Don't yell."

"—uck oo—"

"Your safe word is pinochle."

He pushed his body against me, and I was flooded with desire. We were playing now. I hadn't intended it, but we were in the game. I groaned at the thought, discipline flying out the window.

"I was waiting for you to lie about where you went, and you didn't. You told the truth. I'm going to reward you. Do you want that?" His voice was laced with promise.

Yeah. I wanted whatever he had in mind.

I nodded behind his hand. He moved it away.

"How did you know?" I asked.

"What did you think? I was going to let you drive away and not follow you?" In one motion, he pulled my shirt and bra up, exposing my breasts.

"Why? Why did you follow if you don't care? I don't understand what you want."

"I never said I didn't care. Look at you," he said. "So tough. But your breathing is shallow and your nipples are hard."

"You're leading me on," I said. "You know I love you."

"Maybe you don't." He stepped back. "Maybe you think you do. Pull your skirt up."

I was powerless against him. I wanted him. I wanted to obey him. What he was doing was terrible, and I knew it. Yet my body rushed and tingled at his command.

I pulled up my skirt.

"Get on the desk."

When I was sitting on the desk, he grabbed my ankles, pulling them up and out until I fell backward onto my hands. He jerked my knees open so he could see my soaked underwear.

"I realized yesterday that you couldn't go back." He opened my desk drawer and got out a pair of scissors. "There's no more vanilla Diana."

He hooked his finger on the crotch of my panties and snipped them open with the scissors.

"I won't miss her," he said, thrusting two fingers deep inside me before I could feel anything about what he said. "But I'm responsible for who she became. Probably the most desirable submissive in the city." He ran his fingers along my front wall, circling the hard bundle of nerves he always knew where to find. "And the worst trained. Do you want to come?"

"Yes, sir."

"The answer is, 'If it pleases you.'"

"If it pleases you," I gasped.

"It doesn't." He took his fingers out and laid them on my lower lip. "Clean these off." He shoved them in my mouth, and I sucked my taste off them. "I need to teach you what to expect from a Dom and show you how you deserve to be treated." He removed his fingers. "Now what do you say?"

I didn't know the answer. I just looked at him with my tits and wet cunt open for him, wondering how to please this godly creature.

"You say, 'Thank you.'"

"Thank you."

"Good girl. Now." He rummaged around my drawer. "How do you find anything in here?"

He plucked out two silver paper clips and what looked like a credit card but was a membership to some forgotten store.

He pulled a nipple taut and pinned the paper clip to it. "You're going to repeat after me." He clipped the other. The pain spoke directly to my pleasure. "Then you can come."

"This is a reward?" I squeaked.

He slapped me between the legs with the card. I had to bite back a scream. It hurt like the best hurt. Like the ugliest package under the tree that exploded into sparkles and song when opened.

"The reward is, I'm going to train you. Period." He slapped between my legs harder. I clenched my jaw. "This is not negotiable."

"Yes."

"Yes?"

Slap.

"Yes, sir."

He tapped my clit with the card just a little. I was on the edge of ecstasy. I didn't care if he loved me. Didn't care if I got hurt. I wanted this drug right now, for as long as I could get it.

"Repeat after me. 'You own me.'"

Tap. Tap.

"You own me."

"My body is your toy."

Slap.

"My body, oh God. My body is your toy."

"Until the end of our term." He drew the edge of the card over the length of my clit.

"Until... God. Until the end... oh..."

"Diana," he said, his voice deep, rough, yet so sincere I had to look at him. "You're beautiful like this. You're perfect. I want to fuck the breath out of you. I want to hurt you. Mark you. I want you to beg me to stop and love it when I don't." His fingers slid into me again.

"What pleases you." I couldn't do more than squeak.

"Don't come." He reached behind me and swiped things off the desk. "Lie back and hold your legs open."

I leaned back and put my hands behind my knees. He put his slick fingers in my ass, deep.

Looking at my cringing face, he said, "Does it hurt?"

"Yes."

"What do you say?"

"Thank you?"

"That's right." With his other hand, he plucked the paper clips off my nipples and watched me closely.

I knew what was coming, and I knew he had it under control. I trusted him with my body if not my heart. I trusted him with my pain. The stinging came a second later. He bent away from me, digging his fingers in my ass and putting his tongue on my throbbing clit. When he sucked it gently, he put his other hand over my mouth.

Good thing. Because I was lost, and without that hand, my cries as the burning pain turned into a mind-bending orgasm would have brought in the whole office.

"Stop!" I gasped behind his hand.

He heard me. I knew he did, but he ignored me, licking and sucking, stretching my ass, bringing me to orgasm again until I couldn't breathe and my cries dissolved into tears.

I gulped for air when he stopped and removed his fingers. He went into my bathroom. The water ran. I got up on my elbows when he returned with two hot cloth towels.

"I'm fine," I said, but he picked me up and carried me to the couch.

"I know you're fine." He wiped my face, pressing the heat into my tear ducts. "I'm showing you how you should be treated."

He put a towel on my sore nipples. The warmth soothed them. Then he wiped between my legs. I lay back and enjoyed it, closing my eyes against the hard office fluorescents.

"You're going to make it worse," I said. "Even if we don't have sex. Real sex."

"You may hate me when it's done."

"I can love you and hate you at the same time, you know."

A short laugh of recognition escaped him. He must have felt the same when I left him. He might have even felt the same leaning on the couch in my office, shaking his watch down his wrist.

"What time is it?" I asked.

"Ten."

I shot up, bursting out of my post-orgasmic haze like a diver cutting into cold water. "I have to go. *You* have to go." I wiggled out of my shredded underpants and pulled my skirt down. "Shoo."

"Where are you going?"

I pulled my shirt and bra back over my breasts. "Meeting."

His head tilted ever so slightly and his jaw tightened just enough. I had no intention of telling him where I was going or why. I didn't want him to help or hinder the cause.

"I'm going uptown," he said. "We can share a cab."

"No, thanks." I stood. The skirt was long enough to cover the fact that I wasn't wearing underpants. I smoothed it down, and he took my hand.

"You can't go out like that."

"Yes, I can."

"I forbid it."

"Really?"

"Do you want me to train you or not? This..." He waved at me from knees to waist. "This falls under my oversight. You have to put something on under that skirt."

"You shredded my underwear, first of all. So it's your fault. And second, we haven't negotiated the terms of my training." I slung my bag on my shoulder. "This isn't Montauk. I have plenty of options."

He put up his finger and pointed right into me. "You want me to be the one to train you and you know it."

I did know it. I knew it better than he did. But I wasn't going to be a passive recipient of his demands, and I wasn't just going to let him have full control of my future. The next two weeks were going to be his training as well as mine. He just didn't know it yet.

I put my coat over my arm. "Send me the terms."

Before he could answer, I walked out with my head high and tossed my sliced underpants into the office garbage pail.

Chapter 13

DAY TWENTY-FOUR

He didn't follow me out, as far as I could see, though he was probably tracking my phone the same way I'd tracked his. I could remove myself from the list of devices on the account, but that would change the rules.

Once I got into the cab to downtown, I shut off my phone. That should make him fucking crazy. I felt pretty satisfied with myself, then sad we'd come to this impasse. I wasn't sure this was any better than a long, ugly divorce. We were playing a difficult and intense game with unwritten rules. One we could both lose.

I missed Manhattan Adam. The man who loved me beyond all sense. The guy I didn't love but whose company I enjoyed. His good sense, his easy humor, his daily, unintentional beauty gracing the loft and the office. The daily catching up, the quick exchange of advice about important and mundane things. I'd never felt so utterly alone as I did on that cab ride.

Manhattan Adam was my best friend, and I missed him.

The cab dropped me at Metropolis. Stefan sat at a two-seat table by the window, drawing in a black pad. He closed it when he saw me and pulled out my chair like a perfect gentleman. I didn't know if the sadism belied the courtesy or the courtesy cleansed the sadism.

"I ordered for you," he said with his Scandinavian accent. "I hope this is all right?"

"I understand it's standard Dominant behavior." I said it with a smile, so he seemed to take no offense.

"Thank you for meeting me. I wasn't sure you got the note I left."

I'd gotten the note. *We need to talk.* It had tipped Adam into his fear that I was inside a world that had broken him, even as he never admitted to being broken.

"Adam found it."

"Was it a problem? I meant nothing by it."

"Was that the first thing you meant nothing by?"

"Regarding you?" He shrugged. "Could be. I didn't know he was so possessive with you."

"I'm his wife."

Soon to be ex-wife.

"All right, Mrs. Steinbeck." He smirked, undaunted, unflappable. "I understand. But I come from a place where we talk about fucking very candidly. Frankly, I would have loved to fuck you. If I had permission, of course. I find you beautiful and interesting." He put his napkin in his lap. "I'm not trying to seduce you."

"You're speaking frankly."

"Exactly." He leaned back to let the waiter put plates in front of us. He'd ordered me a pancetta tartine with goat cheese that looked wonderful.

"And how does Serena feel about you thinking another woman is beautiful and interesting?"

"Usually she would want to know the woman and watch me fuck her." He pulled the toothpick out of his turkey sandwich and laid it on the side of his plate. "It's worked very well for us, this arrangement. You and yours don't have the same. I understand, of course. But it wasn't clear in the beginning."

I focused on my tartine, trying to wrangle crumbs and pancetta that didn't break apart easily. I had so much to learn about Adam's world and my own, where they intersected and what I was comfortable with. I wished he was there to help me with it.

My food went down in a lump. Wishes weren't an alternate reality of a life not lived. They were tricks of the mind, fooling us into believing we had control.

"Is that what you wanted to talk to me about? In the note you left?"

"Yes and no." He sipped his water, considered it, then me. I should have been uncomfortable, but I wasn't. "I wanted to continue our conversation, but Serena and I hit a wall on the way home. Figuratively, of course."

"No seat belts required?"

"My heart needed crash gear."

I let out a short, surprised *huh* that I didn't mean. He raised an eyebrow. No beating around the bush now.

"I thought you didn't have a heart at all," I said.

"Ouch."

"I'm sorry. It doesn't look like love. Not..."

Not when you do it that way. Not when it's violent and demanding. Not when you're playing with her like she's an object.

Of course. That was what Adam was reacting to on some level. He should have known better, but the fact was, he didn't. He couldn't separate the violence of his dominance from the love it took to create it.

"Diana?"

"I remember what we were talking about. On the beach. You wanted insight into Serena. She was drifting away the way I drifted away, right? You wanted to ask me things you'd ask her."

"Close enough."

"I'll tell you what I think. But I want you to do something for me." My thoughts were still unformed. I had disconnected words for my feelings.

Risk.

Commit.

Me.

Separate.

Whole.

"Let's hear it," Stefan said.

"Sponsor me for the club."

"Your Dominant is supposed to ask."

"I know, and he will. Or he might. I don't know. He's not even..." *mine.* "Whatever. I need three members, and if you help with the application, I'll get a head start."

"What are you playing at, Mrs. Steinbeck?"

I couldn't answer that because I was sure the game didn't have a name. "Serena. Commit to her. Commit to her alone. No sharing. No group... whatever it is. Just her. See if that changes anything."

"It won't."

"How are you so sure?"

"She demands more every time. She is limitless."

He was in awe of her, that much was clear. What had scared Adam away made Stefan worship her. The ability to engage in sex so rough it looked and felt like rape had broken Adam's confidence in his judgment. What she'd asked him to do had driven him to not only marry a vanilla woman, but keep his relationship so kink-free, he could convince himself he was a changed man.

"Have you reached your limit?"

He didn't answer. He just pushed his food around until he gathered a forkful. "I do like you." He put the food in his mouth, chewed, and swallowed. "You are, as they say, a real pistol."

"She wants my husband. She told me as much. I'm invested in keeping you two together."

"The feeling is mutual."

"Sponsor me, and I'll talk to her."

His face betrayed nothing but doubt. His body told another story. He leaned forward, elbows on the table as if getting closer to me gave him hope.

"What could you say? She's willful. She won't just take advice from you. Nothing personal, of course."

"No offense taken. And I have no intention of giving her advice."

"She won't respond to threats."

"Stefan. Come on. Threats don't work with anyone. Not even masochists."

He smiled from his perfect white teeth to his sparkling, devilish eyes. "At least not from other masochists."

"Just trust me."

"What's your plan then?"

"Tell her the truth," I said.

"I like this plan."

"Will you sponsor me? Or do you need to see if I'm successful first?"

"I will honor the spirit of the favor. Eat now, would you? Adam will get on my case for not taking good care of you."

We finished lunch while making small talk about Sweden, the endless night, New York snow, and the beauty of Montauk in the winter.

He walked me to a cab. "I want to apologize. For the note. If I'd known he'd act like a child, I wouldn't have left it."

"Don't worry about it. If it wasn't that, it would have been something else."

He kissed my cheek and closed the door. Once the cab got moving, I turned on my phone.

If it hadn't been for the note, would things have been different? Would we have stayed together? He'd come home from the city ready to settle into a life with me. Had that one thing not happened...

No.

I wasn't stupid. If it hadn't been that, it would have been something else. A request to go to the club. A call at an inopportune time. Anything. Adam wasn't ready to love submissive Diana, and he would have found a way to run just as I would have found a way to chase.

The phone connected to cellular. Adam's half-hour-old texts buzzed.

—Three guidelines. All other agreements in place, including end date—

—No other Dominants —

—You are not to go to the Cellar—

—You're at my command 24 hours a day unless you're working—

I sent mine without preamble, negotiation, or agreement.

—No sharing—

—I stay in the loft—

—Tell me everything. No lying. No leaving stuff out—

I'd gone from pushing for four redlines to having only two that mattered.

My first was non-negotiable. Whether he thought he loved me or not, letting other people into our relationship wouldn't help my cause. The second was me carving space for myself. And the third was the point of the whole thing. Without it, we had no chance.

—Agreed—

                                    —Agreed—

And thus, he agreed to let me hope that I could fix the mess I'd made.

Chapter 14

DAY TWENTY-FOUR

I worked the rest of the afternoon and walked home after the sun set. The snow had almost finished melting, and the sound of cars passing and the rumble of the subway underground was cut with water dripping from rooftops and flowing through the street.

I was bone-tired. I could fall asleep to the rippling water or the car alarm. I was going to eat ice cream and watch back-to-back episodes of *Law & Order* until I couldn't keep my eyes open.

I got the mail, took the elevator, walked down the hall until I got to the orange door of our... *my* loft.

A package sat in front of it. Four inches square. Brown paper tucked neatly around the edges. An envelope with the words *Little Huntress* printed on it rested on top.

Taking the box inside, I got my jacket off and barely set it on the hook before I ripped open the envelope. I stood in the foyer in my wet boots with the package tucked under my arm and the envelope on the floor.

Diana
You begin tonight.
Do not open this package now. Open it when I tell you.

I could hear his bossy voice in my head and fell into a calm, yet excited obedience. That voice was pure pleasure to obey.

Tonight you will lie down to sleep at nine p.m.

I glanced at the clock. It was six forty-five. Plenty of time.

Until then, you will not watch television or look at the computer. No screens. No books. No phone calls. No magazines. You may write in your journal, eat, and take care of the house. I own your boredom.
You will take your clothes off as soon as you lock the door. Turn the heat up to eighty-two. Shower. Remain naked for the rest of the night. I own your nudity.
Lie down on the floor at the foot of the bed at nine p.m., no sooner or later. You will sleep there. You may lie on the rug or the floor. I own your comfort.
Don't touch yourself. I own your pleasure.
Don't look in the box. I mean it. I own your curiosity.

Jesus.

His instructions were hard and cold, yet I tingled for them. Each claim of ownership was sexier than the last. Each demand made me wet to please him.

I flipped the card.

I intend to come and go as I please, but I don't own the loft. You have control over it. If you need to set a limit, set it now. If I don't hear from you, I'll take it

as permission to enter.
I'll be in touch.
—A

Would he enter? And when?

It didn't matter. I was doing this all the way. He could come and go as if he owned my space as well as my boredom, my nudity, my pleasure, and my curiosity.

I stripped down in a state of joy, snapping the curtains closed while fully nude. Let the people in the department store across the street get a good look before I shut them out. My plan was incomplete and my life was a mess, but inside the loft, naked from head to toe, every inch of my skin was alive. My feet felt the woolen texture of the rug and the creaky bounce of the floor. My nipples felt the brush of my arm when I got a plate from the cabinet.

My lips slid against the fork, newly awakened by the fact that they weren't acting out of habit or survival, but for him. Because he'd told me to, and it pleased him.

My shower had a purpose, the towel drying me had a resolve. Each movement was a scene in a larger play that Adam directed. I was complete as long as I was doing what he asked me to do. I was free to feel my own body in space.

The feeling of contentment and peace remained at eight o'clock, but I had an hour to go before sleep and nothing to fill it with.

And the box started to weigh on me.

I shook it, but it made no sound. I peeled the folds back to see how they were fastened. Just tape. Tiny dots of double-stick. I'd never get it back the way it was.

You could...

I put the box in the cabinet under the kitchen sink and slapped the door closed.

What was in that damned box?

I took it out of the cabinet. Shook it again.

Was he above leaving me an empty box just to test me? No, he was not, but there was definitely something inside. It had weight.

I put the box to my nose and got a slight whiff of him. A little leather. A bite of something I could never identify. I dropped the box and picked up the note, pressing my nose to it.

Licorice.

That was it.

I went to his bedroom closet. It had been mostly emptied, but once I threw the doors open and stepped in, he surrounded me. Leather and licorice. I opened the drawers, filling every corner of the space with him.

So good. So very good.

I got on my knees and crouched with my cheek to the floor, breathing deeply. I closed my eyes and let him seep inside me.

I loved him. I couldn't speak about the future or the past with him, but in that closet, on my knees, I loved him and it was enough.

The throb between my legs was a growing ache as the minutes passed. I rolled onto my bottom, leaned my hands against the floor, and spread my legs for the empty pole and wire hangers he used to have his clothes on.

How was I supposed to get through the night without touching myself?

I put my head back, surrendering to the mundane difficulties he'd set for me, and spotted something on the top shelf.

Bounding up, I grabbed it.

Packing tape.

I could use that.

The wrapped box sat on the kitchen counter. I picked the edge off the packing tape and carefully unstuck a good section. Sticking it to the top of the box, I spiraled the roll of tape around, letting it scream when I moved it, until the box was a cellophane-wrapped mummy. It would take me so long to get it out that I'd have time to stop myself.

Perfect.

Just to be sure it wasn't staring me in my face, I tossed the entire thing into the freezer.

That was that.

I had thirty minutes.

I checked on the box a few more times. Dusted a few shelves while stark naked. Vacuumed. Brushed my teeth.

By the time I shut off the lights and curled up on the floor at the end of the bed, I was exhausted and completely obsessed with my husband.

I wondered if that had been his plan the entire time, then fell asleep.

Chapter 15

In the night, he came.

In the dark, he whispered.

You are beautiful.

You are perfect.

You please me so much.

He put his lips on my fingers, tasting them, and I sighed out of a dream.

I'm going to show you how to live.

I'm going to make sure you're safe.

I'm going to teach you how to be happy.

He picked me up, put me on the bed, and covered me.

I breathed my gratitude and fell asleep with the shape of his kiss burned into my cheek.

Chapter 16

DAY TWENTY-FIVE

When I woke up, the thermostat had been turned down to something less tropical and my robe had been left on the edge of the bed. I put it on. The gunk was still in my eyes when I came into the kitchen. I was alone in the loft, but his smell was everywhere. He'd come to me in the night, said nice things I barely remembered, made sure I hadn't touched myself, and slipped away.

He'd set a robin's-egg-blue box on the counter at an exact right angle to the edge, and the flower on top of it was a surprise. Not a blood-red rose or an exotic lily.

A dandelion.

Where had he found a dandelion in winter?

The square box was still wrapped in packing tape, but it was on a dish that had collected a puddle of condensation from the freezer. A note lay on top.

> *Huntress—*
> *For the next two weeks, you are to have Kayti send me your work appoint-*

ments. Outside of those, I own your time.

Open the blue box. Wear what's inside all day.

Good job wrapping the brown box. It's impenetrable against your curiosity.

Carry it with you.

I'll summon you later.

Be ready.

—Adam

PS: Do what you want with the dandelion.

The dandelion was normal in every way. His grandmother, a second-generation Italian, had eaten dandelion salads made with leaves she pulled from the yard, right down to the flowers and the stems with their milky sap. I couldn't see how that connected with me, but the effort involved in finding a dandelion in winter wasn't easily dismissed. He'd left me a puzzle to figure out.

Slowly, because there was no reason to rush the sensual pleasures of a box that particular shade of blue, I undid the white ribbon that held it closed.

I opened it.

Inside was a pearl choker six strands high, held in place with diamond-studded rows. I went to the hall mirror. The robe was high on my neck, so I ripped it off and let it fall so I could put on the choker.

A long chain with a little ruby on the end came from the clasp, and once I had it fastened, I tried to look down at the gem and couldn't. The pearl rows were high, and the bars that held them held up my chin. It didn't *look* uncomfortable. On the contrary, I looked long-necked and proud, even with my hair in a nest of sleep.

He'd said he was going to show me how I should be treated as a submissive.

This wasn't what I'd expected.

I didn't expect to feel so beautiful.

What could I wear with it? Nothing too sexy, but nothing too plain. I couldn't wait to get dressed. I couldn't wait to start the day.

He's training you to live without him.

Yes, yes, I said to myself as I wrapped the dandelion in waxed paper and pressed it between the pages of a dictionary, he was doing exactly that. And I was going to train him to love me again.

Chapter 17

I wore a white shirt open two buttons and a grey skirt that ended below the knee. I wore white lace garter and stockings under my clothes. I regretted the high heels. I couldn't comfortably look down as I walked down the street to work, so I had to be slow and careful. I had to feel each step, and with every crack in the pavement, every time I couldn't comfortably look down, every time I felt the weight of the extra box in my bag, every moment I felt a few inches taller, I thought of him.

This was a devil of a way to live.

Serena's agent texted me as I was on the way upstairs. I could see the supermodel on set at eleven o'clock. I had fifteen minutes.

Kayti caught me as soon as I got in.

"Oh my god," she said, putting her hand on her throat. "That's gorgeous."

"Thank you."

"Did he give you that? Or..." She dropped the volume of her voice. "You didn't find someone else already, did—?"

"No. It's from him."

She seemed delighted. "Is the divorce off?"

"No."

"Damn."

I went into my office, narrowly avoided crashing into the couch that had always been there because I couldn't look down, and I put my bag on the desk. "Did you send Adam my schedule?"

Kayti closed the door behind me.

"Add an eleven a.m. with..." Who? I demanded honesty from him but wasn't ready to give it. At least not on the schedule. Not at all. No. I couldn't tell him I was trying to wrangle my way into the club. But I had to. It would be great if I could decide one thing at a time. "Just block out eleven to eleven thirty."

"Okay. So, uh... if the divorce is on...?"

"It's complicated. Is my father in yet?"

"He came in then put a bunch of work in a bag and split. He swore he wasn't sick but..." She finished the sentence with a facial expression that relieved her of saying my father was lying.

I almost said, "Sick? Again?" but stopped myself. My opinion of my father's health was irrelevant, but I could turn this to my advantage. Two birds, one stone.

"I'm going to see him at noon, so just block me out until two. Resend the schedule and tell Adam he owns me after two."

She had no idea how literal I was being.

Chapter 18

Fourteen floors above the street, the roof had been transformed into a garden with a patio and a small greenhouse. The chairs had been pushed to one side so the changing booth could be set up, and the wrought-iron table had been repurposed into a makeup station. A forest of white umbrellas on stands surrounded the scene.

Serena stood on the edge of the roof with her legs spread and her hands on her hips while a photographer with a thick Italian accent ordered her to move a little *zis* way or a little bit *zat*. Huge fans blew her dress between her long legs, and her hair splayed out like a wall of vines.

"Back! Lean back!"

She did, just a little, and collapsed over the edge.

I screamed. Everyone looked at me as if I was a crazy person in a courtroom. The fans slowed and the flashing stopped. A man leaned over the edge of the roof, holding out his hand, and Serena climbed back up with a shoe in one hand.

"*Perfetto!*" shouted the photographer. "*Sirty minote!*"

Another guy in a tight Y-shirt showed up to help Serena back onto solid ground. Once she had both shoes off, she came right to me.

"Aren't you cute?" she said, not unkindly. Her face was caked in makeup. It looked awful and unnecessary.

"I didn't know there was a net."

"I mean with your collar."

Maybe it had been said unkindly. Maybe I was just being naïve and stupid to think she'd have anything nice to say. Good thing the choker kept my head high.

"Is it a bad time?" I asked. "We can do this tomorrow."

"No, no." She waved me to the changing tent. "I'm going to Tel Aviv for two weeks."

She pushed the flap open for me. Inside, designer clothes twisted on the floor and draped from hangers. Two women, one middle-aged, one in her twenties, discussed a belt. Serena pulled off the white dress and tossed it aside. She wore nothing underneath. Her body was a song to the perfection of the female form.

"Sit if you want." She indicated a white folding chair.

"I'm good."

She threw the dress on it. "Ruby?"

The younger woman looked up. "Yeah?"

"Can I have five minutes?"

They left us alone. Serena didn't reach for a robe or any kind of covering. She just stood fully clothed in no more than her name and her beauty.

"We've been here since five in the morning without a break." She rolled her eyes.

"We never talked," I said. "I never accepted your apology."

"Stefan made me do it."

"Oh, then—"

"It was sincere," she said. "But I wanted to do it in my own way. Stefan turned everything into a game. It was exhausting."

"He said you guys split up."

"Yes." Her hand drifted across the sleeve of a flowing teal jacket. "Enough is enough." She pulled her hand back and crossed her arms. "I've come to see there are better things out there. I've been eating fruit I don't like because I was too afraid to reach for the apple."

She played with a button on the canvas floor, flipping it with her toe. I realized I wasn't the one who should tell her about changing tastes or the limitations of a fruit metaphor when living, breathing, changing people were involved.

"And you found an apple already?" I shouldn't have been surprised. She'd won the genetic lottery. Her world was littered with apples.

"I just had to reach for it." She kicked the button away. "So. How did you like your trip into our world? Short but sweet? You seemed to be enjoying yourself." She smirked. Or I was imagining it. "You left early."

"Yeah. We had to." I had nothing else to say, but I felt like there should be more. My face probably expressed my search for a feasible response.

"You don't need to tell me why. I told you. He can't love a sub. Don't worry. Plenty of them are capable. Or you'll decide to do without love. But you'll be all right." Serena put her hand on my arm and squeezed it. The gesture could only be decoded one way. Sympathy.

I took a deep breath, laying out the plans I'd made in my mind, and threw them all in the trash. "I came to ask you for a favor."

She put her hands on her hips. It was impossible to not look at her body. I found myself casting my eyes down.

"Go ahead."

"I need three people to sponsor me for membership into the Cellar."

"Do you?"

"That's the rule."

"No, I mean, do you really want that?" she asked.

"What do you mean?"

"If he can't love you now, once you're a member and he sees you there? That's not going to fix it."

I knew that as well as she did, and I feared it. If I didn't get him back, my sexual life was going to get very complicated and very messy. But I wasn't going back to vanilla, and I wouldn't let him. Not with me, at least.

And not with her. Never with her.

That was it. My opening.

I thought I'd pitch her Stefan. Tell her how forlorn he was. But no. She didn't want forlorn. She wanted to be beaten under a bridge.

"We may fix it. We may not." I shrugged. "He needs the sweet as much as the kinky. So we'll see."

Her bee-stung lips parted and her perfectly arched eyebrows went up a fraction of an inch. Surprise.

I'd been right. She didn't want him for sweet. Maybe Stefan was too much and she thought Adam was a notch or two more manageable. But Adam said she hadn't gotten aroused for gentle sex. I didn't think my statement would stop her from chasing him, but it would plant a doubt in her mind. That was all I needed.

And I needed to assert myself.

I probably didn't. But I had to.

"When I knocked my head, I was awake. I heard you, and I remember. You're after my husband. Thank you for being honest with me. Now let me be honest with you. You're probably the most beautiful woman I've ever met. You're intelligent, and you don't have any shame. I have no idea why you're so fucking insecure."

I was a good five inches shorter than Serena. I was softer and riddled with aesthetic imperfections, but when our stares locked, it didn't matter. I had the upper hand. Adam was my husband. I knew him. He was mine.

She wouldn't sponsor me. She wouldn't bring me into the world she shared with him. A world that I couldn't access without him. Fine. Let it be then.

Ruby poked her head in. "Can we come back?"

Serena waved them in. "I'm sorry. These ladies need me. We can talk when I get back. I think we can teach each other a lot."

"Yeah," I said. "I think so."

She was set upon by the two stylists, and I backed out of the tent.

She'd said nothing I could pin down. Admitted nothing and threatened nothing.

Just had to reach for the apple.

Could something have happened already? Had I lost a battle I'd slept through?

The sun had moved the tiniest bit, but it was enough to send the set into a frenzy of moved scrims and recalibrated light. Men and women in black T-shirts carried reflectors, floods, light meters, shouting numbers and pointing at the sky.

I detoured around them, coming up against the greenhouse. I looked inside as I passed it. Mostly orchids, and a long bed of wheatgrass that was probably sold to a local health food store.

I stopped, because the wheatgrass had taken on a few weeds and, against all odds, they'd flowered.

Dandelions.

Chapter 19

I was on 57th Street at midday in high heels and a collar. It was cold as hell, and I felt exposed to more than the elements. Exposed by what, I didn't know. By the insecurity I'd accused Serena of.

Dad's texts speared that exposure, getting right in the crack in my armor, puncturing me where I was weak.

—Guy came with paperwork for Adam. I opened it. Sorry. Probate closed on a property in South Brooklyn—

—I'm home the rest of the day. Kayti taught me how to use the internet. Should I have it couriered to him?—

Fuck this. There was only one reason Dad would go into the office and just turn around and go home. I might be losing my husband to a supermodel. I wasn't losing my company or my father.

"Dad?" I said into the phone.

"Peanut." His breath rattled like an old train.

"I'll give it to him."

"I left it on your desk."

"I was going to come by and tell you this, but I can't. Don't talk. I'm taking care of the company. You can't work anymore."

He coughed, and I cringed at the sound.

"I'm not digging ditches," he said. "I sit on my ass all day and make decisions."

The last vowel came in a wheeze. Shit. The stubborn motherfucker.

"Dad..."

"I stay home when I need to. It's fine. Stop babying me."

"Do you not trust me to run it without Adam? Just say it. Say you think I'm incompetent."

"Peanut, it's a big company in the middle of a lot of change."

"Great. That's just great."

"I'm very proud of you."

I didn't tell him to fuck himself, because he was sick and he was my father. But I was going to. The words were on the back of my teeth and about to break through. So I hung up and waited until the call was cut completely before letting go.

"Go fuck yourself."

Saying it didn't make me feel good. Not even a little. I felt like shit. I stared at the phone, wondering if he'd call back.

He didn't. Good. I wouldn't know what to say to him without fighting. I didn't want to fight with my father.

I caught a cab across town to R+D.

Chapter 20

Adam Steinbeck. My husband. A man I'd shared a bed with for years. A man I would have used fine, fine adjectives to describe a month earlier was now a stranger to me.

If not a stranger, a more evolved form of himself.

Or he was the same, and I had evolved.

Or both/neither/all/nothing.

I'd sat in boardrooms and conferences, obsessed with how I presented myself. Was I strong enough? Confident enough? Was I listening? Talking when it counted? Did I seem bitchy, sharp, entitled?

I should have watched him the way I did from his office. The door was open, and the conference room was across the hall. The blinds were open. He sat at the head of the conference table with four people. Papers everywhere. A whiteboard filled with cryptic lists and notes.

He was everything in his grey suit and red tie. He came from nothing and became everything.

He saw me through the window and the hall as I leaned on his desk. I wasn't being suggestive, but I felt his desire.

The Adam I'd shared a bed with for years was a good man. I would have used fine adjectives to describe him. Trustworthy. Loyal. Steady.

This Adam didn't bring those things to mind. Handsome. Confident. Powerful. Infusing the spaces he touched with licorice and leather.

I'd come to his office unbidden because my conversation with Serena had scared me. She wanted him, and she'd implied... no... I'd *inferred* too much from my conversation with her and the presence of an impossible dandelion. I wouldn't have bat an eyelash at any of this when I was with the Adam I knew before. But now, I wasn't so sure how much of that guy was left or what this one wanted. How much of his confidence let him cover lies. How much of his power would he abuse?

He got up from the meeting, said a few words, held the door open for his colleagues, and stepped through the hall as if he owned the air.

"Hello," I said when he crossed the threshold.

He didn't answer. He closed the door. Locked it. Dropped his folder on the long table in front of the couch. Closed the blinds to the left, then the right. Only when we were fully alone did he face me.

My heart was going to shatter my ribs, but I stayed still, more or less. Even when his eyes removed my clothes and his body hovered in the space like a predator sizing up its prey, I didn't move.

He rested his gaze on the pearls on my throat. "Diana."

I would have responded if I could breathe. I'd come to challenge him, and I didn't think I'd have the strength to do it.

"Get on your knees."

My knees obeyed, bending, holding my weight, while the space between my legs throbbed. I didn't have a chance to think.

"It's not two thirty." He came close to me. His cock was three inches and a layer of fabric away.

I leaned toward it. "I skipped an appointment."

"Why?"

"I want to talk to you."

He took me by the chin and made me look up at him. "Standard etiquette."

"What?"

"Standard etiquette is I put my cock down your throat then punish you for coming here when you weren't supposed to. I make you wait to talk to me until I'm satisfied you understand your place." He let my face go.

"Understand my place?" Even from my knees, I looked down on him and his attitude.

"Yes." He held out his hand. I took it, and he helped me up. "But you're a whole new way of doing things."

"The old way could get a guy throat-punched."

"Speaking of throats." He touched the pearl choker. "This is beautiful. You look thoroughly possessed."

"I'm thoroughly pissed, actually."

"You may be untrainable, huntress. Sit."

I sat on the couch, and he sat on the matching chair perpendicular to it.

"You were supposed to wait for me to call you," he said.

"I saw Serena today."

"At the shoot?"

I was surprised he didn't give me some open-ended answer like "huh," or "really?" He let me know right off the bat that he knew where Serena was today.

"At the shoot."

"Why?" he asked.

"I had to tell her something, and I wanted to do it in person. And you know what? I got the distinct impression she thinks that when you and I are through here, she's taking over."

"Subs don't take over."

"You know what I mean. And I left thinking she was nuts, but then... I have to ask you something. It's the middle of winter. Where did you find a dandelion?"

"Did you like it?"

"I didn't understand it."

"It was a last-minute inspiration this morning. You're all wound up. It's very sexy." He raised his foot and wedged it between my knees, pushing them open.

"Where did you find the inspiration?"

"Dandelions are the most nourishing weed in the garden. You can practically live on them. If you close your legs, I'll stop explaining."

I opened my legs and crossed my arms. He bent at the waist, put both hands under my knees, and pulled me to the edge of the couch.

"I could have left you a hothouse flower. An orchid or something high maintenance. But think about it. This underappreciated weed grows and grows. You can't kill it. You can try, and it comes back time after time like a big middle finger in the lawn."

"You don't even have a lawn."

He put his hands on my crossed arms and exerted pressure down until I uncrossed them.

"We had one when I was growing up. We ate them with olive oil and salt." He slid off the chair and kneeled in front of me. Pulled my skirt up slowly. "They are delicious." He kissed inside my thigh. "They are tenacious and beautiful, just like you."

He kissed between my legs, pressing his lips to the soaked fabric of my underwear. I gasped and dug my fingers into his scalp.

"Hands under your bottom," he said.

I wedged them under my ass. He pulled my panties to the slide and licked the length of my seam.

"I'm not..." I fell into a groan when his tongue flicked me. "A dandelion."

"They come and come and come."

He sucked my clit with a constant pressure, but I wasn't going to give him the pleasure of my pleasure for free.

"Where did you get it?" I squeaked.

"Beg to come."

"Please."

"Beg harder."

He took me with the flat of his tongue then flicked again. I felt every movement, every breath. My body wanted to come, but every fiber of my soul wanted more.

"Please tell me. Just tell me. Please," I said.

"To come, beg to—"

"Tell me, I'm begging you! I forgive you, I promise!"

He worked me like an instrument. I could barely breathe.

"Tell me where you got it. Please."

"I'll tell you. Now come."

His word was good enough. When he laid his mouth on me again, I let loose with an arching back and a scream I had to bite back.

With barely a second to let me come down, he stood and took me by the arm, pulling me to the floor. I was on my knees in front of him before I had a chance to think.

"I own the building the shoot was on. I went this morning to make sure the permits were cleared. The dandelion was in the greenhouse on the roof. You can check the deeds with the city." He tilted my face up to him.

"The owner of the building goes to check the permits? Please. Give me a break."

"She was nervous about the net. She wanted me to look at them. I'm aware that I don't know anything about hanging a net on the side of a building. I know she was manipulating me. But if something happened, I wouldn't be able to live with myself. So I went."

"Did she try to sleep with you?"

"Yes."

"What did she do?" I asked.

"Why are you asking this?"

"I'm curious."

"She got on her knees. I told her to get up. She asked why. I told her I'd had her already. I didn't want a second go round. I was an asshole."

"I don't think it worked."

"That's how it goes with emotional masochists." He stroked my cheek with his thumb. "Open your mouth."

"She thinks when our contract is up, she's going to be yours."

"I said open your mouth." He undid his trousers. "I didn't say talk with it."

His dick was out, and my mouth watered for it.

"Adam, I can't do this if you're making plans for after."

"I'm not making any plans. But Diana, hear me. We can't ever be what we were. I explained this. Do you understand it?"

"If you want my full attention, I need yours."

He took my chin again, pressing his fingers into my cheeks. "You have it. Open your mouth."

I opened, pressing the back of my tongue down for the length and girth of his cock. He thrust into me, taking my throat repeatedly, letting me breathe, then fucking my mouth again.

"Deep breath. I'm coming," he growled.

I took a deep breath and opened up all the way.

He fucked my face, holding me still while he thrust. "Fuck. Coming so hard down your throat. Swallow it." I felt the first spatter on the roof of my mouth, and he slid against it to go deep. "Take it all."

He took his dick out, and I swallowed every last drop.

"There's no one else," he said, running his fingers through my hair as I licked him clean, looking up at his beautiful, satisfied face. "I'm doing this with you. One hundred percent. I'm training you to leave me again."

I took him in my mouth so I wouldn't answer that I was the one who was training him.

Chapter 21

"I put something in the mail for you today," Stefan said. Opera came through the phone as I turned the key in my front door.

"Should I be excited?" I swung the door open.

"You're a third of the way to membership in the Cellar."

"Thank you! One down. Two to go." I flicked the lamps on, bathing the loft in warm light. "I spoke to Serena this morning. I don't think I convinced her of much."

"She saw me today. We spoke. That was all I wanted. Thank you."

We hung up without me telling him Adam might have been the reason Serena saw him. There was already too much personal information flowing between the four of us.

As I circumnavigated the loft, I got back to the front door and made sure it was locked.

Two white envelopes had been slipped under the door and pushed forward when it swung open. I opened the one with the McNeill-Barnes logo. Just like Dad said, it was a judgment blah blah for an address in Brooklyn pursuant to etc etc yada yada.

The other envelope was the size of an invitation. I ripped it open.

The note was in a deeply masculine handwriting, so neat it was nearly generic. The words were underlined in the same felt top pen. I flipped the card, looking for more. Nothing. I put the note on the dining room table and stripped down. Everything came off. Even the pearl choker. I didn't realize I'd been smiling through the whole process until I was putting my underwear in the hamper and caught sight of myself in the mirror.

I would have looked longer, but the lock on the front door clicked. I ran through the big, open space on the balls of my feet and crouched in the threshold between the loft space and the bedrooms, out of the way of the open door.

With my face to the floor and my arms stretched in front of me, I couldn't see. I could only hear his footsteps, the closing door, the lock, his voice.

"I see you were thinking of me."

I didn't want to talk to the floor and I didn't want to move, so I gave him a thumbs-up. He laughed with a tolerance for bad humor I'd never tire of.

The warmth of his hand spread across the middle of my back. "Stand up. I want to look at you."

I stood, keeping my eyes on the floor. He wore his black shoes. The tops were spotted with rain. He picked up my chin and looked at me while he stroked my lower lip with his thumb.

"Did you ever imagine this scene right here?" he asked. "You naked and kneeling when I came in the door?"

"No. Not while we were living together. But since Montauk, it's all I can think about."

He drew the backs of his fingers across my cheek and down my neck. "You took the pearls off."

"Naked is as naked does."

He smiled, brushing his hands across my breasts, tightening the nipples. "Where's the box?"

"In my bag."

He took his hand away and undid his tie. "Do you want to open it?"

"Yes."

"You're not ready." He slid the tie from his collar and came behind me. "Keep carrying it around until I tell you to stop."

He put the tie over my eyes and knotted the back. The world went dark, and I went liquid. Was he going to do the thing I'd seen on the screen? Lead me by his touch?

He put his hands on the sides of my face. I felt his breath and tasted his tongue as he kissed me. Maybe he thought he didn't love me, but his body told me he did. Or maybe together we'd redefined love. Maybe we'd evolved from desire to love to need, because our kiss was nothing if not needy.

He slid his thumb between our lips and put it in my mouth, breaking the lock of the kiss. I sucked his thumb, and he pulled it away. I kept it in my mouth, following into the loft. One step, two, letting him lead me around blindfolded. I trusted him to keep me safe in sightlessness.

The momentum forward stopped and became a right turn, a spin, a disorienting five steps in a direction I couldn't be sure of. Then forward a step. One turn. Two. I was lost, naked, and blind with nothing but his thumb in my mouth to guide me.

I yanked away. "Sorry. Before I forget…"

"Yes?"

"Some legal documents came to the office today. Dad opened them. He was totally snooping."

"Where?"

"Foyer table."

"Don't move."

I didn't. His feet stayed where they were while his hand stroked every inch of my body. I thought he'd forgotten the envelope, but when he'd activated every cell of my skin, making me hot and tingly, he went to the foyer. His heels clicked on the hardwood. Four times. My nervous system sent signals outward, toward his heat as papers crackled, folded, and fell onto the dining room table.

"Lean forward. Hands down. Fingers spread."

Wait. Was I grabbing my ankles? Was I near the windowsills?

As if seeing my hesitation, Adam spoke. "Trust me."

Okay. I was going to trust him. I put my arms out, spread out my fingers, and leaned forward. My hands hit the coffee table, and I laughed to myself. "I thought I was across the room."

He pressed my lower back down, making me raise my ass for the hundredth time. "We're going to really work on your posture. The purpose is to keep you mindful of your body, so... lower back down. Ass up. Legs"—he kicked my feet apart—"at shoulder width. Look straight ahead. It elongates your neck and lets me see your tits."

He pushed me this way and that to get me just right. Every touch was gentle and firm, and when I was perfectly how he wanted me, he cupped my ass and kissed my lower back.

"How is this?" he asked.

"Honestly?"

"Of course."

"Uncomfortable. But if it's what you want, I can remember it."

"You're getting—"

He stopped himself. The table was covered with magazines and mail. I heard a slight ruffle in the space below my chin. I couldn't feel him. He'd made sure at least one part of his body was on mine the whole time, except when he looked at the papers, and without his touch, I felt disoriented and isolated.

"Adam?"

He took the tie off my eyes and held the note in front of them.

Take your clothes off and think of me.

"What?" I said. "Was I supposed to do something with it?"

"What is it?" he said as if he were holding all his control behind his teeth.

"A note? Is there another definition?"

"Who wrote it?"

I stood up. Sexy time was done. "You didn't? It was under the door when I came in."

I took it and looked closely, suddenly recognizing the weight and lines of the writing. It was written in very fine felt tip pen, scored with a straight edge. I'd thought it was Adam. Assumed it was, but wishful thinking had shaded my perception. It wasn't my husband's writing at all. I covered my mouth.

Adam thrummed his fingers on the tabletop. I'd done nothing wrong. I didn't owe him an explanation, but he was going to get one.

"Okay. Just stop looking so mad, okay? I thought you left it. That's the first thing. Stop. Stop looking mad."

"I'm not mad."

"You look mad."

"This is not my mad face. This is my 'what the fuck?' face."

"This is my 'calm down' face." I tossed the card on the table and went into the kitchen, where I snapped Insolent's card off the fridge. I put it on the bar that separated the kitchen from the open area.

Adam crossed the room and took it. "Who gave you this?"

"Charlie. Don't be mad. Look! There's the mad face again."

"Is this the guy you were waiting for at the Greens?"

"Yes. I left him a note saying I couldn't go through with it. I presumed he got it."

Adam plucked my phone from the table and dropped it in front of me. "We have a deal. You and I. No one else."

"I'm keeping that deal and you know it."

"Text him and tell him that."

I unlocked my phone, leaning a hip on the counter. "For a guy who doesn't love me, you sure act like you do."

> —Hi Insolent. Just want to be clear that this wasn't working for me and I've moved on—

"I can't believe you told him where you lived," Adam said as I hit Send.

"He must have gotten it from the driver when I took the car home."

Adam snapped the phone away from me. Looked at my text. "You're too fucking polite."

He tapped the glass. When I realized what he was doing, I came around the counter and reached for the device. He held it away. It dinged with an incoming, and when he looked, I wedged myself in front of him so I could see.

> —My husband is training me. He is my Master. No more notes—

The new text from Insolent jarred me.

—Let me know if it doesn't work out—

"Charlie sent you this asshole?"

I didn't want him to be angry with Charlie, but it was too late. His own phone was out and he was dialing.

Adam, phone tucked between his shoulder and ear, put his hand on the back of my neck and pulled me into him. I let my naked skin feel the safety of his suit and the firm caress of his hand.

"Charles," Adam said, "who did you send my wife to?"

I couldn't make head or tail of what Charlie was saying.

"You bet it was going to bite you in the ass," Adam said. "Do you know this guy? Is he another war criminal?... Because she told him no thank you and he's leaving notes at the house. Under the door. He knows where she lives, and I don't like his tone."

Adam listened for a long time. I tried to get away so I could put some clothes on, but he wouldn't let me go.

"Yeah," Adam finally said. "Dominic is fine if we can get him."

He said his good-byes and hung up, looking at me with a tenderness I hadn't seen since the day before I left him. It might have been an opening. Was it too small for me to get through? Only one way to find out.

"Why not just tell him it's going to work out?" I asked.

"What do you mean?"

"He said to let him know if it doesn't work out." I slid my phone three inches toward him. "Assure him it's going to work out."

"I'll assure him of more than that. In person. Let's get you dressed."

We went to the bedroom, where Adam opened my top drawer and dug around the back, coming up with a pair of Christmas pajamas.

"Are you serious?" I asked.

"It's cold."

I opened the drawstring pants. I'd gotten them when I was pregnant, promising to eat a tub of peanut butter cups and get fat as a house. "They have candy canes on them."

He handed me the long-sleeved top. It had a collar with red piping and red buttons down the front.

"I have a perfectly good nightgown."

"You're supposed to do what I tell you."

"Yeah. Stuff that makes sense like 'get on your knees' or 'suck my cock.' This is just weird." I snapped up the nightgown.

"It's too sexy," he said, putting up his hands. "Give me a minute to explain. Just…" He laid his hands on mine, pushing the nightgown out of sight. "Just trust me."

"You can explain, then I'll trust you."

"What's the point of that?"

"Trust me."

He sighed and shook his head a little. "Charlie knows him. Knows where he lives and what he looks like. He and I are going to visit him. Just to make sure he got the message. Which means you're here by yourself. Do you want to be in the house alone?"

"Not really." I was resigned to the scenario before he even finished.

"We're getting someone to watch you. He's going to stay in the living room. Hopefully it'll be Dominic and he'll be here in a minute."

I picked the candy-cane pajamas off the bed, pensively pushing the red buttons through the holes. "I'm sorry. This is my fault."

"No, it's not. You did everything right. You texted. You met him in a public place. You were honest about your intentions, right?"

"Yes."

"And as soon as it wasn't working for you, you let him know."

"I should have texted. A note on the back of the card? So stupid."

"You had every right to assume it would be delivered. And I'm sure it's nothing and I'm overreacting."

"I'm sure."

He kissed my forehead. "Thank you."

"It's too early for bed."

"I was being unreasonable. Wear whatever you want."

"The little elves are so cute."

"They are." He caught my lips in the tenderest of tender kisses.

I could have kissed him like that for another three or four days without interruption or acceleration, but there was a knock on the door.

"Let me get it," he said. "And I meant it. Put on whatever."

I put on the Christmas pajamas because the elves were cute, after all.

Chapter 22

I met Dominic. He was six five, and when I shook his hand, I felt as if I were grabbing a concrete-filled oven mitt. I put on a movie and invited him to watch with me. He declined and went out into the hall. I checked on him a few times. He stood outside the door, listening and waiting. I invited him in, but he said he was fine. He refused food, took water, confirmed he didn't need the bathroom. I watched another movie in my bedroom and fell asleep in the blue light of the TV.

I woke when the light went off. "Adam?"

He sat on my side of the bed and moved my hair off my face. "Go back to sleep."

I pushed myself to a sitting position. I couldn't see the clock. My vision was cloudy with sleep, but my mind was completely awake. "What happened?"

"I can tell you tomorrow."

The light from the moon and the building across the street surrounded his silhouette.

"I can't sleep if you don't tell me."

He turned on the lamp. I squinted and turned away from it, and he put his hand on mine while I adjusted to the light and wakefulness.

He looked fine. Better than fine. Hale and healthy and ready for a day out. I must have been a sight with my crusty eyes, nest of hair, and candy-cane pajamas.

"What time is it?" I asked, rubbing my eyes.

"Two and change."

"What took so long?"

"It wasn't as easy as we hoped."

"Did Dominic stay in the hall the whole time?"

"He's a pro. The best."

I cleared my throat, tilted my head right then left to stretch my neck, then sat up straight. "I'm ready."

He smiled and patted my hands. The gesture wasn't forced or shallow. He wasn't phoning it in. "We went to the last known address. Me and Charlie. Dominant members of the Cellar have to pass a probation period and interview, and Charlie was part of the vetting process. So we figured it was just a misunderstanding."

"Right."

"We got to the place on the Upper East Side. Poor guy, living alone. It smelled like he hadn't left in months."

"Months?"

"Maybe decades. He had Watergate memorabilia all over the house. He had a 'Nixon Now' poster. Framed and everything. He said his mother put it there when Ford took the White House and he hasn't moved it since."

I blinked a couple of times. "Wow."

"We talked. I think you're safe now."

"Thank you."

I was more than safe. If Insolent was actually a smelly, homebound Dominant pretender living in his mother's old apartment, I'd eat my candy cane pajamas. I'd just heard Adam Steinbeck's fantasy of Insolent, and I wasn't about to burst his bubble. I would let him get away with his lie and give him the gift of my unquestioning obeisance.

"What should I do?"

"Go back to sleep." He stood. "Tomorrow, you're moving in with me."

I jumped out of bed. Maybe not that unquestioning. "Wait, wait..."

"I don't like that he knows where you live."

"Murray Hill might as well be the moon. It'll take me an hour to get to work."

"Forty minutes. And it's temporary."

I crossed my arms in my Christmas pajamas with little elves. I didn't know how I expected him to take me seriously in that getup. "How temporary?"

"Until I'm confident he's gone. Or the end of our agreement. Whichever is first."

"So you'll let me move to somewhere on planet Earth after the thirty days?"

His smile was shaped like an orange slice. "Jesus, huntress. It's just the east side."

"Ugh."

"I have two bedrooms. It'll be just like old times. And it'll be easier for me to train you if you're there."

I brushed by him and opened my top drawer. "I'm awake anyway."

My back was to him, so he couldn't see my excited grin. He was making me a part of his life, giving me plenty of opportunities to prove to him that he loved me. On a day-to-day, married people level, we belonged to each other.

My smile turned into a frown.

He was bringing me further into his life and embrace. He was protecting me and treating me as his own. Of course I should be thrilled. That was exactly what I wanted. The more access I had to him, the more likely he'd realize he loved me.

Unless he didn't.

Unless this all backfired completely and training me was the last thing I should let him do. What if I fell more deeply in love? What if this only got harder instead of fixing the rift between us?

"Are you all right?" he asked.

"Sure." I pulled out some more clothes. "I was just thinking about what I have to do at work tomorrow."

I'd lied through my teeth, just like him. We weren't supposed to lie. That had been the problem in the first place. Lies to ourselves and each other had broken us and they had no power to heal.

"You're not going to work tomorrow," he said.

"What?"

"You're staying with me until I know it's safe."

"It's down the block." I thrust out my arm with its fistful of underwear. "Why don't you just stay here?"

"Because this person knows where you live. He doesn't know where I live. Just work from my place tomorrow."

"No. Here's the deal. I stay with you if I go to work. You stay here if you want me to take the day off."

It made no sense. I was basically inconveniencing myself no matter which option he chose. But I couldn't just give up on one of my redlines.

"You're impossible," he said, a stiff second finger pointing at an irritation somewhere in the southern sky. "You're making it very hard to take care of you."

I opened my mouth to say, "I didn't ask you to take care of me," but that was another lie. I wanted him to take care of me. When we were married, and after we got back from Montauk, I wanted nothing more than to feel the weight of his watchfulness.

But that didn't mean I was going to let him eat me alive.

"It's not my job to make it easy for you," I said, dropping my underwear back into the drawer. "The business is about to be mine. If I'm in the city because you sent me home early from Montauk, then I get to prepare the business for the transfer and you just have to deal with that."

He crossed his arms and set his feet a little farther apart. For anyone else, that signified intransigence. For Adam, it meant the negotiations were about to begin.

"The deal was you submit to me. We never negotiated our feelings."

"Sexual submission. That was the deal."

"Place and time were my call."

"The place was Montauk. Wanna go back? Or is it not as much fun without your ex-girlfriend in the house next door?" I slammed the drawer closed. "You knew they were there, didn't you?"

"I did."

"Why did you put me in that situation? On top of everything else, having them there made everything worse."

"Because you agreed to go. They were there and you agreed and I had to choose between taking you to Montauk or not. I decided to take you because I was dying every day. You have no idea how goddamn desperate I was."

If I hadn't had an idea ten minutes before, I did once I heard those last two sentences. His desperation was still there in the soft rattle of his vocal cords and the forward set of his jaw as he tried to hide it.

"I do. I know it. You looked at me and saw someone you loved not loving you back, and all you wanted to do was save yourself. Right?"

He took a long time to answer. I thought I was in for a rant on what I'd done to him versus what he'd done to me. I expected excuses, defenses, and rationalizations.

I got one word, said with a thick undertone of regret.

"Yes."

"I need to make sure my company survives. This is how I'm saving myself." I could have lost him at any minute. My situation with him was that precarious, but winning him wasn't worth losing myself.

"This was supposed to be easy," he said with a smirk.

"It's not. It sucks."

"Right. Yeah. And there's tomorrow." He rubbed his eyes with one hand while the other was still crossed over his chest.

"I have to work."

"The papers your dad opened? It was a summary judgment. My uncle Bernard—"

"The hoarder? In Idaho?"

"Yes. He accepted a buyout for the house."

His grandparents' house was a beautiful three-story Cape Cod two blocks from the Belt Parkway. His uncle had wanted the house, but Adam wouldn't sell it so he could "fill it with old newspapers and empty Coke cans." The fight had been bitter and long, but Adam was a tenacious fighter and a patient man. It had obviously paid off.

"I'm going there in the afternoon to see how much of a mess I'm dealing with." He took his hand from his face and flattened it, pointing it toward me. "Come with me. Work in the morning, and come with me after lunch."

Sheepshead Bay was the exact last place I wanted to go, ever. It was far away, residential, isolated, a land of freestanding two-story houses with siding and stoops—and it had nothing to do with me at all.

"Why not just go yourself and let Dominic protect me from evil for a few extra hours?"

His shrug was barely perceptible, and it had the weight of honesty behind it.

"I wouldn't mind having you around." He looked at the floor, put his hands in his pockets, and looked back at me. "It's been empty a long time. I haven't seen it since my grandmother died. I don't..." He stopped himself and shook his head a little as if dismissing a thought.

I believed him, and I felt for him. His grandparents had raised him as their own, educated him, and made him into a man after his parents died. Getting the house meant he had to deal with the place he'd grown up in.

"All right. But I'm sleeping here tonight."

"And Murray Hill tomorrow night."

He'd slipped right back into the negotiation. I couldn't help but admire him sometimes.

"Fine."

"Discussion over," he said, his voice steady and sure, half an octave deeper with an unbreakable rhythm. "You mouthed off." He yanked the end of his belt to undo it, and I was wet in an instant. "Put your elbows on the bed. Feet spread on the floor and your ass up where it belongs. We'll start with your pants on. You're going to count until I tell you to stop."

He snapped the belt free and looped it in one hand. I couldn't stop looking at the way his fingers bent around it. When had he slipped from a human man into the skin of a god? Was it when he rubbed his eyes or when I agreed to his last demand? It seemed fast, but the transition was so smooth, he must have been changing right before my eyes the entire time. My knees were so weak with anticipation that I could barely make it to the foot of the bed, but I did exactly as I was told.

He put his hand on my back, across my ass, between my legs, pressing the fabric against me. He didn't correct my posture, just appreciated it.

"Count with me," he said from behind, and I did.

Chapter 23

DAY TWENTY-SIX

The Jag was mine. I'd earned it in the bathroom at R+D a lifetime ago. I'd touched myself when Adam told me to and stopped when his watch beeped. It was the first time I'd heard his Dominant voice outside a boardroom. It was the first time I'd heard him directed it at me and not at an adversary. It was the first time I'd gotten wet from no more than words.

He'd done what he said he would. Signed the car over to me without another word. Though he could have bought himself another car in a heartbeat, he lived in Manhattan. Cars were unnecessary.

Until you wanted to go to Sheepshead Bay, which was a good hour on the B or Q, four stops from the netherlands of Coney Island. Then you'd want a car, and if you were Adam, you'd drive it even though you gave it to your soon-to-be ex-wife when she played with her clit in front of you.

In the underground garage, I handed him the keys when the valet brought the Jag up from the spot we owned. Adam's coat opened to show his jeans and a cashmere sweater with a button-front shirt underneath. That sweater was winter-sky blue and made the color of his eyes surreal. I could barely look at him as he opened the door for me. I was sure he took that as submissive, but the facts were more mundane and more alarming. The more I looked at him, the more I loved him. I could barely stand it. He'd shaken my body to the core multiple times the night before, then he'd slipped out to the guest bedroom while I slept it off. I woke bereft and irritated that my afternoon had been hijacked.

He snapped the door shut and slid next to me.

"Should I take the Gowanus or the Prospect?" he asked, adjusting the mirrors. He'd picked me up at two o'clock because I needed more time at my desk, and he'd done it without disappointment or complaint.

"I like the Gowanus."

"Always the rebel." He put his arm behind the seat and backed up a little, his body stretching gracefully, his neck elongated as he looked through the back window.

"I like seeing how the neighborhood changed."

He faced front and headed into the daylight. "The warehouses?"

I shrugged. The Gowanus went through a neighborhood of shipyard warehouses that had sat empty for decades as the Port of New York's business dried up. "Except the ones some greedy developer renovated into condos."

"I hear he made a killing."

"You know what I hear?" I said with a hint of gossip in my voice.

Adam took us downtown toward the Battery Tunnel. "What do you hear?"

"I hear his wife can barely sit this morning, he beat her so hard."

"He's a real asshole."

"He's amazing." I regretted it before it was out of my mouth. I shouldn't have been complimenting my husband or getting comfortable with loving him, but I couldn't help myself. Like water flowing downhill, my feelings went in the direction of gravity's pull.

"I hear he's only amazing for the right woman."

I had to stop it there. Fold my hands in my lap. Pretend that didn't mean anything at all. He was just talking, right? Just playing the game. I didn't know how to protect myself from him and win him at the same time.

"Are you ready to get the company back online?" he asked.

"I don't know. It's hard without you, and I haven't been able to hire anyone to replace you with the freeze."

"Yeah. I'm sorry about—"

"No, please."

"Well, I am."

"Fine. Zack is back though," I said. "So we can get the editorial acquisitions up and running quickly."

"He wants to fuck you."

I knew my husband. I knew when he blurted out something he didn't want to by the way he lowered his voice a notch mid-sentence.

"Yeah, well. I'm married at the moment."

We entered the Brooklyn Battery Tunnel with its double line of yellow lights and narrow lanes. There was nothing more to say. I'd added "at the moment" to give him an opening to claim me, but the timing was wrong and he wasn't ready, so we just rode the turns of the tunnel in silence.

The fact that there were other men in the world who were capable of loving me was going to be a sticking point for him. I was poking that flaw as hard as I could, but he knew his weaknesses as well as I did, and he was working on repairing them as hard as I was playing them.

We snapped back into sunlight.

"Let me ask you something," he said. "It's hard to ask. It'll be hard to answer. You don't have to."

"Noted."

"Could you ever go back to regular sex? Not sometimes, but all the time. Just vanilla again?"

He stayed left onto the raised platform of the Gowanus. It was pretty empty in midday, and we went on a good clip toward the outer reaches of the Belt Parkway.

"I don't know. I don't think so. I can't see much outside what's going on with us right now. But we broke something in Montauk. I don't know if I can put it back together."

"What kind of something?"

"Some kind of shell, I guess? I was ashamed. Not like I knew it. I thought I was fine. But I wanted to be hurt and dominated, and I thought if I got all that, I'd hate myself. I thought I'd have to give up who I was. The things that make me, me. I don't know what they are anymore, but I don't feel less like myself. I feel more like myself."

"Do you though?"

"Do I what? Feel like myself?"

"Hate yourself."

I thought about it. Searched for the answer. I'd said I felt like myself, but I didn't tell him whether or not I liked it. I'd thought that was implied. "No, I don't. Not for that."

He drove without comment. We passed the warehouses. Blocks and blocks of big casement windows and stonework.

"Here's yours!" I said, pointing at a slate-grey building with white trim.

"You made me do the white."

We'd been together toward the end of the project, when he was putting on the finishing touches. In the first months of our relationship, he'd brought me there to show off.

"Are you glad?" I asked. "It looks great."

"Yeah. It does."

His grandparents' house was another twenty minutes down the Belt, past the Verrazano Bridge, past Bensonhurst and the train yards at Gravesend, in a nondescript neighborhood built for the working class of the outer boroughs. We turned onto his block as the winter sun got low on the horizon.

The gate across the driveway was locked with a chain. Adam pulled the Jag into a spot across the street and put it in park. He sat there.

Adam's grandmother had died years before we met, and the estate went into probate immediately. The three-story house was unexceptional on the outside. White siding. Screen door. Green trim. A plaster statue of the Virgin Mary inside an arched white cocoon sat in the center of the front yard. He'd paid for the upkeep through his property management company, painting every few years and making sure the patch of lawn in the front didn't get overgrown..

"What are you going to do with it?" I asked.

He shook his head. "No clue."

He got out and came around the front of the car. I waited until he opened my door and helped me out. The street was lined with thick-trunked oaks that would shed hundreds of leaves as big as a man's hand. The curb was crusted with week-old snow and ice Adam insisted on helping me navigate it.

He held my hand as we crossed the street. Ostensibly, the gesture was to keep me from falling. But not really. I knew how to walk on barely icy streets. When he touched me, I knew he needed me. Maybe not in life, but in that moment. He needed me.

He put the code in the front gate, and once we got up the steps, he pulled out a key. "Ready?"

"I've never seen where you grew up."

"It's nothing special." He jiggled the lock, and the door opened with a *creak* and a *whoosh*.

The hall was dark. A stairway led up. A closet on the left and a door to the right. A coat rack had a single fedora with a little feather in the satin band.

"What's that smell?" I asked.

"Sulfur. There's a coal furnace. It stinks up the whole house. My guy came yesterday and started running it. Still works." He took off his coat and helped me with mine. "My grandfather cut the house up into three units. The stairs go to the upstairs unit, which is two bedrooms, and an attic studio. The rent helped them pay for my school."

"Real estate speculator runs in the family."

"Yeah." He hung up my coat and handed me a handkerchief. "It's going to be dusty."

I took it. "Thank you."

He opened the door on the right, and when I went through, I was transported back in time. Not just to Adam's childhood, but to another era. An era of wood paneling and molded pile rugs. An era that was dated even when he was a kid. Pictures of him spanned the hall, broken by a doorway to a room with plastic-covered furniture and a console television. He took my hand again, pulling me so fast I couldn't get a good look at the photos of the handsome boy in the plaid tie with his hands folded in front of him.

Adam went to a larger room with the dining room table. The chairs had mustard velvet cushions covered in more plastic. The fabric matched the drapes.

"They had to really chop this floor up to get it to work," he said, playing tour guide.

He was concealing some anxiety I couldn't pinpoint. I hadn't been around when his grandparents passed. I only knew his grandmother hadn't lasted more than a month without her husband.

"They built this wall and put their bedroom right off the dining room." Adam continued with the tour. "The living room, we passed on the way in. My room used to be the porch." He snapped open the blinds and opened the window.

"Yeah," I said. "Let's get some air in here."

I did the same to the window next to it. I went left and he went right, opening windows and doors. The dust was its own ecosystem, and the sulfur smell had probably gone right through the plastic covers and permeated every porous mass. I opened the windows in the kitchen, and he went around to the porch. We met in the master bedroom with a king-sized bed in front of huge bay windows. The bedspread was silver blue with diamond stitching, and the pillows were stuffed into a hard tube.

"It's like a time capsule," I said.

He snapped his fingers as if remembering. "I had the water turned on."

I followed him into the kitchen, where he stood watching a faucet run pure brown.

"Yuck."

"Toxic," he said. "My grandfather wouldn't switch to copper pipes. He thought lead made you stronger."

"Oh my God. What did your grandmother say?"

"She believed what he told her to believe." He turned away and changed the subject.

He opened the fridge. It stank. A line of brown water came from under it. We looked up. The ceiling was leaking and dripping behind the ancient yellow refrigerator.

We went into action. Adam gripped the appliance by the sides and scooted it one way, then the other to pull it out. I went looking for a pot.

Couldn't find one.

"I think something died back here in 1987," Adam said.

I listened as I looked for something to catch the leak.

"Or when Grams died, latest," he said.

Some cabinets were totally empty, and some had odd things in odd places. I opened a cabinet to the left of the sink. On the bottom shelf were wine glasses, above them were dishes, and on the top shelf was a big blue bowl.

Adam continued. "She couldn't do a thing without him. He died, and everything went to shit. This leak could have been here and she wouldn't have gotten it fixed. Not without him."

The blue bowl would do.

"The bills." His voice came from behind the fridge with a particular muffled echo. "The tenants. How she cooked. What she cleaned on what days. I don't know how she made it fifteen minutes without him telling her how to breathe."

I slid a kitchen chair across the linoleum and situated it in front of the counter so I could reach the bowl. I stretched and reached it with both hands as Adam told me more about the dynamics of the people who had raised him.

"I bet she died because he told her to cook him dinner from the grave."

I balanced the ridge of the bowl on the tips of my fingers and lowered myself.

"Stop!"

I froze with my knee on the counter. Adam was half in-half out of the back of the fridge. He held a tea towel in his right hand that was loaded with brown behind-the-refrigerator gunk, and his left was held out to me like a flashing sign at the end of a crosswalk.

"What?" I got my other knee on the counter. "It's for the leak."

I held out the bowl, but he wouldn't take it.

"Not that bowl."

"All right."

He opened the oven. The pots were in there. Obviously.

He took a sauce pot and wedged it behind the fridge to catch the brown drops.

"Adam?"

"This is what I'm talking about. This is exactly what I'm talking about."

"What are you talking about?"

"Just get down. Just..." He held out his hands, one empty, one clutching a gunky tea towel. "Fuck. Where would a normal person put the garbage?"

"Under the sink." I got down so I could reach it, but Adam yanked open another cabinet where an old plastic garbage container was upside down on the shelving paper.

He slapped the tea towel in it. "Nothing ever made sense."

"People get set in their ways." I sat on the counter with my feet on the seat of the chair and put the bowl in my lap.

"You see that bowl?"

He was upset. I didn't know why, but something about that kitchen had set him off.

"This one?"

"We used that every day. And every day she had to have my grandfather get it. Did she ever say, 'Let's put it on a lower shelf instead of the wine glasses? Because, you know, we drink our fucking wine out of fucking jelly glasses?' No. Because he *wanted* it that way and what he wanted he got."

When I was a kid, I used to stand under the light switch and flick it as slowly as I could to see if I could discern the moment the light went from off to on. I never caught the moment. It was too fast. But that moment was happening in the kitchen where Adam grew up.

"And you know why?" he continued, even as the idea solidified in my head. "I figured this out when he died and she didn't know how to do shit. He did that and a billion other things so he'd be indispensable."

"He needed to be needed," I said.

"He didn't want her to function without him."

"He needed to dominate her."

"What?"

"Not sexually. Or maybe. I don't know. But he needed her to submit, and she did."

He cocked his head a little, and I jumped off the counter. I handed him the bowl.

"And when he died," I said, "she had to go too. Right?"

He took the bowl gently, as if he didn't want to break my thought. I didn't let go. "What are you trying to say?"

"You always said she died to make him happy. I never knew what you meant. But now I do." I let the bowl go. "I'm not going to die without you. I'm never going to be so dependent on you or anyone."

"I never said it was like that for subs. You're confused."

He didn't use his Dominant voice to object. He said the words without conviction, as if he wanted me to prove otherwise.

"Intellectually, you know that's the truth. But you can't unsee what you saw with your family. In your heart, Adam? In your heart you can't love a sub because you're afraid they'll forget how to live."

"That makes no sense."

"That doesn't make it false." I put my hands on his arms. I needed to touch him. I needed to feel him connected to me, because I knew I was right. "Your problem isn't that you don't love. Your problem is you love so much it scares you."

He pulled away, and when I went to grasp his hand, he snapped it away.

"This is ridiculous."

"What's—?"

"Everything. All of it. Just..." He curled his fingers into fists and closed his eyes. "Just give me a minute."

He left and didn't look back. Through the dining room and down the hall, past his childhood and the plastic-covered furniture in the living room, onto the front porch, where he'd slept as a boy.

Chapter 24

He'd asked to be left alone, so I left him alone. Stranded in an isolated corner of New York in the winter, in a house that hadn't been inhabited in years, with a man who took up more room than space, I didn't know what to do with my body.

Pushed against the wall, the kitchen table had two chairs facing the window. I'd moved the one at the head. A black-and-white TV took up much of the tabletop. Dust coated everything like snow. I opened drawers for no reason. Inexpensive but sturdy silverware and servers, plastic measuring cups worthy of a hipster vintage store. A chrome plate was set into the wall. It had three parallel slits with teeth. I pulled it open to find wax paper, tin foil, and paper towel rolls behind it. I pulled out the paper towels, found some blue liquid in an unmarked atomizer, and squirted the table. The paper towel was black after one swipe. Half a roll later, a third of the table was done, it was getting dark, and I hadn't even gotten to the crevices.

I couldn't clean all this up myself. I didn't have the tools or the time.

Putting down the paper towels and squirt bottle, I followed my husband's path.

Adam was sitting on the bed, leaning on the wall. It was shingled and painted with outdoor paint. When I put my hand on the doorframe, I noticed how thick it was and how it had a big hole for a deadbolt. The light from the wide window was a flat grey that made him an opaque silhouette.

"It's dark in here," I said.

"There's a light switch in the hall."

I leaned out and found it. The switch clacked loudly when I flipped it. An outdoor light by the doorframe went on, bathing the room in yellow. The blue of the crocheted bedspread looked military green, the woods looked like cheap veneer, and the world outside looked dark and unknowable with reflections of us painted on it.

"Yuck," I said.

"Piss was all the rage when I was a kid."

"Has that bedspread been sitting out for five years?"

"Just got it out of the drawer."

I shut off the light, and we sank back into deep blue. The school globe looked rounder, the books and blotter on the desk looked more mysterious, and as Adam faced me, he looked more three-dimensional.

I crawled onto the bed next to him and put my back to the wood siding.

"Definitely got a nice indoor-outdoor thing happening," I said.

"They used to sit on this porch every afternoon. Watch the kids get home from school. Say hi to the neighbors. I remember them being happy on this porch. My grandmother brought Grandpa tea in the winter and iced tea in summer. If you look under the window, you can see the ledge where he rested the glasses. There's still a ring in the paint."

I craned my neck, but though I could recognize that the little shelf in the front of the room used to be the ledge of the porch railing, I didn't see the ring. It was too dark.

"When they took me in, they just closed this thing up and chopped up the house to support me. It was what they did because that was what they did. Not an obligation. Maybe it was cultural. But they had no choice. I was their business. They were close to sixty when they took on a five-year-old orphan. Their entire lives revolved around me, but my grandmother's life revolved around my grandfather. She did a figure-eight around the both of us. When he died, I thought she'd be free. I thought I'd offer to make the porch a porch again. She could sit on it and be happy."

"Why didn't they just take this room out when you moved out?"

"He got set in his ways. They had routines and God forbid one thing was out of place. She was miserable. But when he died, she went right after him. Like she forgot how to live."

The sun had set, and the streetlights came on. I didn't press the point with him. Didn't mention his grandfather's dominance or how it had affected him. A car with a loud stereo drove slowly along the block to the Belt Parkway service road.

"He pissed me off," Adam said. "Sure. But by the end, I was pissed at her too, for letting him destroy her."

"But you loved them."

"Yeah." He rubbed his lower lip. "And she could really cook."

"What was your favorite thing?"

He smiled absently. "You'll make a face."

"Maybe."

"Snails."

I made a face. "Ew."

"She'd make them in this big pot." He flicked his hand to the kitchen, or wherever the pot was, as if he was visualizing it. "But only on my mother's birthday, because she'd loved them. Every year in July. Ten pounds at a time with tomato sauce. We'd pick them out with straight pins, and Grandpa would grouse around the house. Like making something he didn't like was a personal insult and not a way to honor my mother. It was the only thing my grandmother ever put her foot down about. It was for me. Because when I moved out, she stopped doing Mom's birthday because of *him*." He jerked his thumb back at the house as if his bossy grandfather was still there. As if he was physically connected to the stories made in the house.

"Fuck him," I said softly.

"Yeah. Fuck him." He took my hand, putting it in his lap as if it was finally home. "What are we doing?"

"Screwing up."

"Like it's our job."

"If you're going to do something, I say, do it all the way."

He squeezed my hand. I was jarred by the way he looked in the direction of the window, but not through it. He didn't look like the commanding Dominant who had been my partner for the past few weeks. He was as handsome as ever, and graceful and sharp, a leader and a decider, but not the same.

He faced me. "I don't know how to fix this."

The light from the streetlights glinted off one eye. His jaw locked, catching things he'd never say. He looked like a man I knew and abandoned. Manhattan Adam.

"We can't fix it," I said, putting his hand in my lap, watching our clasped hands make a new form. I rubbed the outside of his thumb with mine, feeling its familiar shape, the strength of the knuckle, and the texture of his skin. "We have to build something new. And we can." I looked up from our hands to his face.

Could I make him feel my optimism? Could I take a piece of it onto a fork and lift it to his lips? Would they part? Would he let me lay it on his tongue? Would he chew and swallow, saying "I do. I do believe we can, I do."

He didn't say that. He didn't believe, but his lips needed to touch my belief and his tongue needed to taste my hope.

I didn't know if I kissed him or if he kissed me, but it felt like a first kiss, with full quivering that left me paralyzed by his nearness. The act of two tongues tasting each other was so intimate between strangers, so taken for granted over time, and so rarely was the wonder of it felt through to the bone.

He was licorice. Fennel and leather. And he moved like cool water, reacting to my movements, countering with his hands and his mouth, wrapping me with his attention. The kiss was the sway of sex, the smell of it, the carnal desire without the promise of anything but another dance.

He pulled me on top of him, my knees on either side of his hips as he pushed them into me. My body reacted as if the shape of his cock was new.

I was blind. The world was pitch black.

But him. In a tunnel of light.

We pushed against each other. Our clothes got moved aside, unbuttoned where necessary and no more. We released our bodies from bondage and joined them. Right in the walled-in front porch built just for him, we made together what couldn't be made separately.

If only for that moment, in that bed, in that dusty old house. We built something as permanent as the night breeze. Something that would go away too soon but would return like the seasons.

I forgot the latent desires and sexual exploration for a minute to look into my husband's eyes and see all his anxiety, his growth, and his intentions. I saw everything he didn't want anyone to see.

He loved me. He was terrified, but he loved me.

I closed my eyes. Felt the strength of his hands as they caressed me. Listened to his tender whispers. His movements under me were as familiar as the sound of my own voice.

Manhattan Adam was still there, and he loved me.

I wanted to cry but couldn't. I was flayed, spread out, raw red, and bleeding. Reality was a serrated knife separating muscle from bone, sinew from skin. It cut away the truth of me from the truth of him.

We were on perpendicular paths. We were crossing at a ninety-degree angle, and soon we'd be traveling on different axes.

Manhattan Adam loved me, and I still didn't love him.

Chapter 25

In my teens, I was infatuated with drawing. The idea of being an artist appealed to me, and since I was forgetful and flighty, I figured I must be the creative type. Music was a lot of work and required a lot of attention. So at fifteen, I signed up for a class at the East End Artist's Studio.

I sat around a platform with twenty other teens. The teacher's name was Len Bellinger. He sat on a stool in the center of the platform. He was big and bellicose with a pencil moustache and combed-back black hair. He held up a soup can and spoke in a European accent I couldn't pin down to any single region.

"What shape is this?" he asked.

"A cylinder!" we chanted.

"Correct. In the third dimension, this is a cylinder. But drawing is in two dimensions. So!" He slapped the can right side up on the stool. "What shape?"

"Rectangle," some of us said, unsure.

"Yes. Now. If I do this... what is the shape?" He held the end up to Hanlon Speck, a foot from his face.

"A circle?" he said.

"Yes!" Len replied. He put the can in front of each of us, and each of us dutifully said it was a circle.

"So!" He placed the can back on the stool. "To draw, you need to live in the second and third dimension. You need to see the circle and the rectangle. You need to know they both exist even if you don't see them." He bent his elbow and made a fist as if catching a fly midair. "You must hold opposite things in your mind at the same time, and you must *believe them both*."

Chapter 26

DAY TWENTY-SIX

He pulled onto the Gowanus and home to Manhattan. Traffic was light, and I was confused about my intentions and my feelings. I felt as if he was going too fast, and I didn't know what I wanted out of him or the next four days. I didn't know if he was going back to being a man who could train me, or if his needle had found the groove of his old self. I held onto the edge of my seat.

He rubbed his bottom lip as he drove. Had he done that in Montauk? Even one time? I couldn't remember. My eyes had been on the floor half the time, and the other half was spent getting my bearings around a stranger.

"You're looking at me," he said with a smirk. Not the devilish smirk that betrayed plans for my body. Just a plain smirk on a devilishly handsome man.

I turned to my window. He was in the reflection. A half mask of blue dashboard lights.

"Sorry," I said, apologizing for nothing.

I'd never finished the drawing class. Never learned to hold two ideas in my head at the same time. Not about soup cans and not about men.

"What happened back there, Adam?"

"Back where?"

How deep was I going to go? Was I really going to shred this thing? Yeah.

I was.

"What happened? In your old room?"

He looked away from the road for a second, taking my temperature. "We fucked. Why?"

"It was the old way."

"Diana." His voice went deep and slow, but it wasn't the voice that made me feel safe. "Did you think regular sex was against the rules?"

"I want to talk about it."

"Okay."

Wrong answer. Wrong answer a million times. He was just rolling over. He was supposed to tell me that he'd fuck me how he wanted, when he wanted.

Even as my anxiety grew from a pinprick to a full chest pain, I knew I was being unreasonable. I was expecting him to read my mind, and I wasn't respecting his need for five minutes off from bossing me around.

"You're supposed to be training me. Twenty-four seven. That's what you said."

He exited the parkway, eyes drifting past me as he looked behind him for traffic. We were right by the grey building with the white trim. The one he'd bought whole and sold in pieces.

"Did you not want to have sex?"

"No, I mean, y—"

"Did I rape you?"

"No!"

"What's the problem exactly?"

"It's..."

"You think it has to be a power exchange every time?"

"No. I... no, not that."

He pulled up to a metal gate and pushed a code into a panel. "What is it then?" The gate rolled open.

I felt silly. I had nothing concrete to say. I had feelings and intuitions and assumptions. What was I supposed to say? *It felt like you loved me, but you also seemed like the guy I wanted to divorce, so which are you? Because I need to know if I love you or not?*

"Where are we going?" I asked.

"Is that literal or rhetorical?"

It was as if he'd read my mind.

"Both."

He drove into the tiny alley behind the converted warehouse. It had a few reserved parking spaces that surely cost a fortune to rent. The loading bay had been converted into an outdoor eating area with strung lights and big doors leading inside. He parked in front of three garage doors.

"Literally," he said, "here." He put the car into park and looked at me.

I swallowed hard as if that gave a woman strength against a man who loved her.

"Rhetorically? Fucked if I know."

He got out before I could respond, came around the front as always, and helped me out of the passenger side. He didn't make eye contact, but walked to the garage door.

"Adam!"

"What?" he asked over his shoulder, not looking back around.

This was the man with half his attention on me. This was the man who patted my shoulder when I was in pain. The one who made love to me like a nice guy.

I leaned on the garage door so I could see his face as he put in another code. I was in his sight, but he didn't look at me. He was all avoidance and internal energy. Locked away like the crown fucking jewels. Had it been being in his old house?

Had it been the memories of his grandparents? The vanilla fuck? Had his love for me turned him back inward?

"Step back please," he said as if speaking to an employee.

I got off the door, and he yanked it up. I was assaulted with the smell of old grease and liquid chemicals. Adam flicked on a light. The garage had room for one car, and it looked to be under a tarp. Adam walked around it, unsticking Velcro tabs, then he whipped the tarp away.

"Wow," I said.

"That's exactly the word," he replied, rolling up the cover.

"What year?"

"67. V8. 450."

The Mustang's paint was perfectly red. Not too blue. Not too yellow. The interior was clean white leather and exposed by the convertible top, which had been removed entirely. It had been placed on a ledge by the four wheels, which hung on the wall.

"I took it when the garage started leaking and put it up on blocks. Uncle Bernard never knew. But hell if I was giving up this car." He ran his knuckle along the side. "I figured since you had the Jag, I might as well use this one."

"That's a good idea."

It was a great idea if we were divorced. If we were together, it was stupid to have two cars in the city. We had the money to keep two cars, but we didn't drive enough to make putting the wheels back on the Mustang sensible. And what was the point of having a car like that if you didn't take it out?

Or the point of having a husband who only loved you when you didn't love him?

If this man standing in the flood of yellow light was Adam, we were getting divorced because I didn't love him even though he loved me. I could love the man in Montauk, but this one? No.

I wanted to love him more than I wanted to be loved.

I felt empty without that love. Crippled. A speed machine drained of gas and up on blocks for the preservation of its uselessness.

"I can't…" I stopped myself. I had an end to the sentence, but not the one after it.

"Can't what?"

Deal.

Decide.

Understand you.

Leave you.

Be with you.

I couldn't fight to be loved and be true to myself. But I could fight to love.

I dropped my bag and took off my coat, which I threw on the hood of the car. The cold air bit my skin and my nipples tightened.

He didn't say anything. He didn't make a move toward or away from me.

I dropped to my knees, keeping my eyes on the concrete floor and my hands to the side. I heard his soles against the floor's grit, and his shoes came into my vision.

Bending at the waist, I put my hands flat on the floor and my forehead between them. My hair spilled around his shoes. My heart thrummed. I stayed still, even as I panicked. On my knees, unable to see him, I wasn't protected. I was vulnerable to emotional hurt. But I didn't know how else to say what needed saying. That I needed him to be Montauk Adam. I needed his control and his dominance. I needed to love him.

"What are you doing?" he asked.

"Whatever you want." My breath hit the floor, and dust blew back up against my chin.

He moved. Grit scraped. He walked far. Then near. To my left. To the other side of the car.

"What if I want you to get up?" he asked from far away.

"I'll get up if it pleases you."

"What if I don't know what pleases me?"

I had a moment of confusion, then I remembered my husband of five years. The man who was afraid to do what he liked to do because he didn't want to lose me. What had he done when he was fearless? When losing me was a foregone conclusion?

I brought my hands around, and with my forehead still on the floor, I unbuttoned my pants and pulled them down, exposing my ass. The shame of it was overwhelming. To talk to my husband by showing him the ways he could fuck me was a deep humiliation, and the only option I had.

The garage door was wide open, and I could hear the *hoosh hoosh* of the expressway. He came around behind me. If he told me to pull up my pants and get in the Jag, I was going to cry, because if I couldn't reach him with this, we were finished.

Doubling down, I put my hands on my cheeks and spread them apart.

He moved. I felt it but couldn't see him. He did it slowly. He knew I was in a dark tunnel. I knew why. To keep me unsure of my own choreography. The garage door rattled down, cutting off the coldest of the wind and revealing the rumbling white noise of a heater.

Forever. That was how long he let me kneel like that. Until I was hyperaware of every sound from the apartments above. The sting of the floor on my knees. The cold air on my sensitive parts. The sound of his breath, revealing his position next to me, on one knee.

"Are you wet?" he asked.

I was so relieved I almost wept. "Yes."

"Yes?"

"Yes, sir."

"I know you're wet. I was checking to see if you still had the ability to answer questions. I asked you something you didn't answer."

"I'm sorry." My breath hitched. I was going to cry. "Sir. I'm sorry, sir."

"Do you want to answer?"

"I forgot the question."

"You said, 'I can't,' and when I asked you to complete the sentence, you didn't. So why don't you tell me what you can't do?"

"I don't remember."

"What do you want, Diana? In the next four days, what do you want?"

I swallowed a lump of cry gunk and sniffed hard. What did I want? I wanted to love him and I wanted him to love me. I wanted the impossible.

"Everything," I sobbed.

"I can give you everything. But not all at the same time."

I nodded by pressing my head to the floor harder. He stood up and slapped his hands clean. I swallowed the rest of my tears. I couldn't break down. Not now.

"Get up on the hood."

Was he back? Was he the man I loved? When I stood and saw the way he took up more space than a normal man and how his posture was perfect and confident, I knew I had him back. He regarded me with curiosity and care, but not love. I was relieved and I despaired at the same time.

I took two unsure steps back with my pants half down, then I got up onto the cold metal of the car.

"Legs out," he said, standing in front of me. When I straightened them he got his hands under the heel of my boot and pulled it off. "Just because I fucked you like a husband this afternoon doesn't mean you're in charge." I was left with a sock half off, and he left it there to pull on the other boot. "You don't kneel to force the issue. I see right through that." The other boot slipped off, the sock with it.

"You were sad and unhappy," I said.

"What makes you think that?" He took my pants by the cuffs and pulled, whipping them off. His erection pushed against the front of his pants.

"You looked... I can't explain it."

He took my underpants down and put them and my jeans over the car door. "Spread your legs."

I did.

"Wider."

I tried.

He grabbed my ankles and pushed them up and out. I fell back onto my elbows, unbalanced on the uneven car hood. One foot leaned on the car antenna.

"You look wet." He put his fingers on the base of the antenna and twisted. "Tell me how I looked."

"Like you were hiding something."

"I'm not hiding anything."

"Not a secret. Not a thing, exactly."

The antenna came out, and my foot fell outward. I thought he was getting it out of my way, but when he swiped the air with it and it hissed through space, I knew different.

"I know you think you successfully psychoanalyzed me back there." He whipped the antenna through the air again, landing it inside my thigh.

The pain was scaring. I yelled and closed my legs.

He jerked them open and leaned into my face. "It's not that simple."

What was he trying to defend, when I hadn't accused him?

"Yes. It. Is."

"It doesn't change anything." He spoke through his teeth, as if opening his mouth all the way would let out something he wanted to keep inside. The truth. The fact that maybe something could change.

"Not today."

"What did I look like?"

He really wanted to hear it. Well, I wasn't ready to tell him. I put my head back, exposing my neck, and spread my legs. I felt him stand straight, but all I could see were the yellow lights and the spider webs on the ceiling.

"You want me to break you?" he asked.

"I want to please you. I want you to use me."

I heard the whipping sound before the pain buckled me. Involuntarily, I closed my legs and rolled. He pushed me back and open, whipping from knee to center as if moving the sensation to the core of my desire. It felt good to hurt. So good to focus away from myself and into the immediate moment. I was untouched by worry, and my only desire was for relief from the pressure of my arousal.

He stopped and threw the antenna into the front seat.

"You're the one who's hiding something." He laid his hand inside my thigh and squeezed the raw flesh. I sucked in a breath. "What is it?"

"Yes."

His hand moved, hurting with a promise of pleasure that had to overcome such pain. He opened his pants. Cock out. Fingers inside me. Had I ever been so wet?

"You like it when I hurt you." He tapped my clit with the pad of his finger, and I arched and twisted.

"Yes."

Pulling me forward, he put his dick in me. My mouth opened to scream in gratification, but nothing came out. He gave me two thrusts. I thought I was going to burst between the pressure of the pain and the nearing orgasm that complemented it.

"Are you going to come?" he asked from deep in his throat.

I nodded, unable to form words.

He pulled out and rested his head on my clit. "You don't run this show, Diana. I top. You bottom. Got it?"

"Yes," I squeaked. "I'm sorry. I wanted to talk and I didn't know how else to get to you."

I wasn't sorry. I would have done it again exactly the same way. Either he intuited my insincerity, or he wanted to punish me. Maybe he had some other motivation. My brain was too soaked in sex to discern why he pulled his body away.

"Don't stop!" I gasped. "Please."

He wasn't going to. I could see the satisfaction of control in his face. He almost looked peaceful and content. Gratified with his denial.

I turned to one side so I could get off the car, but he pushed me back down and leaned over me until his face was an inch from mine.

"You want to fuck?"

"Yes."

He flicked my clit with the head of his dick and buried himself inside me, pushing so deep it hurt, then deeper, until his root pressed against every fold and knot.

"I looked like what?" He pulled his full length out and thrust in again.

"God, it hurts. Yes." I clawed at his shirt.

He wrangled my wrists together, crossing them and pressing them against my chest. "What did I look like?"

"Like you loved me."

He slammed me, and it was so good, so painful paired with such a rush of shuddering pleasure that words broke down into syllables, then individual sounds.

"When?"

I had to organize the sounds. Had to do what he told me. "Porch." I spit it out.

Holding me down, he took my body on the hood of the car. He took my will, timing his movements perfectly, as if he knew what I needed and how to deliver it.

"Do I look like I love you now?" he said through his teeth.

I could barely see through my own pleasure or speak through the pain. He'd never driven so deep it hurt. Never ripped through me like this.

"Answer," he demanded.

"I'm. Come. Going—"

"Do not come. Answer. Do I look like I love you now?"

"No." I thought it would come out in a shout, but it was a whisper.

"Good girl. Come for me. Say my fucking name."

His name boiled in my core and flowed past my lips. Pleasure exploded, overtaking the pain, mating them into a blinding whirlpool of soul-shaking ecstasy.

He put his free hand on my face, pushing me down with his weight on my wrists, sternum, head, possessing my body completely, holding me still so he could use me.

With a jerk, he came inside me. Framed by his fingers, his surrender was visible in his hooded eyes and slack lip. His dominance was in his clenched jaw and the ropes of strain in his neck. He was both in that moment of ultimate vulnerability.

He chanted my name as if it were law, then fell on me, his chest rising and falling with mine.

In one second, he'd shift his weight.

In three seconds, he'd get up.

In ten seconds, he'd look me in the face.

In thirteen seconds, he'd speak.

In fifteen seconds, I'd realize he didn't love me.

"Get off me."

He propped himself up on his hands so he could see me. I was right. He was Dominant Adam, with nothing but confusion in his heart.

He stood back and got his dick in his pants. I snapped my underwear off the convertible door. He grabbed it.

"I have it." He held out my underwear so I could get my feet in the holes.

I pulled the sock off and put my feet in, then I jumped off the car to get them up my thighs.

"No. You don't." I snapped my jeans away from him. "All the tender shit is lies. You shred me then take care of me like it was an act of love. But it's not. Not for you. You're just playing a part."

I hopped into my jeans. He stood back with his arms folded as if he was passing judgment on my delivery.

"When I'm gentle, it's a lie? Is that why you can't stand it?"

"The problem is this. When you dominate me, I'm in love. But when I submit, your love dies." I got my jeans around my waist and buttoned them as if I were trying to fling the sides together. I missed and slowed down to fasten them correctly. "We are the two most incompatible people who ever lived." I bent down and got my other ball of a sock and poked the toe through the ankle. "Do you agree or not?"

I snapped the sock, trying to uncurl it. It wouldn't go. I did it again, getting frustrated. Adam took the sock.

"You have a lot to answer for," I said. "With everything. Lying the whole marriage and taking me to Montauk to get over me."

"I didn't think you'd love me."

"I know. I believe you."

"This is not what I wanted." He held out my untangled sock. "It's an unmanageable clusterfuck."

"Epic." I snapped the sock away. "And I wanted that old Adam back so he'd love me, but I just..." I shook my head and studied the stitches in my stupid sock. "I'd only hurt him again. I can't do it all again. It's too much."

He put his hands on my shoulders. I didn't look up. If I looked at him, I would love him or not depending on who I saw.

"Do you think I can't love someone who loves me?" I asked.

"Huntress."

"I mean it. Because if that's the case, I am royally fucked."

"And I am too."

A teardrop fell on my sock. I wiped my eye with my wrist and sniffled loudly. He put his hand on my jaw and made me look at him. He didn't look dominant and assured, but he didn't look locked up like Manhattan Adam either.

"I need you," he said. "I don't know how to love you, but I don't know how to live without you either. For now, can we just need each other?"

"I don't want to get stuck. I don't want to wake up in a year in this weird in-between place. We need to finish this the way we planned, when we planned. It's not going to be easy, but it's the only way."

I wanted him to fight for me, but he wasn't going to. A sinkhole of despair opened up inside me.

Don't say it.

"You're as trained as I can get you in the time we had."

You're saying it.

"If I ever love a sub, it's going to be you." He stepped close to me and put his fingertips on my collarbone, brushing my skin with a light, preoccupied touch. "Today I felt close to you. Very close. And at the same time, I can't. I've tried. Every time you submit to me, it's like I'm waking up from a dream and the reality is that I'm fucked up."

He hurt me. Every word opened me to hopelessness. But my overriding emotion wasn't self-interest. It was compassion. He was truly pained and utterly confused. He couldn't explain it to himself any more than he could explain it to me.

I felt sorry for him.

I also felt a responsibility to him.

And though he could hurt me worse than any other human being could, I decided to put my own pain away for a minute. I'd feel it later. I'd feel his lack of love like a punch to the chest. Later.

I pounded my feet into my boots. Later.

I'd left him once. I knew what it took to admit the bond was gone. To say it out loud. To be responsible for the vacuum where love used to be. Even if he left me on day thirty-one, his suffering was greater than mine.

I reached down for the garage door handle and yanked it up. It rattled, and the whoosh and white noise of the expressway filled the room.

"We should stop," I said. "We're just making it worse."

I didn't want to see his reaction. If he agreed, I'd choke on my loss. I couldn't bear it, so I walked out to the Jag without looking back.

He got in front of me, wedging himself between the car and me, holding my elbows with an unexpected intensity. "Give me a chance. Give me the days we have."

I held two things in my mind. He was making me crazy. He was confusing me. He was yanking me toward him and pushing me away at the same time. I was angry, frustrated, vulnerable, defensive, and broken.

And I saw this for what it was. The obfuscation before clarity. Everything had to come out of the closet before it was rearranged. This was the mess where every emotion was strewn on the carpet, waiting to be put back in an orderly fashion. Through all my confusion, I made the calculation that this was a necessary stage.

Fear was hitched on the back of that calm assessment, because the emotional certainty that was to come might include love and it might not.

"What are you fighting for?" I asked, pushing him toward the lucidity I feared.

"Us. Me. I don't know."

"You just said—"

"I know what I just said. Then you walked away and I thought it might be the last time you left, and I made up this thing in my head that if you got to the car before I caught you...I got scared."

He didn't recognize his own scramble of emotions, and I didn't recognize the woman who made the calm assessment that this was part of his journey either toward me or away from me. But though she coexisted with a hysterical panic, she was in charge.

"What were you afraid of?" I asked.

"That I'd never see you again."

"That's not love?"

"I don't know what it is." He drew his hands down my arms pensively. "Maybe it's just the opposite of indifference."

Can a body survive on scraps?

Can a woman pick the meat off dry bones and live?

How long would we do this to each other?

"Four more days," I said.

Love or bust in four days.

Chapter 27

DAY TWENTY-SEVEN

I got to work at ten.

The night before, Adam had helped me pack things, take perishable food out of the fridge, and lock up. We took a cab to Murray Hill, where I reacquainted myself with the apartment he'd had when we met.

Three bedrooms with casement windows and a four-foot-wide wraparound veranda that wasn't good for much more than standing. He'd done it to flip then kept it, so the fixtures and finishes were flashier than what we'd chosen for the loft.

After he fucked me on the rug, leaving me more sore than I'd ever been, I went to the room closest to his, just like in Montauk. Alone. I tried to cry. I tried to feel the pit of my grieving and sadness, down where it was the thickest black. I'd tried to dig it out, but I couldn't find where it ended, and I'd fallen asleep before touching bottom.

"Dad," I said when I walked into my office. "How are you doing?"

"Fine," he wheezed, hunting and pecking at his email.

"I moved temporarily, just so you know. It's temporary, so—"

"Where?" He barely looked away from his screen.

"Murray Hill."

He peered at me over his glasses. If I'd hoped he had forgotten where Adam lived when I was single, it was dashed with that look.

"Temporary," I restated.

"Why?"

Because a Dominant I contacted to train me as a submissive makes my Dominant husband nervous for my safety.

"There have been security problems at the loft." I put my bag on my desk and unraveled my scarf. "We're just being safe."

He turned back to the screen. Hunted. Pecked. Two pointer fingers tapped keys like a sparrow seeking seed in the grass. "That's pretty far east. You going to make it on time for the thing at the Intercontinental?"

The thing the thing the thing... ooh. The thing. The Literacy Project event. McNeill-Barnes donated big. Mom used to be the development chair. Mom and Dad had gone to the black tie gala at the end of the campaign for years, then Dad took me until Adam came along. Then he and I went. It was a family tradition.

"Can you come with me?" I asked.

"Yeah. Sure. Am I doing this right? What do we do on invoices from states with no sales tax?"

He tapped the screen, and went to help him. I'd never teach him as much as he'd taught me, but I spent the rest of the morning trying.

• • •

—What are you doing right now?—

Adam texted the question at four in the afternoon. Dad was gone. Since McNeill-Barnes had been legally mandated to do nothing but tread water for thirty days, my to-do list was short and boring. All task, no work.

The phone rang. It was him.

"Is the office door closed?" he asked without greeting.

"Yes."

"Blinds to the hall? Shut them."

I got up and twisted the rod that closed the blinds.

"Are you done closing the blinds?"

"Yes."

"Good. Put the phone on the coffee table and put me on speaker."

"Done." I hoped he heard the anticipation in my voice.

"Pull up your skirt."

"I'm wearing pants." I unbuttoned them.

"Down all the way then. Bend at the waist and put your hands flat on the table. Do all the things we talked about. Put your ass up and your knees apart."

"Yes, sir," I whispered, letting my jeans fall around my ankles. I bent over the table and spread my feet apart. The exposure was enough to arouse me, and when he spoke, I rubbed myself against the sound of his voice.

"How does that feel?"

"I wish you were here."

"I have to go to Philadelphia tonight."

No.

I didn't give voice to the cry of my heart. We didn't have time for a night apart. *I* didn't have time. Not a minute to spare.

"I know we only have a few nights," he said, reading my mind again, "but I have to go."

"I understand."

"I'll make it up to you."

"You better."

"You're getting five strokes for that." I wished he could have seen my face, be cause it reacted to a strong flow of tingling pleasure that ran from my waist to my knees. "And you left the package home," he said. "You're supposed to carry it with you."

"I'm sorry."

"I want you to open it, but you have to earn it. Do you understand?"

"Yes, sir." I bent my waist more and leaned close to the phone, whispering, "packing tape is sexy."

"Not as sexy as your ass. So listen to me carefully. Tonight, don't take a shower. Take a bath. A hot bath. Use your fingers between your legs until you're wet and you want it."

"I'll be wet already if I'm in the bath."

Did he chuckle? I heard nothing more than a pause, but he might have.

"I'll clarify, but you're still getting punished for the wise mouth. When you're wet with your own juice, make your fingers wet, and I want you to put one in your ass."

I stopped breathing. "I—"

"Yes, you can. When you're loose, put in a second finger. When it's all the way in, you can come."

Suddenly aware of my exposure and position, I curdled. I wanted to pull my pants up and stand. I must have waited too long. He knew I was balking.

"Huntress?"

"Will it hurt?"

"The first time? Yes. But it's nothing you can't take."

I rested my cheek on the table.

"You like it when I hurt. Why?"

"Because you do it for me. You hurt for me. Because I say so. It means you trust me, and there's nothing like that. It makes me want to push your pain harder and keep you safe at the same time."

"I don't want to hurt there."

"That's why I'll make it as pleasurable as possible." He cleared his throat. "This is training, Diana. And you're doing great, but you need to get more comfortable with that part of your body. Get dressed. Dominic will be outside to take you home."

"Adam," I said, getting halfway straight. "I think it's fine. With Insolent. I really think he got the message."

"I'll see you tomorrow night."

The screen went black.

As I pulled up my pants, I wondered if I could get away with skipping the bathtub exercise.

Chapter 28

What freaked me out most wasn't the pain, but the violation. He'd used my mouth for pleasure more than once, and I enjoyed the feeling of being no more than a convenient object for him. The submission involved in removing my personality and desire from the equation was almost spiritual.

That was probably an exaggeration, but at the same time, it wasn't. I was focused on nothing but him and my objectification.

Anal was a different thing entirely. The size of his cock wasn't a joke, and he was bound to rip me open. Anal wasn't just about submitting to him and his desire. I was submitting to the risk of damage and pain.

He was going to tear me apart for his pleasure.

As much as pain and blood and shredded tissue scared me, what scared me more was the sight of him enjoying it. There was more than a touch of sadism in his appetites. This could be where we found the limits of my masochism.

I knew I could refuse him. I could take as many redlines as I wanted. But I wanted to be trained. I wanted to do it right, and yes, I wanted to finish.

A thousand years before, when I was engaged to a man named Brian, I'd agreed to anal. It was the night of our engagement party, and I was a little more than a little drunk.

The night was winding down, and as we were kissing and stumbling down the hall, he pushed me into the men's room. There were five stalls with heavy wooden doors. We went into one. I sucked him a little. He got under my Lacroix gown and fingered me until I came. Then I put my hands on the door and bent for him. He pulled my underwear down, and when he said he was going to fuck me in the ass, we both laughed.

A big gob of spit landed in my crack. That was all the lubrication I got, and I didn't know any better. Neither did he. He shoved his dick in my ass, and the pain was brutal. It came from inside me. I screamed and told him to stop.

He did. He pulled out and apologized, but the pain in my gut stayed for another five minutes. We agreed to not do that again.

And that was that.

Now here I was being trained to take anal for someone else's pleasure.

Yeah. I was scared.

"Diana?"

I jumped. Kayti stood in the doorway.

"What's up?" I asked.

"We're going to dinner. Wanna come?"

"God, yes."

"Awesome! We were going to catch the N up to 49th and go to Gerdie's?"

"Yes, yes, yes." I was already closing windows on my computer. "I'm starving."

"Great."

"Wait." I closed my laptop. I couldn't take the train with her. Adam had gotten me a bodyguard and a car. Because he was afraid I'd picked up a rogue

Dominant. Who I'd called. Because Adam hadn't wanted to train me. Even though I was submissive. And we were still getting divorced but were acting as if we weren't.

I couldn't seriously explain half of that.

"Meet me out front," I said. "I have a driver."

Kayti; Frank, her fiancé who worked around the corner; and Zack piled into the back of the car. I got in the front next to Dominic.

"Do you know where Gerdie's is?" I asked when the back door slammed shut.

"Sure do." He glanced at me sidelong.

I was supposed to go to Murray Hill, but I was hungry and with friends. So I shot him a look back, and he pulled away, turning uptown.

"What's with the private car, Di?" Zack asked.

"She's the boss, Zack," Kayti protested. "It's the boss life."

"No hack license," Zack continued. "That's not a driver." He changed his tone so it reached Dominic. "You a bodyguard?"

We loved having Zack at McNeill-Barnes because he was sharp and perceptive. That was the exact reason I didn't care for him in the car at that moment.

"Zack, you're being an ass," I said, turning halfway. "If I say he's the driver, he's the driver."

What was that tone? I heard myself as if I were someone else, and I sounded like Adam Steinbeck telling me to get on my knees.

And Zack heard me loud and clear. He actually nodded and shut the fuck up.

I could get used to this.

Gerdie's was packed, but Kayti had magical mystery reservations. Zack to my left. Kayti to my right. Frank across from me, and Dominic somewhere in midtown. He'd said he'd "stay close," but he had to put the car somewhere, and this was not a neighborhood known for legal parking spaces.

Everything was normal on the surface. We talked about work. Kayti showed off her ring. Frank blushed like a schoolboy. Zack leaned two inches too close to me and I jabbed him with my elbow while I brought the fork to my mouth. As the courses came and went, I started to think about taking a bath when I got back. I wondered what my fingers would feel like, what position I'd put myself in. How silly I'd look. I wondered if I could get away with not doing it and saying I did.

I'd missed the last three jokes and I was now laughing because everyone else was. I was ready to get home and just do this thing.

I got up and handed the waiter my card.

"I'll get this ready," he said.

"Where's the bathroom?"

"Downstairs, to the left. Ladies' is the last door."

—Dominic says you're out—

Adam's text came as I pushed open the door to the single toilet.

—Dinner. Why? Do you miss me?—

—I need you to be careful—

I wanted to be careful, but I also wanted to eat. I texted him as I sat.

—I'll be careful. I'm getting the bill and going home—

—And taking your bath?—

—Yes—

I stood, straightened my clothes, and washed my hands. The light was terrible. Blue green and dim. I looked like a ghoul. Had I stopped thinking about Adam since I'd gotten there? Had I laughed with my friends freely or been fully present for one second?

No. I hadn't. I wasn't finished. I was incomplete. In process. Waiting. And I hated it. Maybe that was why I never finished things. The in-between place where the marriage got hard, or school was a drag, or the project was in production were empty and easy to leave.

I couldn't this time.

—I'll be thinking of your fingers—

—I'll be thinking of your ass—

—~~I need you to love me, I'm going to die if I do all this and you still leave. There's no one else, Adam. No one I'd let do what you want to do. I've never loved another man and I promise I've never trusted another. I can't live without you. If we split up after you train me I'll set myself on fire I swear~~—

Highlight>select all>delete.

—My ass is yours—

· · ·

I crawled into bed victorious. Slowly, I'd gotten two fingers in. My ass stretched with the second finger, then closed around them like a vise. I brought myself to orgasm with the other hand, and the involuntary pulsing around my inserted digits shocked me.

Ten o'clock. Was he back at the hotel? Or was he exploring Philly's scene?

I scooted under the covers with my phone.

—I did it—

The reply came immediately.

—Good girl—

—I'll take it easy on you tomorrow night—

—I have to go to the Literacy thing at the Intercontinental —

—That's tomorrow?—

Nobody's perfect. Not even Adam, who never seemed to forget anything. He'd probably scraped the event from his mind when he moved his stuff out of McNeill-Barnes. In his bones, he was a real-estate mogul, not a publisher.

—I'm going with Dad, then we'll probably go back to Park and I'll crash there—

Not that I was looking forward to sleeping in my old room, but that was how it usually worked when Dad and I went out. Even when I was married.

—I'm taking you—

—No—

—(...)—

Whatever he was typing, I didn't want to hear it.

—If we're seen together they're going to say the divorce is off. And so if we split up after the 30th day it's going to hurt to have to tell everyone again—

—(...)—

—Just let dad take me—

Fight for me, Adam. Fight for me.

I thought he'd never answer. The dots crawled on the bottom of my screen, but whatever he was typing, it didn't make it to my screen.

Fight. For. Me. You fuckwad!

He was taking too long to answer. Way too long. What was the problem already? All he had to do was fight the tiniest little bit.

Maybe this wasn't worth it. Maybe I was climbing a tree without a foothold.

—Just talked to Lloyd. He doesn't want to go.
Be at the apartment at six. I'll help you get
dressed—

I practically danced under the covers and, I admit, I squealed with happiness. He was fighting for me. Maybe it was one night and not a lifetime, but he was fighting.

—Put the box on the night table. And carry it

with you tomorrow. Got it?—

—Yes, sir—

Yessiree-fucking-bob.

Chapter 29

DAY TWENTY-EIGHT

Long white ones for high cholesterol. *Click click.* Yellow once a day as a last resort to keep it from getting worse. *Click click.* Aspirin for blood. Albuterol inhaler—full.

"Then Jesse Helms tells her he'll be a dead man before he puts a woman like that on the NEA committee." Dad snapped the paper.

He had the ability to read something and talk about something completely different at the same time. I could barely count pills and have a conversation at the same time.

"He was a bastard," I grumbled, recounting the little pink pills.

"So I'm glad I don't have to go."

"Just want to make sure, Dad. Adam can be pretty persuasive." I shook the bottle of cholesterol meds. There weren't enough.

"I like seeing you two together."

"You're running out of yellow ones," I said. "You should have another week."

"No," he said with a cough and a short wheeze. "I took what I was supposed to."

"Are you sure?" I was alarmed suddenly. I'd asked him to take over the company and done nothing to help him manage his meds. "When I was gone, are you sure?"

"Loretta's a professional."

His nurse came once a day and she wasn't his daughter. She was a hired hand. Yes, a professional, but what the hell did she know?

I stood and flipped through the calendar by the back door. He'd gotten a new bottle just when I remembered, and a new prescription had been called into the pharmacy in the meantime. Besides, the idea that he'd taken double the dose of his medication was ridiculous. He would have noticed.

I kept counting the weeks, not because I distrusted Loretta or my father, but because something about the way the time had passed stuck in my throat. Why did it matter? I knew when the thirty days ended, so why did I keep knotting my brows about the calendar?

I dumped his yellow pills and counted. Those were a week short as well. I'd carefully counted the days in Montauk, but the weeks before had blended into one.

"Dad?"

He looked over his half-moon glasses. "Yes?"

"I have to go." I slid the pills back into the bottles. *Click click clickclickclick.*

"Everything all right?"

"Yeah."

Dad didn't have to say a word. I stopped at the door and looked back at him. His belt held up his pants, and his shirt folded under the arms. He was soft around the middle and thinner than he used to be.

"Did you..." I took a sharp breath before getting on with it. "Were you happy with Mom?"

He took off his glasses and leaned back. "Why are you asking me that?"

"Because. I don't know."

"I loved your mother. She was better than me, and I blamed her for that, but I loved her. She forgave me. Which proved she was even better. But I still loved her. I wasn't self-destructive enough to let her go for loving me."

I kissed him on the cheek. He grabbed my wrist as hard as he could, which wouldn't have held me if I didn't want to be held. He didn't have that kind of strength.

"And I love you," he said. "I won't lie and say that didn't factor in."

"Got it."

I ran out, grabbed my coat, and didn't slow down until I got back to the loft. I ran so fast I felt scared and excited at the same time, balancing them on opposite sides of my brain without worrying about dropping them.

Chapter 30

I was supposed to go to Murray Hill right after my dad's, but I didn't. The loft was a short cab ride, and I could make it in time.

I ran in, slammed the door, and stripped my coat and scarf, leaving them in piles on the floor. Kicked off one boot. Took a step. Kicked off the other boot. Unbuttoned my pants. Got into the bathroom. Ripped the package open. Skimmed the directions, which were printed in four-point type. Yanked my pants down all the way, sat on the bowl, and peed right onto the stick.

What do you want?

I knew what I wanted. I wanted to have a baby before I got cancer. I wanted to just do that one thing, then they could remove every body part that made me a woman. They could turn me into a flat-chested Barbie doll. I was all right with that. Take it. If it made me live, just take it.

And what about Adam? What about the knot of conflicting feelings we both had? What about the compounded opposites? The love that flicked off like a light switch for one of us just as the other's flicked on? It was a disaster. A complete disaster. I couldn't bring a child into the mess we'd created.

I sat on the toilet with my hand trapped between my closed thighs. I couldn't look.

What did I want?

Was it important to know before I looked at the stick? The result wouldn't change.

But I had to know what to hope for. I had to believe something before I knew something. How else would I know how to feel?

I didn't want to be pregnant. I didn't want a baby now. Of the dozen reasons a woman could miss a period, I didn't want it to be the most likely. Anything but. I wasn't ready. *We* weren't ready.

"One line. Just please, give me one line."

I opened my legs and lifted the stick to eye level. The wet, grey wave had passed the first line in the little window and made its way to the other side in a serrated procession, passing where the second line should have been, to where it never would be, to the edge.

No happy second line appeared.

One pink line.

Not.

Pregnant.

A sob shot out of my lungs like cannon fire. I threw the stick in the trash as if I could break it. It just made a cracking noise against the plastic bag. So ineffective. Everything was ineffective. Everything I tried to do was a goddamn joke. Even the things I didn't try failed. Even when I was handed everything in life I barely made it work and here I fuckingwasinthisfuckingbathroom—

I stood and kicked the bottom of the pail. It upended and spilled toward me, dropping a couple of cotton swabs by my socked feet and a failed pregnancy test on my foot. I kicked it off, lost my balance with my pants around my knees, and fell ass-first on the bathroom floor.

Tears came. Breaths hitched. I had a decent amount of snot happening. I let it go for a long time, but no matter how hard I cried, I couldn't touch the bottom of the pool.

I stayed there, curled up, and cried. I pulled out all the stops. I dipped deep into the well of pain to find I was emptying the ocean with a slotted spoon.

• • •

My phone dinged. It was getting dark, and I was still on the bathroom floor. My back pocket was folded under my waistband, tucked somewhere behind my knee. I wrestled the phone out.

—Where are you?—

I was mad at him. I was mad that he'd given me a broken baby last time and hadn't gotten me pregnant this time. I was mad that he didn't love me enough to be a father to the non-baby. Or that he would be a fine father, but not on terms I understood. I was mad that I loved the wrong parts of him, and that I felt closer to a sadist than a kind man. I was mad that he'd opened me up and I couldn't close the wound without him. I was mad that I could only really cry when he hurt me.

—At the loft—

I wasn't ready to tell him why I'd run to the loft, but I felt the compulsion to explain.

—I had to get shoes —

Lies. The marriage had collapsed on an underpinning of lies, and there I was, trying to set that same foundation again.

My reasons were irrelevant. Lies were lies.

—Come here before we go to the Intercontinental —

Dominant voice through the text. I sat up on the tiles. My eyes throbbed from crying, and the muscles around my mouth hurt from an hour in the weeping grimace.

Was it wrong that I wanted to please him? That in my misery, the idea of satisfying him was comforting? In obeying him, giving him that pleasure, I could soothe my own pain. I could stop worrying about the future for a few hours and do nothing but make him happy.

—Yes, sir—

I scrambled up and got my pants back on. I put the test and the bathroom junk back in the garbage can. I had this. I pulled my hair out of its clips and brushed it down, taking a good look at my face.

My eyes and lips were swollen and puffy. The whites of my eyes were webbed with hot red. He'd know. He'd ask. I couldn't lie to his face. I'd tell him about the failed pregnancy test, and he'd be relieved. I wouldn't be able to bear it.

—Bring the box—

Apparently my curiosity was about to be sated. Well, that would be a nice distraction.

If I just focused on pleasing him for one night, I might not be sad tomorrow. I could let it all go, and tomorrow I could be the adultingest adult in New York City. I could tell my husband, lover, Dom, ex, everything, and he could soothe me or not. I'd have it under control by then. I'd be able to see a way forward.

We had cold packs in the freezer. I took the softest and pressed it to one eye, then the other as I went about the house, gathering a long slate-blue dress and matching shoes. Navy lace garter. His pearl collar, just in case. I pressed the pack to my eyes the whole ride to Murray Hill.

Chapter 31

I'd gotten complacent. I let myself think I'd won him back. That our separation was over and we were about to open a new chapter in our marriage. I'd let the idea of a future with him get real when I took the pregnancy test, and he was so perfect, so comforting in his dominance, I let the hope solidify.

Because who could be so intimate and still walk away?

What kind of person played a woman's body like a well-loved instrument without caring about the woman inside it?

I had him. He wasn't going to say good-bye. I couldn't imagine being without him, and in my little cocoon of self-reflection, he felt the same way.

Complacency is the prologue to calamity.

I was going to be diligent. Stay on task. This wasn't the time to get distracted by a pregnancy test that changed nothing.

The strategy was to make sure he understood that he loved me. The tactic was to submit. To show him that even in submission. I was still the woman he loved.

Buck up, buttercup. There's work to do.

. . .

Him: Trousers open. Shirt buttoned. Tie draped, not knotted. Socks. Watch big as a dinner plate.

Me: Wet hair. Stockings. Garter. Bra. He'd taken away my panties. I wasn't clothed in much more than his stare.

"Where's the box?" he asked, doing up his cuff. I'd seen him do it a hundred times, and it was never as sexy as it was that night.

"In my bag, sir."

"Get it and present it to me."

I padded out to my bag in my bare feet. As soon I was out of his sphere, I remembered the single pink line. What it meant. The years I'd have to wait to start a family. As soon as I was back in the bedroom with the box, those years fell off me. He didn't make me forget, but his presence protected me from myself. Even saying nothing, he gave me permission to not worry. I needed that or I was going to cry again.

I got on my knees, looked down, and held it up to him. The corners were blunted and the tape had curled at the edges, but I hadn't opened it. I was proud of myself.

He plucked it out of my hands. "You did good with this."

"Thank you, sir."

"You all right, huntress?"

"Yes, sir."

Seeing outside myself, I was saying sir more than usual. I was more compliant in attitude as well as action. If I kept this up, he would realize something was wrong before I had the empty, clear feeling I got from making his will my own. That would be a lot of wasted sirs.

He took a small knife from his pocket and slashed the paper and tape off an edge, then down at a right angle.

"You conquered your curiosity." He handed me the slashed box. "Go on."

I opened it to find a small velvet box with the top on a hinge. I creaked that open. The shiny chrome object inside was a four-inch-long bulb with a ring on the end. I took it out, hooking my finger in the circle.

"Is this what I think it is?" I asked.

"What do you think it is?"

"A Christmas ornament."

He looped his finger inside the ring and took the toy from me. "Exactly right." He put the end against my lips, running the curve of the object along them. "Lick it." His voice was so soft and so stern at the same time.

I put out my tongue and tasted the hard metal.

"Open your mouth." When I did, he slid it in and out along the flat of my tongue until it went all the way in without gagging me. "Close it."

I sealed my lips around the base, leaving the ring outside my lips.

"The way it's in your mouth is exactly the way it's going to fit in your ass. You'll want to lubricate it with your spit. Be generous."

I tried to swallow my fear, but the plug kept my throat from closing. Adam took my hand and led me to the bed, guiding me onto my back. He opened my legs and pushed my knees back, squeezing the flesh of my thighs to expose me to his eyes.

My throat hummed, but I kept my lips locked and my tongue curled around the bulb. I eased into submission, and sexual pleasure merged with a rightness that washed away pain.

Adam bent down and licked the length of my seam. He sucked and kissed me without reservation or pause. He used his fingers to move the lubrication to my ass and back again. I groaned, eighty percent of the way to orgasm.

He stood and slid his finger in the metal ring. "Open."

I opened my mouth, and a thick line of spit tethered the plug to my tongue.

"Hands and knees." He slapped my bottom as I complied. "I'm putting this inside your ass."

"Then what?"

He couldn't fuck me if there was a plug in me. Right? I didn't know how it was supposed to fit in the first place.

"Then we're going out."

"With it in me?"

"Yes. Trust me."

He slid it across my ass, back and forth. There was plenty of lubrication on it, and the twenty percent of an orgasm I had left pounded at the gate.

"I'm going to take this slow," he said. "If there's more than a little pain, you need to speak up. It shouldn't hurt. Just breathe."

"Okay."

He slid it in my ass so slowly it felt as if it wasn't moving at all. I pushed against it. It went in a little, stretching me.

"Breathe," he whispered, putting his hand on my lower back and guiding me toward him. I stretched farther. "Does it hurt?"

"No. It's definitely something. But no pain."

"That's the widest part," he said, and with one last push, he got it all the way inside. My body closed around the base. "It's in."

I twisted around, looking at him over my shoulder. He had his cock in his hand.

"Make it hurt," I whispered.

He drew his hand down my back, considering it.

"Later," he said, sliding into me.

He fucked me hard from behind. I'd never felt anything like it. The weight. The stretch. The way his cock rubbed it through a membrane wall. I was completely full and fully complete, reaching orgasm with my whole body. He bent around me, his hand on my throat, gentle and firm as he came inside me.

His hoarse whisper seemed involuntary, straight from the gut, bypassing heart and brain. One word.

"You."

I closed my eyes and let him kiss my neck and whisper in my ear. I was perfect. I was beautiful. I was so very good.

One pink line perfect.

One lonely line beautiful.

One single line good.

I didn't feel inadequate for not being pregnant.

I felt inadequate for not creating a marriage worth being born into

Chapter 32

The event at the Intercontinental was the same as always. Bright lights. Little bronzed nametags. Red carpets that looked good on video but, in real life, were worn and gum-spotted. None of it mattered. He was on my arm and in the core of my body was a solid weight of shiny silver metal, stretching me for him.

"How's that thing feel?" Adam asked once we were out of range of the flashing lights.

"Not bad." I pulled him closer.

He gazed down at me, and what should have been a long, warm look into my soul ending in a kiss was actually short and interrupted by his need to talk to someone across the room.

We'd been married business partners long enough for me to regret the loss of that warm moment at the same time as I understood it. The nametag on the end of my ribbon lanyard said McNeill-Barnes Publishing, and it meant business. I could still play company owner. I could still be a business-woman. I was always the heiress to an iconic publishing house. Even with a butt plug inserted in my ass.

I had to bite my lips to keep from laughing. We were talking to Giulio Fenestro, who was a shoo-in for a Pulitzer. Not the time to giggle about walking around pretty-as-you-please with a hunk of precious metal in my rectum.

Do. Not. Laugh.

Adam yanked me to the silent auction tables.

"What's so funny?" he whispered.

"Nothing." I snapped up a clipboard.

"I've punished you today already. Am I going to add more for lies of omission?"

I wrote my name and a number on the sheet. I didn't even know what I was bidding on.

"Put my address. You'll be there for the duration."

"So sure, are you?"

I put down the clipboard, He took me by the chin and looked deeply in my eyes. I tried to hide the pain of the pregnancy test. First, with defiance, then submission as I looked away. I couldn't bear to look away for long, When our eyes met again, he wasn't looking at something that pleased him.

"Talk to me."

"I'm nervous about later, I guess."

He let my chin go and broke eye contact.

"Well, well," he said. "Look who's here."

I followed his gaze to Stefan, who was talking to Thalia Jonson from Breakneck Books.

"Krovite published his catalogs, right?" I asked. "That must be why he's here."

Adam didn't wait to answer but approached the pair with his usual confidence and grace. He didn't take my hand or give me his arm. His fingers didn't brush my neck as they often did when we were at a party together. He just went, and I dragged my butt plug behind.

Five minutes before, I would have had to stifle a laugh, but now I felt small and infantile with the sophisticated humor of a twelve-year-old boy.

I shook Thalia's hand and did a double-air kiss with Stefan. We talked about the future of plated art books versus art textbooks for a few minutes before Thalia excused herself.

"Just like old times," Stefan said then turned to me.

"Are you moving to Breakneck?" I asked quietly. "They just bought Havershim's old plant in Norfolk."

We engaged in a light, gossipy business discussion about Breakneck's color plating abilities, during which Adam didn't touch me or look at me. I could hold the conversation, but the weight of his inattention kept me from breathing right. Kept me from thinking clearly.

"Can you excuse us?" Adam said, offering me his arm.

"Of course."

He pulled me away from the crowd in the ballroom and up a set of beige marble stairs. My stockings felt saggy and my shoes bit the soft parts of my ankles, but I continued. I needed to focus on pleasing him.

We slipped past a velvet rope, into a narrow hallway lined with paintings of beautiful Victorian women and a deep blue carpet. He wasn't looking at me. Just walking fast and looking ahead. The avoidance hurt more than my shoes.

"Stop," I said. "What's the problem? Wait—" I interrupted myself, looking at the floor and putting my hands up to fend off his voice and his face. I'd melt for either. "You're going to ask me what I'm talking about, so let's just skip that part." I stood straight and took a deep breath, balling my fists and girding myself against his brutal charms. "If I thought you were taking me to fuck me, I'd follow. No problem. But I'm getting the sense there's no sex at the end of this walk."

My voice sounded shrill and desperate, and everything about him was simply rock solid and right with the world. Even in his confusion, as all the things he could say flashed across his face, he was perfect and I was a little girl who wanted to rip a piece of metal out of her ass.

"Just say it, Adam. Whatever it is."

"Your eyes."

"What about them?"

"They're swollen. Just a little. You probably put ice on them before you came, and now they're swollen again. You were crying. Don't deny it. I want to know why, and you haven't told me. So that means one of three things. Either it's something you don't want me to know, it's someone you don't want me to kill, or it's me."

My eyes swelled up again. My palms became as wet as my mouth. I was going to explode in a cyclone of spit and tears, so I clamped my lips shut.

"And I know it's me," he said. "It's what I said. It's what I didn't say. I don't know which. I can't get this right. I mean, at the Sheepshead house, when I made love to you, I felt it again. I thought..." He closed his eyes slowly and opened them again, looking more composed. "It doesn't matter."

"It does. It matters."

"It makes me crazy when you cry."

"Why?"

"I want to hurt whoever hurt you. Then I realize I might have to hurt myself. And I would. I will. Why were you crying?"

My feet hurt and my shoulders were suddenly stiff. Remembering the bathroom floor, I felt like a brittle statue in a fancy dress. I was made of shell and soft tissue. No lie I told would change that.

"I thought I was pregnant."

His eyebrows went up, and his face took on an urgency I'd never seen before. Part confusion and part smothered joy. "You—"

"I'm not."

"Ah."

"But it made me think. This baby. It doesn't exist, but it had parents. And I don't know if his parents have a future, so those babies won't ever exist. I feel like I killed children."

"What does that mean?" He brushed a hair from my cheek. The gesture was tender and sweet, somehow protective, existing in a land between Manhattan and Montauk.

"I didn't want it," I said fiercely. That was the only way. "I told myself to hope I wasn't. I know hoping one way or the other didn't affect the results, but the hope told me something. I don't want to be pregnant. But when I wasn't, I was disappointed. And that told me something too."

"You wanted to be pregnant," he said. "But not with me."

"I want children with you, but not in this situation. I don't know whether I'm coming or going."

"Maybe you're doing both." His fingers caught the ribbon lanyard, stroking to down to the nametag. Diana Steinbeck. Our names were merged on my tag.

"I don't know how to fix all this."

"It's amazing that you left me in the first place without thinking about how terribly inconvenient it would be."

"I'm impulsive. If it didn't take three sponsors to get into the Cellar, I'd be —" I cut myself off, but it was too late.

He increased the downward pressure on the lanyard just a little. "Excuse me?"

Fuck it. I had to stand by my actions or dance around them like an adolescent trying to get away with adult behavior. He wasn't my father.

"I started the process before you redlined it." I didn't say how many minutes before, or how easy it would have been to halt. Maybe I was an adolescent. I yanked my lanyard away. I wouldn't be physically threatened by him.

"Did Charlie write a letter?"

"I asked Stefan and—" Fuck it again. We said no lies of omission. He couldn't hurt me anymore. "Serena."

Adam let the tag drop, took me by the hand, and pulled me behind him.

"Adam, wait!"

"Don't let go."

He held my hand so tightly I couldn't have let go if I wanted to, then he slapped open the door to the main hall and cut into the crowd. He didn't slow down long enough for me to say help to someone I knew or cut a turn on my high heels.

"Adam! The floor is marble!" I barked after I slipped, avoiding a fall but not shame.

He stopped and, with the force of inertia that kept me moving forward, wrapped his arm around my waist. Then he kept crossing the room as if he were saving a life.

"What are you doing?" I hissed.

"Stefan. That's what."

"It's not his fault."

"The fuck it's not."

I followed more readily in an odd, unbelievable need to protect Stefan. "You introduced us. You made it possible."

"Exactly," he said. "I'm the only one who can undo what I did."

"It won't go through until after the thirty days."

"Irrelevant."

"You're being unreasonable."

He couldn't lodge an objection because Stefan came into view. I didn't know the man he was talking to. Looked like an old-school publishing guy with a comb-over, a five-thousand-dollar suit, and red tie.

I smiled at him as we approached, and since we were about to bulldoze his conversation, I mouthed the word, "Sorry."

"Isn't it funny how I don't see you for years and now you show up here?" Adam said the second he was in earshot.

"Nice to see you too," Stefan said. "Adam Steinbeck, this is—" he indicated the man with the comb-over but didn't have a chance to make the introduction.

My husband was made of fuel and fire. "And the Greens too. Everywhere she is, you show up."

Comb-over excused himself. Not that anyone noticed.

"It's nice to see her." He directed his words to me. "Do you want to see me?"

Adam didn't let me answer. "No, she doesn't."

"I think he's kind of interesting," I said.

Adam leveled a finger at Stefan. "Rescind your sponsorship."

"Is that what this is about?" Stefan faced me. "Are you all right?" He seemed genuinely concerned. He deserved an answer, but Adam didn't give me a second.

"She's fine."

"That's enough!" I said, pushing Adam's arm off me.

"She's mine, you understand? I'll decide if she's in or out." Adam growled it as if it were deadly true, but we'd just had a conversation about how I wasn't his. About how he could never love me and be happy at the same time.

"I am not." I was flat serious. Not yelling, almost too quiet for Adam to hear through the rage in his ears.

"I'm watching you," Adam continued. "And I'm watching her. So—"

"I'm not yours."

"—if I ever see you near her again—"

"I'm not yours." I raised my voice just a little.

"—I'm going to make it my business to —"

"I'm not yours!"

The ballroom gallery fell silent. The string quartet hit a speed bump and played again. Interrupted conversations continued. The world spun on its axis for everyone else, while I stayed suspended in time. Gravity stopped, and I floated in the space between us, where the tension between his shock and his rage vibrated.

"I'm not yours," I said. "We talked about this."

"For two days, you are."

I shook my head slowly. I couldn't utter the words releasing him from his last half week with me, but it was done. Something inside me had snapped under the weight of his words, the pregnancy test, and the burden of keeping love alive for the both of us. The charade was ending.

I held out my hand. "I need me coat check ticket, please."

He gave it to me. "I'll get you home."

I snapped the ticket away and pushed through the crowd. He would follow. I knew him at least that well. If I turned around, I'd encourage him. I just wanted my coat and a cab—alone. Then I wanted to go to my father's place and cry for a few hours. Maybe I'd cry hard enough to excavate my grief. I wouldn't tell Dad why I was crying. I wouldn't tell him how I knew we were finished. I wouldn't talk about the submission or my own needs. I'd only tell him how bad I felt for fucking this up.

"Diana." Adam sidled up to me when I handed the girl my ticket. "Let me take you home."

"No. Just no."

"Why not?"

My coat came. I pulled it over the counter. "Because I'm sad. And I feel hopeless. And trapped."

"By me?"

"You want me to answer that?"

He guided me away from the coat check window. His jacket still smelled like Montauk snow and his body smelled like fennel as it pressed against me.

"Don't answer," he said. "Just listen. We have a few days. Only a few more before things get even more complicated. Will we be together? Apart? Some middle thing? Something so painful we can't even imagine it? These few days we have, they're precious. It's all unknowns after that. So let's just lock ourselves away. You and me. We trust each other. We'll close the door on love and celebrate trust."

Running my fingers along his lapel, I avoided meeting his eyes. He pressed his lips to my cheek, then my neck.

"I want to tie you down one more time."

"What's the point?" I was arguing about nothing. I was going with him. I just wanted him to work a little harder.

"The way you try so hard to stay quiet when I hurt you. That moment of hesitation before you get on your knees." I felt the line of his erection against my thigh. "I want it as long as I can get it. I can keep you on the edge for fifteen minutes. I want to see if you can stay quiet before I let you scream." His lips traced a line across my forehead.

"I hate you."

"But you trust me."

I pushed him away, looking into his eyes. "I do. And if you break that trust, it's broken forever."

"I won't."

I walked past him, pushing my arms into the coat sleeves, tying my scarf, my heels clopping and echoing in the cavern of stone. A doorman opened the brass doors, and I went out into the cold.

Chapter 33

I got into the cab with the word *trust* written on my heart. But it wouldn't stick. Trust didn't want to be on the heart. It was in the mind. Maybe it was in the hands or voice, but though I knew we trusted each other, it wasn't the same as love written on the heart.

We got to Murray Hill before I decided what to do about it. So I abdicated to complicity. Trust would have to write itself wherever it wanted.

When we got into the apartment, he took my coat like a gentleman.

"Go into the bathroom. Take the dress off and put your hands on the vanity."

All the command and dominance were there. All the confident intonations that ensured my obedience were present. I should have hopped off to the bathroom to do his bidding.

If it were Montauk, I would have.

The day before, I would have.

But it wasn't Montauk or day twenty-three. It was the night of day twenty-eight, and something had changed. I went to the bathroom with my chin high and my shoulders back. Not to please him, but because I wanted this dead weight out of my ass and I didn't know how to get it out myself.

Naked, leaning over the vanity with nothing but the French stone countertop in my sight, I laced my fingers together and bowed my head. The diamonds on my wedding ring pressed hard against my fingers. After the first meeting with my lawyer, I'd put it back on. He'd had his ring on, and it seemed disrespectful to take it off before papers were signed, or he took off his, or we both agreed that the marriage didn't exist any more.

It was as if my world had always revolved around his pleasure.

He came in behind me. We made eye contact in the mirror. When he put his hand on my lower back and pressed down to get my ass up, I turned back to the top of the vanity, pressing my forehead against the cool stone.

"You're perfect. Don't let anyone tell you otherwise."

"Not even you, sir." *Sir* was marbled in sarcasm. Damn. I didn't want to show my hand. I didn't want my words painted in four coats of my feelings. I wanted to hide, and didn't.

He wasn't stupid. He heard it, but he chose to ignore it.

"When I take this out, you're going to be open for a few minutes. I'm going to lubricate you." He leaned down and whispered in my ear, "It won't hurt when I fuck you. Not more than a few seconds, maybe. You're going to come like you've never come before. Are you ready?"

"Yes, sir," I whispered back with my eyes closed.

He stroked my skin, warming me, then tugged gently on the plug. "Push out a little."

I did, and the thing slid out. He wrapped it in a towel and snapped up a bottle from the cabinet.

"How does that feel?"

It felt odd. It felt as if my body was doing its own thing. I felt stretched, empty, as if I'd made room for something that wasn't there anymore.

He squirted lube on me.

I wasn't scared. I thought I'd be tense at the prospect of getting fucked in the ass, but it wasn't the fear of pain or humiliation that caused my anxiety.

His buckle clacked and his zipper hissed.

"Do I say pinochle, or can I just say stop?" I asked.

"Don't think about that yet."

"No. I mean *now*."

"Why are you safeing out?"

"I just am. I'm not in the mood."

He continued to massage my bottom. "The sub doesn't get moods, Diana."

I stood up straight. Naked in the mirror with him behind me, we looked like normal people. But we weren't. Everything was wrong.

"Pinochle." I said it without question. I said it like he said *get on your knees*. And just in case he missed it, I repeated it. "Pinochle, pinochle, pinochle."

"Why?"

I faced him. "Because this is too intimate for how I feel right now."

"Diana, I—"

"I'm moving back to the loft. This..." I put my hands on his lapels. "This is a complete waste of time. I mean... it's not. It's fine. It's what I signed up for. But I'm just saying pinochle to the whole thing."

I gave him a little push and brushed past him to get to the bedroom. The afternoon's jeans hung over the back of the chair. I couldn't wait to get into them. I couldn't jam my legs in fast enough. My foot got tangled in the fabric and I nearly fell before he jumped to steady me. His hand on my arm, perfect pressure, just enough to hold me up but not hurt. His posture and expression were pure concern for my bodily well-being.

Oh, to be taken care of by a man who loved me. Something I'd never desired because I never wanted to be taken care of was now a lofty and far away fantasy.

"Let go," I said. "Let me fall, okay? Just let me fall." I stood straight, buttoning my jeans. I was still naked from the waist up, but his only interest was my face.

"Stay," he said. "Stay tonight and go tomorrow."

"No. I'm getting a cab." I snapped a shirt out of a drawer and pulled it on. No bra. Didn't care. The coat would cover me. "I'll come back for my stuff in the morning."

"Wait."

I didn't wait. I went to the front door. A pair of boots and the heels I'd worn to the event were under my coat. I stuck my bare feet into the boots.

"Diana!"

"What?"

In his nice blue suit, tie halfway undone, sock feet, and unbuttoned trousers, he looked like a man falling apart at the seams. He looked the way I felt.

"I want you to stay with me." The desperation in his voice was new, and I was upset enough to be immune to it.

"Whatever." I got my coat on.

"You're acting like a brat."

"I'll be one by tomorrow."

I turned the knob, but he leapt for the door, pressing his hand on the seam between the door and the jamb.

"Adam. Let. Me. Go."

"Stay tonight. Please."

"Look, if you can't love me, I get it. It's fine. I can save you the trouble. Just save me the trouble too. Save me the heartache."

"Just stay."

"Why? What's the difference?"

"I want you to finish what you started."

He said it with all the Dom bells and whistles, but it landed like a squib, not a bomb.

"I'll decide what's worth finishing. Me. I'll decide. Now let me out."

I yanked the door with all my might. His hand came off it, and I swung it wide with everything I had. It slapped the wall so hard the bell rung. I didn't waste a second, getting out into the indirect, warm lighting of the hall just as he put his arms around me. They grabbed nothing, sliding away like a scarf that wasn't wrapped tightly enough.

Chapter 34

DAY TWENTY-NINE

The rain sounded like a percussion section. I wrapped myself in my covers, alone at four in the morning. Wide awake after three solid hours of sleep.

I'd walked out on him to save my dignity. He'd made sure I had a car home, but I could barely look at the driver.

I'd reveled in feeling like a piece of meat with Adam. Rejecting my identity for a few hours. Existing for his pleasure. I didn't know what had changed. Something enormous and abstract. I couldn't put my finger on it. I got on my stomach and put my arms between my chest and the mattress, trying to squeeze out the panic that Adam and self-respect were incompatible.

I took my journal off the night table and scribbled in the half light.

At some point, it was going to come to this.

There was never hope for it. I'm running west to chase the sun. It's going to set, no matter how fast I go.

I'd stopped writing questions in my journal. I was making statements. I didn't even notice the change for the first two pages. I didn't realize something had broken until the third page, when I was unable to get the stream of consciousness back to questions.

Take a page from Adam's book. He didn't need love all those years. I don't have to love a man to get satisfaction from him either. Maybe. What would it be like?

Finally. A question. And yet, it was unanswerable because I couldn't imagine it. Couldn't sink deeply into a fantasy about some Dom I'd never met, seen, spoken to.

What was it like for Adam? How did he give himself to that intimacy without being intimate?

Practice.

Maybe.

Maybe peeling Serena and subs like her down to the core built him up until intimacy wasn't intimacy anymore.

The valid, even productive train of thought veered off the rails as I imagined him fucking Serena. Eating her pussy. Pulling her hair. Pretending to rape her by a creek.

My heart was a spool of emotions spinning as the thread was pulled faster and faster. She wanted him. She could have him again. I'd known it before, back when I was confident that I'd win him back, but all my imaginings of them weren't an imagined past, but a possible future.

I grabbed my phone.

His green dot was planted solidly in Murray Hill, in his kitchen, if the satellites were dead on.

That should have helped, but it didn't, because Montauk Adam wasn't limited to a single room. If he could take me anywhere in the house, he could take Serena too. She'd said she was going to Tel Aviv, but wasn't she back already? Or he could be with someone else. Or texting her. Or thinking about how he was going to get her in bed.

"For the love of God, Diana. Get control of your life," I said, tossing the phone back on the table. I hugged my pillow. It was a sad substitute.

Get control.

All right. Well, the first thing I had to get control of was the next few hours. Because sleep wasn't in the cards, and I wasn't going to lie in bed and mope like a freaking loser. If I was awake, I was going to do something. I put on sweat pants and a hoodie, laced up my sneakers, and went for a fucking run in the fucking rain.

The utter, blanket stupidity of this move wasn't apparent until I got around the corner and stepped in a puddle that left one sock soaking wet. The other didn't meet the wetness challenge until the next block.

Yet I felt better. Cold. Wet. Slipping every dozen steps, I still felt as if I'd gotten control of a few minutes of my life. All I needed to do was tack together more minutes, hours, and days.

I heard splashing footsteps behind me about four blocks from home, on a cobblestone stretch of Crosby. New York never sleeps, but it does go into a fugue state in the wee hours. A few cars splashed past. The bakery lights were on. But I didn't see another soul on the street. I turned. A man jogged half a block behind me, but not jogging. Not really. He was in jeans and a T-shirt. His hood shadowed his face.

What a pain in the ass.

I wasn't afraid. Not at first. At first I took the normal precautions. I turned onto a wider street with more traffic. He was still there. Then I had the good sense to be scared.

My heart raced. My vision closed up in the rain. I picked up my pace, but not that much. Not enough to force him to run. I wanted him to be complacent, because I had to think.

Assume it's not a coincidence. Assume it's not a random guy minding his own business. Run into a public place. Except there are no public places at four in the morning.

Run home. Then he'd know where I lived.

The thunder cracked and the rain picked up as I chose home. Crosby Street was narrow and dark, but I could get behind a locked door.

Headlights from a slow-moving car lit up the sidewalk, and I avoided another puddle. As I turned, the same headlights shone ahead. I turned. The man in jeans was still behind me, and astride him, a car kept pace. He glanced at it. Stopped as I kept going. When I turned back again, the man in jeans was running away from me, and the car sped ahead.

What the hell?

Had the driver chased the man away? I hadn't heard anything. Was it just the presence of the car? What had just happened?

You know exactly what happened.

I got under a scaffold and took out my phone, quickly opening the phone tracking app.

Adam's green dot was two blocks ahead of me, turning off the street I was on, left onto Crosby. Must have been Dominic's car. Or a hire. Something he'd grabbed fast when he saw me move. Something he could park by the loft and wait in, because according to the dot, that was exactly what he was doing.

If I started jogging, I'd get home from the other direction. He'd already be watching.

I could have gone and gotten a hotel room just to fuck with him. But I wasn't feeling spiteful. Having taken the run, I was truly tired.

I jogged home, looked at the car long enough to note it was Dominic's, and went into the lobby without even waving at my husband. I didn't want him to know I knew he was there, and I wanted to give him the gift of thinking I was safe because of him. Whether it was true or not, whether he deserved it or not, the gift was still mine to give.

Chapter 35

DAY TWENTY-NINE

I tried to work. I had an essay to read, a box full of emails, and checks to sign.

Though I'd slept soundly for a few more hours, my adrenaline was pumping by the time I got to work. Pictures of Adam and Serena danced in my head like sweaty, grunting sugarplums. I didn't want that shit in my brain. I felt violated by my own thoughts.

So of course I had to check his green dot.

It was like an addiction. I craved the rush of anxiety. I was both miserable and comfortable in the heady, unpleasant pain of panic.

It was day thirty. If I was going to get him back, my last best chance was during the next sixteen hours. After that, we'd live on the same planet, but we would be unbound.

And yet, it was over.

He loved me and couldn't admit it. He could chase away stalkers in the middle of the night, throw a fit about another Dom's advances, but he couldn't admit he loved me. Did I even have time for this? With or without

Serena breathing down my neck, how was he serving me as a lover? Was I chasing him out of fear that she'd scoop him up? If he was wrong for me, what was the damn difference?

My hands shook too hard to sign the checks. I answered emails. The essay was good enough. I sent it to Zack for further review.

Nadine's son wasn't in, but his little space was carved out, waiting for him. I wished he was there. He cheered me up.

Dad sat at the desk across the room. I could hear his wet breaths behind the mask. Humidity was tough on him, even if it was cold. The air became a solid thing.

"Dad?" I said.

He said *yes* from behind the mask and kept his eyes on his keyboard.

"Do you want to go home?"

He tapped a few more keys then pushed the mask to the top of his head. His grey hair got caught in the strap and stuck out at odd angles. The shape of the mask left a red oval around his nose, cheeks, and chin. "Why would I want to go home?"

"You don't sound good."

"You always tell me that, and I'm always fine."

"I'm sorry, I just don't want you to feel obligated."

He shut off the oxygen tank in three angry turns. "I am not obligated. Stop it. You make me crazy. Like you got nothing better to do than henpeck me your father."

"You're fine. I know."

"You don't. I taught you everything you know about this business before you were sixteen, but I haven't taught you everything I know."

I put my elbows on the desk and folded my hands. "Fine. Tell me something you know that I don't."

"Tell you something?"

"Yes. Tell me something. Surprise me."

"Management rule number one." He stuck his pointer finger at the ceiling. "If the person sitting next to you isn't complaining, don't ask them to. They're probably very happy to be working." He slipped his mask back down and turned on his oxygen.

Zack knocked and poked his head in.

"Hey," I said. "I just sent you the camorra essay."

My email beeped, and I looked as a matter of habit.

"I don't think it's expandable," he said, closing the door behind him. "Not unless you want to do historical forensics, which is fun but doesn't sell."

"Forget it." I opened the email and read it. "Oh!"

"Good news?"

"I won the silent auction. I forgot I even bid."

He leaned into me. I could smell his cologne. "Dinner for two at *Le Bernardin*. Very nice." He smirked and looked me up and down in a way that was wholly inappropriate.

"Yeah." I didn't want Zack to ask me who I was taking, because I wasn't taking Adam and I wasn't taking him. "Dad?"

He pushed his mask back. "I'm fine! Stop asking!"

"I know. Do you want to go to dinner with me?"

Zack stood, getting his breath off my neck. He really needed a good poke in the ribs with a very sharp stick.

"When?"

"I don't know. I haven't gotten the voucher yet."

"Sure." He looked from me to Zack and took the snap out of his tone. "Fine. Yes." He put his mask back and got to work.

"He really is a fun date," I said, and Zack and I laughed.

With a knock on my desk, he said, "I'll take you some other time." He winked and turned to leave before I could gracefully decline.

But then, why should I? Why not go with Zack? He was handsome and smart. He'd taken care of his mother when she was sick. He didn't seem particularly broken or so whole he was boring.

Wasn't I happy enough before I started crawling?

Why not just live? Why make it all so complicated? Why make every single thing about sex? Why not just fuck like a normal person? Was it so antithetical?

I couldn't stretch my limited experience over the drum of the question.

Two birds lined up, right then. And I had a stone.

All I had to do was throw it perfectly the first time.

Chapter 36

DAY THIRTY

I'd never been to the Cellar outside a tryout night. Without the amateur population, it was much emptier and had the feel of an exclusive gathering place, rather than a nightclub.

Stefan met me in the lobby, wearing a sweater with his collared shirt and a pair of slim slacks. He'd told me to wear whatever I thought would help me achieve my goal for the evening. I didn't tell him my goal. He was trying to get it out of me.

I'd chosen a long silk skirt and heels. The skirt covered me to the ankles but was so tight my goose bumps showed.

Adam had started texting me at four thirty.

—When am I seeing you tonight?—

I didn't answer the first time.

—Diana? I can still punish you—

                                                             —No, you can't—

I hoped he felt his power waning. I hoped he felt the weight of day thirty. I hoped he wanted to make it the most memorable day of the past month and I was thwarting him by not giving a shit.

Which was untrue. I gave a shit. Just not the same shit.

—Stay there. I'm coming to the office—

**—I'm leaving now,
so have at it—**

I called Stefan, and after I spoke with him, I did the hardest thing I could imagine. I left my cell phone in my desk drawer. Adam could track it all night long. I didn't do it to be cruel, but I needed space, and since this was the last day of our arrangement, I wasn't going to get any without a little subterfuge.

Stefan signed me into the Cellar as a guest.

"I want to tell you something," I said in the elevator ride up to the Cellar's sixth floor.

"Yes?" Stefan answered, hands in his pockets as if it were the only way he could keep himself from using them brutally.

"Serena's after Adam. She thinks she can make him happy where I failed."

"And vice versa."

The elevator doors opened, and we went to the bar.

"You knew?"

"I know her. Inside and out."

Could I say the same of Adam? Did I know him inside and out? I did, but it hadn't helped me one bit.

"You can stay close to me," he said.

"Okay."

Stefan pulled a chair for me at a little table by the window and ordered two ginger ales. At the bar, I recognized the young Dom from my first visit, when I'd gotten pulled into a dark room to watch a woman get paddled. He was in a crisp white shirt open at the neck and a grey sports jacket, talking to a woman in a business suit.

"If you have any plans," Stefan said when he saw me watching the young Dom, "consider me first. For your own safety."

Stefan was still Stefan. He still didn't care for Adam, yet he tied himself to a man he didn't like in an obsessive knot I didn't understand. If I could hazard a guess, Stefan didn't understand it either.

"Really? Safety?"

"I'm less of a wild card than you think."

I'd have to consider it. If I was going to continue experimenting in this world, I would have to weigh my options. Stefan was attractive. He respected me. He was probably more hardcore than I was ready for but—

"Well," I said, sitting up straighter. "You might want to turn around."

He raised an eyebrow, finally turning when I nodded.

Serena stood in the doorway, looking so confident a normal person wouldn't believe she was submissive. I wanted to look that confident. I wanted to fully submit and fully dominate at the same time, just like Serena.

Stefan only had eyes for her.

I didn't want what they had. Their relationship walked too many wires, was too high maintenance, too brutal and servile.

Locking eyes with her, Stefan grabbed my hand across the table. "Now. Please."

The *please* was more of a command than appeal. She turned her head away and went to the bar.

Stefan took his eyes from her and met mine. "I can give you what you want, however you want."

"Are you trying to make her jealous?"

"Come." He stood and held out his hand.

His Dominant voice had no effect on me. He was good, but he wasn't Adam.

I stood without his help. "Listen to me, you need to try something different. She's not coming back to you over sharing. Give her a reason to want you."

"I know her," he hissed.

"Apparently not. You're invested in keeping Adam and me together so she comes back to you. Get her back because she loves you."

Stefan and I were locked in a dead heat when an Australian-accented voice came from behind me.

"I just got the most interesting text." Charlie leaned on his cane.

"Let me guess," I said, letting Stefan watch Serena get a drink. "*Is my wife there?* You said yes. He said he was on his way. How long do I have?"

"This is getting old," Charlie said, leaning on Stefan's chair.

"At some point, he's going to have to just deal with the fact that I have a body and I'm going to do what I want with it."

"This is his club, missy." Charlie's voice was unusually sharp. "This is his safe space."

"Missy?" I sat so I could be eye-to-eye with him. "Who the fuck do you think you're talking to?"

"I'm talking to one half of a hot mess. The closer you get to what makes you happy, the more miserable he's going to be. And the only way for him to be happy is for you to forget all this and be miserable. What you two need is a few miles between you. Indefinitely."

Fuck him. He was butting in where he had no business butting. I sipped my ginger ale to hide the tension in my mouth. Scanning for Serena, I caught the eye of the young Dom in the white shirt. He raised his eyebrows just a little. Enough to let me know he wasn't looking at me by accident.

"He's like an alcoholic." I looked back at Charlie. I could have made a speech about my explorations and self-actualization, but I didn't. Couldn't. They were too abstract. "He's addicted to ideas about who he can love. You know the best thing for an alcoholic? Hit bottom."

Hit bottom. Make it worse by far. Take it as far as it would go. Was that the answer? Or would it make reconciliation impossible? And if it did mean Adam and I were finished forever, did that also mean that was best for both of us?

"People break up all the time. We're not inventing anything new."

"On the contrary." He leaned both hands on his cane. "You two are definitely inventing something new."

"Then let's not pretend to follow the old rules." I picked up my bag and coat and walked past him.

He laid his hand on my arm. Not a hard or threatening gesture, but it made me stop. "Where are you going?"

"Winning the race to the bottom."

I walked to the bar before he could ask me to explain. I made sure the young Dom saw me, but he was talking to a woman. I couldn't approach directly.

I needn't have worried. He met me halfway across the room.

"Hello," I said, folding my coat in front of me.

"I was hoping I'd have a chance to talk to you."

"About?"

He didn't pause a beat. "About where our needs intersect."

"I have a need."

"Tell me."

"My husband."

"Your husband?"

"You might know him. Adam Steinbeck."

"Adam Steinbeck?"

"Is there an echo in here?"

He laughed a little. Nice smile. Nice face. I convinced myself I could do this.

"You intrigue me past original thought," he said. "Tell me more."

"I was with him when you paddled a sub in one of the rooms back there."

"And?"

"And it looked like fun."

He raised an eyebrow, tilting his head slightly. "I like fun as much as the next guy. Adam hasn't been around in years, now his wife shows up wanting a paddling? Is he allowing it?"

"No. But he doesn't want me. He dropped me. So I can get my paddlings anywhere I want."

He crossed his arms. "What's your end game, Mrs. Steinbeck?"

"Honestly?"

"Honestly."

"Get him pissed enough to do it himself. He won't because I'm his wife. I need him to address our intersecting needs, as you say. If you do it, he might wake up out of his stupor."

"You know how foolish that is, right?"

"He's on his way."

His grey eyes lit up, and he put on a mischievous grin. "We'd better get to it then. My name is Chris."

"Diana. Nice to meet you."

He led me to the back. When I looked back, Charlie was no longer at the table. Serena was at the bar. I turned the corner with the vision of Stefan five feet from her, standing stock still as if afraid to approach. Three weeks earlier, I wouldn't have believed Stefan was afraid of anything, Serena least of all. Maybe it would be a night of shattered assumptions.

Chapter 37

If I ever love a sub, it's going to be you.

Desperation was a terrible mentor. Desperation covered the pitfalls in soothing colors, made everything outside of itself look more sensible. Desperation pretended to be calculation, but it was terrible at math. Desperation denied it was desperation until it hit bottom.

I can't love you.

"Your cheeks are red," Chris said when he closed the door behind us.

He'd led me through the long hallway with the rug of naked bodies to the same viewing room I'd seen him in last time. It was smaller from the inside, dimmer, both cleaner and more run-down than it looked from the other side of the mirror. Cables ran from the back of a box to a beige power strip with a red light at the end. The door on one of the cabinets didn't sit quite flush with the frame. The upholstery in the luxurious wingback chair had a tear that was shaped like an eye.

I felt close to you. Very close. And at the same time, I can't, Diana. I've tried.

"I'm nervous."

"Let's take away as much of that as possible. Let's set limits. One. You're a married woman."

"For now."

"I'm not going to touch you."

"Okay."

"And you can keep your clothes on."

"I want it hard," I said, surprising myself. "Don't waste my time with love taps."

"I wouldn't worry about that." He slid a paddle out of a leather case. The same one he had when I'd seen him before. Light-color wood. Three holes. Worn leather handle. He placed it on the table. "Ten strokes."

I nodded. "Yes."

"Yes?"

"Yes, sir."

When I called him sir, I was hit with the gravity of what I was doing.

Every time you submit to me, it's like I'm waking up from a dream and the reality is that it's just not there anymore.

"Lean against the edge." He tapped the table. I did it. The height came right to my waist. "Now, bend."

I did, getting my elbows under me. The paddle was right below my face. He crouched by my feet and fastened my ankles to the legs of the table. I had to stay on my toes to stay forward, creating a forward thrust to my posture.

When both were fastened, I got scared. I wasn't supposed to be scared. I was supposed to be aroused in anticipation.

Chris came up and looked at me. "You all right?"

"Yeah."

"We're playing a game, Diana. It's not more serious than that. And no matter how hard you say you want it, I don't know you well enough to really get in there where it hurts."

"Just don't bore me, okay?"

He laughed again. I was torn in ten places. He wasn't Adam, but he seemed all right. He was safer than my husband in a hundred ways, yet he was as dangerous as they came.

"Kiss that paddle," he said. "And spread your arms out."

I put my lips to the paddle and opened my arms. He pulled leather cuffs from under the table and tied down my hands.

"Now, if you want to stop, just say stop."

"I can remember that."

"Pick your head up."

I did, and he slid the paddle out from under me.

"Back down."

I put my forehead against the warm wood of the table. He tapped my ass with the paddle, and for the first time, I felt vulnerable and exposed. My heart pounded, and I took a deep breath.

"Count with me," he said.

He tapped my bottom again.

"Count," he said.

"You're joking. I'm not even counting that."

"Mister Adam Steinbeck has his hands full," Chris said before thwacking me good and hard.

I grunted. "One."

Again, harder. *Whoosh-thwack*

"Two."

"You really meant it."

"I got this."

He hit the breath out of me, *whoosh-thwack* sending waves of pain from skin to core.

"Three," I counted through my teeth.

"That's your sweet spot, right there."

Again, *whoosh-thwack*, a little lower. I let out a deep *unh*.

"Four."

I wasn't turned on sexually, but I was on fire with challenge. I could take this. I could take whatever he dished out.

I could finish. But that was all it was. He couldn't break me. He couldn't find me. He wasn't my master, and I wasn't his property. Not even for a minute. All he could do was test me.

On the wall above, a red light I hadn't paid any attention to turned green.

"You're doing great," he said before he hit me again.

Multiple strokes made each one hurt a little more as fresh pain laid itself on top of old pain.

"Five."

The next *thwack* came without a *whoosh* and the pain arrived out of cadence.

"Six."

The sound of the last *thwack* hadn't been a *thwack* at all, because it repeated itself. Deeper, more resonant, farther away.

Someone was pounding on the mirror.

"Well, well," Chris said. "I suspect—"

"Don't stop."

Whoosh-thwack.

Harder. I curled my toes and strained against the cuffs. "Seven!"

"You sure?"

The pounding was accompanied by shouting, but it was all muffled a million miles away.

"Yes!"

Whoosh-thwack. Searing pain.

"Eight!"

Again. Tears shot from my eyes, but someone else was crying. Someone who didn't care if she ever got to ten. A woman in the moment. I wasn't that woman for the next stroke. I was the huntress, and completion was my prey.

The pounding on the mirror stopped. The green light on the wall went back to red. Had he gone away? Had it been someone else? Did he decide to stop trying to love me?

"Nine!"

So busy in my thoughts, the last stroke came as a surprise and I cried out.

"Ten." It came out as a groan.

"Good girl."

Chris laid the paddle down and came to the side of the table. Past my tears and the limitations of a head resting on a table, I couldn't see much besides the full-sized boner under his trousers.

He undid a cuff then crouched to meet my eyes. "You're really beautiful."

"Thanks."

He walked around the table again and undid my other cuff. "If it doesn't work out with your husband, I'd really like to hurt you sometime."

On the wall, the light went from red to green.

"I know where to find you."

My wrist came free just as a crash deafened me. I twisted, wobbling to feet that had been paddled for ten strokes, to hear another crash as a garbage pail came through the two-way mirror, opening a three-foot-high hole.

Adam was on the other side of it.

My husband looked like a savage. Borderline feral with his jaw clenched and teeth showing. His jacket was open, exposing a chest that heaved with breath, stretching his shirt. His hair was askew, and his fists were clenched. The fire in his eyes was directed over my shoulder, at Chris, who I'd stupidly gotten involved in something that didn't concern him.

"I asked him to," I said.

"I'm going to kill him anyway." Adam stepped through the hole in the mirror, swiping the cracked edge of the opening. A spray of broken glass clicked to the floor.

"She was lovely," Chris taunted. "Too good to throw away."

"Chris," I said, turning slightly, "thank you, but can you go? Please?"

Chris backed away. Adam lunged at him in one fluid move. I put my hands on my husband's chest and pushed as hard as I could. The moment when his body parted with my fingers was the moment I realized how sore my bottom was.

Chris grabbed his case and his paddle. He didn't seem bothered at all. "Take care. And I mean that."

He left. I pushed Adam as he tried to charge out the door after him.

"Back off," I said.

Finally, he looked at me.

"Blame me," I said.

"What were you thinking about?"

"My future. My life. What I want."

"I won't watch you become a whore."

When rage surged from my glands, it bypassed my heart and mind, going directly down my right arm, which shot out and slapped his face with every bit of strength I had. His face moved with the velocity of the blow, but not enough. I swung again with the same force, but he grabbed my wrist mid-stroke.

"Diana."

The rage wasn't done flowing. It rerouted through my left hand, which caught him by surprise. I slapped him again. And again, when my left hand went to slap him a second time, he grabbed it midair until he was holding both of my arms up by the wrist.

I wasn't done.

I'd been raised in privilege, but I was still a New Yorker. When I spit in his face, the aim was as perfect as the thrust, and a formidable mass of throat gunk landed right between his eyes.

"Stop it," he growled though his teeth.

There were voices in the hall on the other side of the broken mirror.

"Fuck you, Steinbeck. Fuck you. You made me like this. You woke me up. You dragged me out of the darkness and now you don't want me in the light. Well, fuck you." I jerked away, and he let me go. "I don't fit in that box anymore, and you don't love me outside it. Fuck you. Either love me or set me free. And if you let me go, don't think for a minute you can dictate how I live without you."

He pulled a handkerchief from his pocket and wiped his face, and I took the opportunity to spin on my heel and walk to the back door, grabbing my coat and bag. I walked fast as I pushed my arms through the sleeves, into the back hall with the rug decorated with nudity. People looked at me, or I thought they did. I was a stranger, but for how long? Forever? Or was I already kin?

I was nothing. Nowhere, in the middle of a jump from one world to the next, midair, legs pumping at nothing above the chasm of in-between-ness. Neither-nor-ness. A yawning gape of indecision. A life without an identity.

The hall was a tunnel, soft and out of focus at the edges like a vintage portrait.

Only forward.

I had to make it to the other side. The other side of who I was. The other side of my life. The other side of the hall.

I clung to the million paths to success and came up with a chest full of anxiety. Go back to vanilla. Go full bore into kink. Get another Dom immediately. Remain faithful until death. Be present at the Cellar. Move to Tahiti.

Every path was a fantasy. A road not taken because it didn't exist. I couldn't decide what to do with my life based on how he'd react, but I couldn't imagine doing anything without loving him.

He'd asked me for much more than I thought I could give. He'd asked me to love him when what awakened my love was the very thing that killed his love. There was no path to reconciliation. They weren't just less traveled, knotty, bracken-blocked road. They'd been demolished by our crossed purposes, and we had so much work to do to find our way back. The thought of it made me tired.

Adam's fingers hooked in my pocket, and when I turned, he looked so anxious I could feel the coil twisting around his lungs, squeezing out all the air. He was trying to get to the other end of something, but our paths were perpendicular. We'd cross once and never meet again.

"Please." He took his hand from my pocket and held both out as if showing me he had nothing left to offer. "I love you."

His words blocked my forward momentum, and the bucket of my heart filled with rage.

"Don't you dare pull that trick. I'm over it, Adam. I'm over not knowing which end is up. I'm over letting you control me. I'm over being a puppy dog to your moods. I can't play any more. I'm done. Finished."

He put his arms around my waist, his lips on my shoulder, then my chest, his arms around my thighs as he kneeled before me and held me still.

"I love you, Diana."

"No, you don't."

In the hall of the Cellar, with his peers playing their parts as props on our stage, Adam knelt in front of me, hugging my thighs, wrapping me in his need.

"I'm sorry, Adam. It's midnight. Day thirty. Time's up."

Adam

Chapter 38

The first time the garbage pail crashed into the glass, the window shattered like a windshield. A hole in the center webbed out in a series of tempered glass cracks that looked like her eye, ocean blue, trapped in a white net. I smashed it again, breaking the web.

I was supposed to know how far to push a sub before she broke, but I didn't. I'd misjudged. I loved her. I knew I loved her. I didn't know how to express it, but she knew. She knew.

She knew everything. She'd intuited it in my old bedroom, even before I digested it. The path closed behind me, and if I stopped, the inertia of the past would run me down.

I'd realized my error too late, because it was the first of so many.

Up to a point, I'd been honest with myself and Diana. That point had been in my grandparents' reinvented porch in Sheepshead Bay. I'd gone to hell after that. Right to hell. I didn't know what to tell her, because I was barely on speaking terms with myself. I kept my silence to buy time. If I'd bought enough, there wouldn't have been lies, only delayed truths, but the mistake went from emotional to tactical. I'd made the mistake of not recognizing that my love had never left and a second mistake of not telling her.

I'd wanted to be sure. I didn't want to lead her down a path she couldn't finish walking without me.

When I saw her in that room with Chris, I broke.

I was jealous. When her toes curled and I could see the bottoms of her feet, I pounded the glass. Fuck the glass. It wasn't stronger than I was. It wasn't thick enough, tough enough. It was a thin layer of bullshit.

If I could just talk to her. Tell her I got it. I was jealous. I'd admit that. I'd cop to a ton of shit. Paddling Serena because I thought Diana didn't even care. Stupid. I'd opened that door with my own actions. Me. My fault. All of it. I'd drop all my shit and apologize. I knew how it felt. And I'd tell her, for a goddamn second if I could, that the jealousy was bad but not the worst of it. I could handle jealousy. It was seeing her hurting herself that broke my heart. She was a new sub. An open wound. I'd let her down, and she did what any sub would do. She tried to find an answer, and for the love of fuck, there was no good end to this for her.

She was in that room because of my failures. She was trying to preserve her dignity with indignity.

As I stormed out of the dark room, I understood it all. I saw inside her because she was my sub, and she saw that I still loved her because of a bond I'd forged and ignored.

We were in sync. I got it. Now to destroy the thin layer of glass between us.

Heaving the pail, I hit the glass so hard my arms vibrated. It cracked into an eye-shape. I couldn't let that cracked eye bore down on me for another second. I smashed the window again, and it came apart in a layered symphony of glass cracking, breaking, falling. A jagged hole opened from knee to chest height. I walked through it ready to connect with her. Ready to tell her I loved her. I'd always loved her. I'd fight for her.

"She was lovely," Chris taunted. "Too good to throw away."

The little fucker just had to poke me. I went in with the best intentions, and he'd picked at the scab like a toddler, flicking away the healing so the wound bled. I would have done something stupid if she hadn't stopped me long enough to let him leave.

"What were you thinking about?" I asked as if I didn't know. She was working on her own wounds.

"My future. My life. What I want."

"I won't watch you become a whore."

I had more to say. Nicer things. How she didn't have to hurt herself. That I'd take care of her. Take care of everything.

But I lost control. She was the sub. I was the Dom. For fuck's sake, why did I lose control with her constantly?

She hit hard. I'd give her that.

"Diana," I said as I held her wrist.

She wasn't a lefty, but she hit like one. I held both her wrists. I could explain this. I could tell her what the fuck was happening if she'd just stop slapping me for a second. Then she spit in my face. I should have been enraged at the humiliation. Any Dom would have punished her hard or broken it off right there. But she was more than a sub at that moment, and I was less than her Dom.

She was the huntress, and I admired how she'd found a way to slap me without her hands.

"Stop it." I maintained a deep control of my voice, but she wasn't receptive. Couldn't say I blamed her.

"Fuck you, Steinbeck. Fuck you. You made me like this. You woke me up. You dragged me out of the darkness, and now you don't want me in the light. Well, fuck you." She jerked her arms. I let her go and went for my handkerchief. "I don't fit in that box anymore, and you don't love me outside it. Fuck you. Either love me or set me free. And if you let me go, don't think for a minute you can dictate how I live without you."

I heard her. Every word. She'd said similar things before, but I hadn't heard her the way I heard her then.

I opened my mouth to tell her, but in the moment I closed my eyes to wipe off the spit, she was gone.

I had to tell her the most important part first, but she was walking so fast and there were people everywhere. I hooked my finger in her pocket as if her clothes might accept me where her body wouldn't.

"I love you." I'd said those words before, but I was sure that was the first time I'd understood them.

"Don't you dare pull that trick. I'm over it, Adam. I'm over not knowing which end is up. I'm over letting you control me. I'm over being a puppy dog to your moods. I'm done. Finished."

The moment when I crashed and all my resistance broke into sorrow, I had nothing to do. I didn't have a plan to execute. The frustration of that note on the counter went from sharp as newly-broken quartz to smooth as a rock pounded by the sea for millennia.

Tell her. Tell her everything. Stay up all night picking it apart.

I just got on my knees and held her as if she was a buoy in a rising tide.

I had the same urgency to make it right, to do *something*, but I was powerless to do anything, and despair filled the space where determination had been. My attempts to love her kneeling form had worn away the need to get her back, and the intensity of my need to protect her pounded away at my ability to leave her.

Both. Neither. All.

She put her fingers in my hair as I knelt in front of her. I was going to have to get up, stand. Walk down the hall. Deal with the broken mirror and leaving my wife. I was going to have to get her back. Keep her. Turn my back on her. Let her go. Insist on possessing her. All of it at the same time.

I was exhausted. I needed her, and denying it had tapped me. I was empty. I had no will outside her anymore.

When she stepped away, I stood and walked briskly behind her without slowing down until we faced the closing elevator doors. It was full of people, and we had five floors to go. I couldn't wait..

"Please." I hissed through my teeth.

She didn't answer. The doors slid open and more people got in. The floor got light as we began our descent.

"Stop playing around," I said. A Domme looked at me, then Diana. I didn't know her and I didn't give a shit.

"Not here," Diana said, watching the numbers flicker on and off. When the doors opened on the first floor she burst out and I rushed behind her. She and I burst into the cold, wet air of Gansevoort. Cabs waited in a line of coward yellow. She opened the door of one without looking at me. Panic gripped me when she sat and reached for the handle to close the door. I held it fast.

"What do you want?" I asked.

She started to answer, stopped herself, shut her mouth, moved her jaw a little as if she needed to chew and swallow what she had been about to say.

I shouldn't have asked. Shouldn't have put it all in her lap. And the question was meaningless. What is it to want? Wanting is compulsive. Want sneaks up in the middle of the night and infests the soul with dissatisfaction. Want becomes an obsession. Want isn't real.

I needed her. My need was physical. It came in chemical bursts of sexual desire and protective rage. Did I love her? Did it matter?

"It's midnight," she said again. "Day thirty. Time's up."

What could I say to that? I couldn't argue that she needed to finish her training or that we needed to stop this disaster before we both did something even more stupid.

"I don't care," I said.

"I can't live like this."

"Me neither. But I can't live without you. I can't live with how I acted. I was trying to break what we had, but I didn't. I made us better, and I couldn't see that. Please forgive me. You have to forgive me."

"Okay." Her voice was husky in those two syllables, as if the word was made up of half-digested pieces of other answers.

The cabbie's voice came from the front seat. "I'm turning on the meter. Where to, lady?"

"Come back to Murray Hill," I insisted.

"Out or in?" the cabbie said urgently.

Her eyes, the color of tempered glass that shattered when I cared about her more than myself, had never looked more opaque.

"In." She tried to close the door, but I held it.

"You shouldn't do this alone."

"Let go." Her voice came in the loudest whisper I'd ever heard. "I mean it."

"Please!" the cab driver begged. "Out or in? Pick one!"

"Let go," she said.

"Come to my place. I'll make you believe I love you."

"No, you won't. It's not about how much you say you love me. I'm ashamed of what I just did. I won the game but at what cost? I degraded myself. Not sexually. I degraded myself morally. I used to be better than that. Now I'm an awful person. I hate what I've become. I hate being a winner and I hate playing games. I can't do this any more."

"We're going!" The cabbie shouted. The car jerked forward as he put it in drive. The door came out of my hand and she slapped it closed. The cab took off.

The car jerked forward as he put it in drive. The door came out of my hand, and she slapped it closed. The cab took off.

Maybe I should have chased it, but I thought a few hours away from me would be good for her. I'd let her stew, then look for her little green dot on my phone. I'd go wherever she was.

As Rob and Carol came toward me, I took out my phone.

"Mr. Steinbeck," Rob said, "there's a big mess in observation seven. Serious damages. Your name came up."

"Yeah." I smiled at him while my tracker app opened. "That would be me. Let's settle up."

I went inside without a fight. I'd pay through the nose for the glass then go to Diana. The green dot of her phone appeared on my screen, making a turn east onto 14th street.

I was about to put the phone away as I entered the darkness of the club, but before I could, the green dot disappeared. She'd cut me off.

Chapter 39

The sun rose with me alone in my bed and Diana half a city away, I just didn't know in which direction. The green dot hadn't reappeared. I stood outside the loft, but the lights didn't come on. I went up to Riverside Drive, but I didn't see her in Zack's window. I went past her father's building on Park. The doorman said he hadn't seen her.

The thirty days I'd demanded had been more crowded than I'd intended. I'd planned to fall out of love with her but hadn't planned on her falling back in love with me. I'd planned to leave her but hadn't planned on wanting to stay.

—**What do you want to do?**—

My finger hovered over the send button. If I asked her like this, I'd find out when she woke up in a few hours. Yes, no, maybe, or a torrent of a hundred texts slicing what had happened between us and what it meant for our future.

But it could be no. A flat no.

Until I got a flat no, I had hope, and I needed it. I wouldn't forgive myself otherwise.

So she wasn't going to decide through the phone. She was going to tell me to my face, and I was going to remind her why I was the only man who could dominate her.

It was five in the morning. I had a couple of hours to answer some emails, go for a run, make myself presentable, and ask her what she wanted face to face.

Chapter 40

I waited in her office.

Our office.

I got there early and sat on the couch, answering email from my phone. I felt strong and sure. Ready to grab her, hold her, convince her that I was back one hundred percent.

But she didn't come. I built a tower out of Legos and still she didn't come.

Kayti didn't come.

The office was empty as a church on Monday. A temp sat at reception. She was as surprised to see me as I was to see her.

"Where is everyone?" I asked, tapping my watch.

"Don't know. Just got a call from the agency. Should I get someone on the phone for you?"

McNeill-Barnes was my company and I didn't need a temp receptionist to find out why the fuck no one was in the office on a weekday.

I called Diana while I waited for the elevator and called Diana. No answer. Got in, hit the button and sent a terse text asking after her whereabouts.

Undelivered, naturally, because I was in a fucking elevator.

By the time I got down the block to the loft, I'd texted three more times and none had been delivered. All my calls went to voicemail. She'd been in my sights eight hours before, but she'd disappeared. New York was playing a shell game with me, picking up all the cups one at a time only to reveal she wasn't under any of them.

I was about to open the door of her building when the city turned the first shell again, and there she was. Through the glass, wrapped like a Christmas present in light refractions from the moving doorway, she stood near the elevators.

She was with a man. He was so close to her, I thought he was moving past her to get to the elevator. But he wasn't. He held her in his arms. I couldn't see well. Was it a hug or a kiss? Or, in other words, did I want to kill someone?

Which I'd wanted to do the night before.

I craned my neck to see who it was. If it was Chris, I would break another window. I would break windows all over Manhattan. I would pave the sidewalks in broken glass.

It wasn't Chris.

If it had been Chris or any other Dominant in the known universe, I would have done harm to myself and others. If she was going to have a Dom in her life, it would be me. But as the light refraction moved, I was relived of that burden. It wasn't a Dominant I knew of.

It was Zack.

Chapter 41

TWO DAYS LATER

I walked to work every morning. Two mornings since I'd seen her, but it felt like a year. I kept intending to hop the subway or grab a cab, but my legs kept moving, rotating the wheels in my mind with a push-pull-push-pull.

Push—She was mine. She'd always be mine. Even as confused as I was about what love meant between us, she'd never stopped being mine. Not for a second.

Pull—I couldn't compete with vanilla. I could never go back. If she wanted the old me—but not *me*—I was powerless to change her mind. And though the feeling was much the same as the day I'd found her note on the counter, there was less I could do about it.

I texted her and heard nothing. Her green dot didn't reappear. She'd blinked out.

I'd lost the love of my life. I had to accept that.

Acceptance was freedom. I went with it for two days. I pushed down a pain in my chest that said *wrong wrong wrong* until I couldn't bear it. Couldn't sleep. Ate nothing. I was sucked dry. I texted again. No answer.

Freedom sucked. Freedom wasn't more than losing the fight. Signing a treaty of complete surrender. Giving up the homeland to the opponent and watching it burn day and night from a foreign land.

I said my good mornings at R+D. Push-pulling down the hall through a tunnel that led to my desk.

I didn't like losing. I wasn't used to it. Not in business and not in the personal. Losing this fight was like walking the length of a swamp and coming out on the other side covered in leeches. Each one had to be pulled off painfully. My pride. My sense of self. My imagined future. My culpability. My love might never come off. That one would bleed me the rest of my days. I'd hemorrhage love.

I closed the door to my office and opened the top drawer, where I'd put her divorce papers. They clearly outlined her ownership of everything. She'd earned it. She'd tried to make it work. She'd come back from her own swamp, gone through it again, and come out the other side. I'd thrown her efforts back in her face.

Well, fuck me.

I clicked my pen and hovered over the dotted line. I had to release her if I was ever going to be free.

I didn't want to be free, but she did.

A knock came at the door, and Eva poked her head in. "Adam?"

"Yes?"

"I set up a meeting in half an hour. We're doing the Theesen property projections. Have you looked at them?"

"No."

She stepped all the way in and closed the door. "Are you all right?"

"Not really."

"Is it Diana?"

"That's a personal question. We don't do personal questions."

She wasn't put off. She came deeper into the office, pink from head to toe in a wide lapel jacket and flowing silk pants. She was a beautiful woman I couldn't be attracted to. How many more would there be?

"If you didn't want me to ask a personal question, you would have said you were fine."

"I'm not lying anymore. But that doesn't mean I'm explaining."

She sat on the chair in front of the desk and crossed her legs. Her pumps were pink. "Noted."

I signed the divorce papers. Dated next to my name. Initialed by the tabs. Folded the pages in threes. Regretted it then let it go, then regretted it again.

"Do you know why I decided to work with you, even though you were younger and had shit for brains?" she asked.

"My acumen?"

"You had no fear. You pitched me projects so risky, no one had even thought of them."

"I was young and stupid."

"And lucky. But I didn't know that yet. What I did know was that you had real upside. You were a winner."

"Well, you were right. Up to a point."

"You're still a winner. Even when you lose."

There were a few occasions over the years when Eva had tried to be a big sister to me. I hadn't been able to let her go there because I needed to be her equal in the office. Had the distance been necessary? Had I distrusted her with my confidence, or myself?

"Thanks," I said. "Can you have Britt send these?"

She took the papers and tapped them on the heel of her hand. "It's hard to see now that this can be a new start."

"Noted."

"You can make your life whatever you want from this moment."

"What if I don't know what I want?"

"You can figure it out. You're handsome. Successful—"

"Are you making a pass at me?"

"You're too good a catch. I prefer pathetic losers." She stood. "It's a weird fetish."

"You can make your life whatever you want from this moment."

"Touché."

"I'll review Theesen and see you in the meeting."

"Good."

She went out and left me alone with a life of infinite choices, minus one.

Chapter 42

I couldn't sleep. A full glass of whiskey didn't cure the insomnia. I went to Crosby Street and watched the loft window for signs of life, but even at eight in the morning, four hours into my vigil from the coffee shop, I saw no sign she was even there. I asked the doorman if he'd seen her and he hadn't.

I was supposed to be letting go. Signing the divorce papers had done nothing to quell the anxiety that screamed *wrong wrong wrong.*

I went back to the coffee shop and ordered another. I just wanted to see if she was all right. That was what I told myself. But by nine thirty, I knew she wasn't coming home. I went back to Murray Hill to get ready for work.

So much for being free. So much for the breadth of choices. So much for giving up on her. Maybe I was tired, and in the exhaustion, I fell back into old patterns. I was married. She was mine. My wife. My lover. My sub.

Even though I felt the truth, I knew another truth. Equally accurate yet diametrically opposed.

She was less mine than she'd ever been.

When I got out of the shower, I took off my ring and put it in the medicine cabinet. My hand didn't feel any lighter. The skin at the base of my finger was pressed smooth and shiny. Even after I rubbed it, an indent remained. Even in winter, the bottom of my finger was a lighter color than the rest, as if the metal was gone but the ghost of the marriage remained.

I got dressed. I didn't have the energy for formality, so I put on jeans and a sweater. Then I decided that maybe today was the first day of a new life, so I put on a charcoal-grey suit that was narrower in the shoulders. Back when I dressed for Diana, I'd avoided it. It was time to stop caring what she liked. It was time to be alone with my preferences.

Single Windsor knot.

Shit.

Wrong shirt for that. It looked dinky with the wide collar, and the wide collar wasn't right with the jacket.

Double Windsor or change the shirt?

Jesus Christ, asshole. Get it together.

The doorman buzzed the intercom.

"Yeah," I said into it, pulling off the tie.

"Good morning, Mr. Steinbeck. I sent a guy up with a package."

"Thanks."

I made coffee. Fuck the suit. Fuck the whole thing. Let it all unravel. Maybe I'd just go to Tahiti for a year and wear nothing but cut-off jeans and puka shells. I could learn to surf. Sit in the sun and tan this white ring off my finger. Let it burn this pain out of my chest. Maybe I could throw away this damaged soul and grow another. One that worked right.

When the bell rang, I went to the door. I signed for a small package, not looking at it until I'd tipped the delivery guy and closed the door.

Mrs. Steinbeck - Congratulations! Your silent auction prize is enclosed. Thank you again for supporting the Literacy Project.

I'd forgotten she'd bid on something at the event. What had it been? Who even knew? I dropped it on the front table. I could send it to her. Or I'd deliver it personally. I could ask her how she was doing. See if she was with Zack. Ask if that meant she was going vanilla. Pretend I was all right with whatever she said. Look right into her eyes and see if she was lying when she said she was fine. Maybe I'd see Zack at McNeill-Barnes and commit murder. Get myself arrested before noon.

Talk about a new life.

As I finished getting ready, going back to sweater and jeans, I decided using the package as an excuse to see her wasn't in line with starting fresh without her.

Having used my entire store of willpower in the decision to send the package rather than deliver it, I was powerless against my desire to see what was inside the box. Maybe she was sending me a message. Hope could be in the bottom of that box. I opened it. A certificate lay on top.

Dinner for two at *Le Bernardin*. I knew the place. Sauces swiped across white plates like impressionist pigment and cooked scallops placed back in the shell. Lighting so dim the menus came with little gold-plated flashlights. Nice. Great. She'd probably take Zack. Maybe her father, but if she was sleeping with that weasely little motherfucker, she'd have every reason to take him.

I didn't have to deliver it at all. Then she couldn't take Zack out to a six-hundred-dollar, pre-fuck dinner.

Maybe she hadn't won this thing. She had no way of knowing, and I wasn't made of stone. The money would go to the charity whether she went out for dinner or not.

I was being an asshole. I was being petty and immature. I was jealous. Ravenously jealous.

I folded the voucher to remove it from the box. I was throwing it out. I only had so much patience for this shit, and it had just run out.

If she wanted to go back to vanilla and it had just been me she didn't want vanilla sex with, I would let her have that.

I hated it.

The thought ate at me.

I had no choice.

Like a bell from a heavenly host, my phone dinged. It had buzzed and dinged all day long. I didn't stare at it or answer it when I was doing something else, but this time, I looked at it.

Hello,

Sorry for the mass email. This is going out to all contacts.
As some of you know, two days ago, Lloyd Barnes passed away from complications associated with emphysema. He was a fearless leader and a shining light. We will miss him.
The wake will be at Costa Bros. Funeral Home. Address and viewing schedule are enclosed.
Thank you so much for your constant support.

~Kayti McTeague

PS: Business at Mc-Neill Barnes Publishing will continue on Monday. Please forward all inquiries to this email.

Chapter 43

Lloyd Barnes had had a long life. He'd made hundreds of friends, and every single one of them seemed to have shown up at his wake.

The funeral home was huge. Located in a double-width brownstone off Lexington Ave., it was a study in small rooms and dark woods, still life paintings and noise-absorbing carpets. She'd be in the front, by the casket. I had to push through a press of people and perform a thousand niceties before getting there.

Lloyd was laid to rest with a rosary in his folded hands. I'd forgotten they were Catholic. They had too. Even when Diana and I were married at City Hall, no one had brought up a church even though I was Catholic too.

"She's not here," a voice said from behind me.

It was Zack. His hand was out to shake. I looked at it. Considered ripping it off. But it was a funeral for fuck's sake. I shook his hand. I could break his face another day.

"Where is she?"

"I don't know. No one does. Apparently she didn't go to her mother's funeral either."

"What did she say?" My throat burned with bile to ask, but I had to swallow it back. Let it burn again. None of this was my choice, and it wasn't about me. It was about Diana. "Anything? Last night? This morning?"

"Nope."

"Why aren't you trying to find her?"

"I don't know what you think—"

"This is her father. He was everything to her. And you don't know why she's not here?"

"I'm not her keeper."

"Yes, you *are*." My promise to keep my shit together was falling to pieces. I gripped his elbow as hard as I'd ever gripped anything. If I didn't, I was going to rip off his balls.

"What are you doing?" He tried to wrench away but was as cognizant of the crowd as I was.

"You're supposed to take care of each other," I hissed. "If you don't hold up your end—"

"I'm not fucking her. Jesus."

I loosened my grip enough for him to get away.

He rubbed his elbow. "You're a damn psychopath."

"I saw you in our lobby." I was as good as calling him a liar. I was also starting to doubt he was lying at all.

"A few days ago? Lloyd was sick, really sick, and I took her home. Look, I tried. I admit it. Her ring was off, so I tried. But she's all yours, okay?"

"It's not..." I stopped myself and straightened my cuffs. I didn't want to be misunderstood. "It's not that she's mine. She needs to be treated right. That's all. No more than that."

"What do you want me to say?"

I looked around. We were being watched. They'd seen my vise grip on Zack's arm. I felt like a criminal.

"Ask around, all right? See if anyone knows where she is. Please," I said.

"All right. For her. Not you, because you need help." He tapped his temple, saying I was crazy. Which I was. Completely out of my mind.

"I'm sorry about your arm."

He waved it off and went to talk to a group of three young women Diana had known in college. I forgot their names, but I knew they wouldn't know where she was.

I looked at Lloyd, painted in repose. The middle-aged woman kneeling in front of him made the sign of the cross and got up. Before I could think twice about it, I took her place, putting my knees on the pink velvet bench and my elbows on the brass bar.

"Lloyd, buddy," I said so softly I didn't know if the dead could hear me. "I'm sorry I couldn't get her back. It's complicated."

She missed her mother's funeral too.

I felt stupid, but I couldn't keep myself from talking to a dead guy. I was out of control, but not in a frightening way. "She's going to be really broken up about you, and it's not going to kill her. I know. But I don't want her to be alone."

She missed her mother's funeral too.

"I'm not a praying guy. I don't believe in miracles. But I want to make sure she's okay. So—"

She missed her mother's funeral too.

I didn't have to finish the sentence. Of course. I knew exactly where she was. Finding her there was a shot in the dark, but darkness was all I had.

"Lloyd. You're all right for an in-law. See you on the other side."

Chapter 44

I was aware she was an adult woman who was perfectly capable of taking care of herself. That unimpeachable truth sat in my consciousness right next to the fact that she needed someone to take care of her. The best someone for the job was me, but if not me, someone. Even adults who could take care of themselves needed to be taken care of.

I didn't try to make sense of it. The two ideas would never sing in harmony. Fuck it. I could own them both.

Manet's *Luncheon In The Grass* was in Paris. She could have caught a flight. The airport was my next stop, but first I had to check the Impressionist gallery at the Met. It was a short hop to Central Park.

I didn't get past Madison Avenue because I ran right into the beating heart of a protest.

The street was blocked by blue sawhorses so police could keep traffic away from the throngs of people holding signs (Christians Against Blasphemy! Some Art Is SIN!) and chanting slogans I couldn't understand.

"Go around 84th," a female cop told a family of tourists. "Back that way. Left. Left. Straight. Can't miss it."

"What's going on here?" the father asked.

"New exhibit. People don't like it. There're pamphlets all over the street if you want to grab one." Not wanting to get embroiled in a discussion, she held her arm out to someone lollygagging. "Move along. Move along, everyone."

I picked a pamphlet off the ground.

IS THIS ART OR BLASPHEMY?

Under the headline was a color picture of Serrano's Piss Christ.

I smirked. The Piss Christ was a big joke on everyone. Maybe. A photo of a white plastic crucifix that was (possibly) in a glass of (what could have been) urine meant to drive everyone batshit while the artist sat back and watched. Pure genius.

I wasn't an art guy. Not the way my wife's family was. Pieces like Piss Christ made me laugh, because they didn't put food on the table. Didn't solve any problems. Didn't make money for more than a couple of people. It was art. A conversation starter. You want to poke everyone? Say you're defiling the crucifix.

Holding the pamphlet over a trash can, I stopped. The photo glowed red and orange. If you forgot it was supposed to be urine, it was beautiful. If you didn't think about the corruption of purity, the oranges and reds had a hallowed life of their own.

As if the cross made the urine holy.

And I thought, why did I think it was my filth that ruined Diana?

Why did I not think Diana purified me?

Why wasn't *she* cleansing *me*?

Like a checkerboard that you always assumed was black on white, but once you saw the possibility that it could be white on black, you couldn't unsee it. The mind goes back and forth with the opposites, melding them into an agreement of inverses. The way a grown woman could take care of herself and need to be taken care of, she and I could ritually defile and purify each other, black on white, white on black, spinning like a pinwheel faster and faster into constancy.

I let the pamphlet drop into the garbage. She and I were linked like black and white as long as the world spun, and I knew that on the day of her father's funeral, she wasn't in the museum.

Chapter 45

"I don't have the key," I repeated to the doorman. "Look at me. You know me. I've never needed a key. I've been coming in and out of Lloyd's co-op for five years and I haven't raped or killed anyone."

The doorman knew me. He also knew Lloyd had died and had admitted Diana was in her father's apartment.

"Tell me what you're checking for and I'll look for it," he said.

"My wife. Please. She's not answering the phone, and I know she's upset."

He didn't know I'd signed and sent the divorce papers. He didn't know I hadn't seen Diana in days or that I'd given up on us. But he knew I wasn't going away, so he unlocked the little cabinet behind the lobby desk and took a key off the hook.

I followed him to the elevator and up to the front entrance with the plant in the hall.

He knocked, waited forever, knocked again, waited an eternity, then shrugged. "Sorry, Mr. Steinbeck, but I can't open it if—"

"The back way. She could be in the kitchen."

He looked at me with narrowed eyes. "I have to get back to the lobby."

"If she's hurt herself and you didn't open the door, I'll do worse than sue you."

"Fine."

We walked down the hall, around the corner, and through the door to the back stairwell. We heard a muffled, high-pitched squeal.

"The teapot," I said, knocking before he had a chance to raise a goddamn objection.

No answer.

"Open this door," I said. "At the very least, the stove's on."

He opened the door, revealing a kitchen washed in twilight, the blue flame of a gas burner, and a violently whistling teapot that rattled. It must be almost empty. I reached for the knob. That was when I saw her.

She was no more than a shape under the window, barely visible in the darkening room. Knees to chest, back to the wall, arms around legs.

"Adam?" Her voice was soft in disbelief.

"Ma'am?" the doorman said. "I'm sorry to bother you."

"Get the fuck out." She said it softly, but with conviction.

He left, snapping the door closed. I crouched to see her. She was cast in twilight shadows. Blocks away, a car alarm went off. A crosstown bus ground the brakes with a deep grumble a New Yorker would barely hear unless they were trying to listen to their wife's soul cry out.

"Can I turn a light on?" I said.

"No."

"Were you going to leave the teapot on there all night?"

"I meant to get it. Did you go to the wake?"

I sat on the floor with my back to the stove and one leg bent. "Packed. Wall-to-wall people."

"I should have gone."

"Why didn't you?"

She played with her fingers in the dark, worrying at corners that weren't there. "They'd all wait for me to cry, and I can't. I don't want anyone to see."

"See what? That you're not crying?"

"They'll think I'm a monster."

"Everyone knows how much you loved him. They'd think you had superior self-control."

"That's me. Self-control girl."

"Are you hungry?"

"No."

"Do you want me to finish making the tea?"

"I don't know what I want."

"I'm making you tea." I got up on a hand and a knee. "I don't even care if you drink it."

After standing and straightening my jacket, I put the teapot under the faucet. When it was full and the sound of the water left us in the semi-silence of New York, I heard her whisper.

"Get out." Her voice had a flat conviction, almost dominant in its command.

"I'm going to stay here and take care of you," I said, flipping on the burner. "You don't have to like it. I'm staying. You've gone through too much alone already." I shifted the teapot as if it would make a difference. "You had no support in Montauk. None when you got home. Maybe Lloyd was here when you got the signed divorce papers. I don't know. What I do know is I'm depleted. If I had to face something like this right now, I'd have nothing left."

She sat on the floor, unmoving, staring into the middle distance.

"You need me," I said, "and you're taking everything I can give you."

She blinked. No more. Watching the teapot had the expected effect, so I kicked off my shoes by the back door and sat in front of her. I took her bare foot in my hands and rubbed it, digging my thumbs into the soft part. She groaned and woke up a little. I dug harder, pushing out the tension, letting her know I was there. She flinched from the pain but came around, making eye contact in the dark room.

"I love you, Diana."

"I don't want you to."

"Tough."

The teapot hissed. Her head moved so slightly I could barely perceive her saying *no*, as if I'd misunderstood.

"I want you to hurt me," she said.

I dug my thumbs in harder. She didn't resist or react.

"Take it from me." She pulled back her foot.

"What do you mean?"

"What you did to Serena. Give it to me. Take it. Make everything hurt. Make me do things."

The teapot whistled, and my dick swelled.

"Do you know what you're asking?"

"Yes. I'll say pinochle if I have to. But no means yes."

I stood and turned off the burner. I hadn't gotten a cup or a teabag. I hadn't made a plan or a list of limits. We hadn't had a cold, honest discussion to protect us from each other.

"It'll work out better this time," she said from below me.

"No." I had to put my foot down. She was in no condition to give up her will so completely.

"Do you know why you scratch an itch?" she said, getting on her feet.

"It's still no."

"Because an itch is pain." She peeled off her T-shirt. She wasn't wearing a bra, and the streetlights on her nipples cast long shadows across her breasts. "A scratch is greater pain. It drowns the itch out."

"Diana. What you're asking for takes hours of negotiating and talking."

I didn't want to talk. Didn't want to turn on the lights. I wanted to give her what she asked for, and though a part of me cried against it, I couldn't help but play the scene in my mind. Her body was so beautiful in the soft light, her skin satin, waiting to be marked. I could destroy her utterly and put her back together.

"I trust you." Her voice was a velvet blanket I wanted to rip into a scream.

"Do you?" I reached for a hard nipple and pulled it.

Her eyes fluttered closed when she gasped. She couldn't have known how bad it could get. She couldn't have foreseen it. "Yes."

But I could play it out. I could give her what she needed. But I couldn't.

"Please," she implored. "Make me."

I could.

I twisted her nipple until she grimaced. I ached for more, and I was going to get it. I took a deep breath of acceptance. I was a sadist, and a masochist was asking to be hurt. I loved her with every bone in my body, and if giving her what she needed broke that love, I could at least give her what she needed.

As if she knew I'd come to a decision, she pulled away and pushed me aside, dodging to get to the door.

The first move was the hardest because it set the tone, and without preparation or discussion, I was playing it by ear.

I took her by the throat before she got past me and pushed her against the refrigerator. She clutched my arm.

"This what you want?"

"Fuck you," she spit.

"No, huntress. Fuck you." I stuck my free hand down her sweat pants. She was soaked.

She fought me. She fought hard, twisting and punching. So hard I wondered if this was what she wanted. Wrestling her to the floor, I got her on her stomach and put my knee between her shoulder blades, gasping for breath. I pulled my erection out but left my pants on.

"What's your name?"

"Diana. Get off me."

I grabbed a handful of hair and jerked her head back so I could see her. "How old are you?"

"Twenty-eight-fuck-you."

I held her hair, moved my knee, and got her pants off. She hit me so hard I saw stars. She made it two steps before I got hold of her wrist and threw her over the kitchen table.

"Self-defense advice," I snarled. "Don't end up on your stomach."

She growled and twisted. I had control of her for a moment, but I knew I'd let her get away again. It was how I exerted control and how she surrendered it.

I could do this.

I could keep it safe. I could be the master. I could play the game. I had no rules, no contracts, no list of hard limits, but I knew her. I knew her better than I knew any other human being. All I had to do was trust that.

I jammed my hand between her legs, sinking three fingers in her. "You're so fucking wet. I could just fuck you right now like a nice guy. Just fuck your cunt sore and make you come. But that wasn't what you wanted, was it?"

A rack of cooking supplies sat by the fridge. A bottle of oil was stuck sideways between soy sauce and salt. I grabbed it and opened it with my teeth, spitting out the cap. I dumped it onto her lower back, letting plenty fall into the crack of her ass. She'd need it.

"We could have done this nice. But have it your way."

Two of my wet fingers drove into her ass. She held back a scream. I pushed her face into the table, stretching her ass. I didn't have plugs or tools. I didn't have time or cooperation. This wouldn't be painless, but it wouldn't be without pleasure either.

"No!" she said.

But no meant yes, and though I thought I'd stop when she said it, I didn't. I trusted her and myself.

"You're taking it. All of it. I'm going to tear you apart."

She rocked back and forth violently, kicking and flailing.

I let her go before driving her to the floor. She crawled out of the kitchen. I snapped up a towel, throwing it around my neck.

I found her in the dining room with her back to the table. The front door was steps to the right, but she backed away in the other direction.

"Get on your knees and I'll take it easy on you." One step forward.

"No."

One step back.

A horn honked outside. She got distracted, and I lunged. Her foot slipped on a bead of oil on the floor. I caught her and drove her to her knees at the same time, pushing her face on my erection. When she opened her mouth to scream, I shoved my cock in it. Her face went beet red as I pushed down her throat. Her hair was a mess. Her fingernails dug into my thighs. When she looked up at me, her eyes were webbed with red and she was so close to utter submission, I almost came in her mouth.

She gulped air when I pulled out. Before she could get away, I was on her, twisting her onto her side. I put my forearm on her head to keep her still. Her leg flailed over my shoulder. With my other hand, I put my dick at her ass. Held her still. She bucked. This was going to rip her up if she didn't stay still.

I could feel her heaving for breath under me.

"Get off me," she gasped. "Fuck."

I'd stopped to think too long. She was getting restless. I needed more control, and I wasn't continuing without it. I snapped off my belt and buckled it around her neck as she cursed at me.

Grabbing her ankle, I stood and dragged her across the dining room floor. Her free foot kicked.

"How old are you?"

"Twenty-eight. Let me go."

She grappled with the belt, but the buckle was in the back and she didn't have enough time to undo it before I got her into her childhood room. It had been stripped of posters and photos. The full-size bed with the white wood head and footboard was dressed in a white, pink, and blue duvet I hoped she wasn't too attached to.

Closing the door behind us, I got my hand around the front of the circle of the belt and put our faces close together. "Be good."

"No."

I let her go and pulled an extension cord out of the wall. The next five minutes were spent tying her hands together. She was slippery and strong, but I was stronger. I got her on the bed and bound her hands to the headboard, above her head. I could turn her front or back while keeping her more or less still.

I got off the bed and undressed while she watched, lying on her back.

"You've got to calm down," I said, pulling her ankles apart. "You might even like it."

"I won't relax. I won't let you."

The fire in her eyes said otherwise, and I had to trust that. I put my knees on her thighs, keeping her motionless with my weight.

This wasn't about getting my dick in her ass. It never had been. This was about taking her so low she could let go of her pain, and it would take more than a fight against penetration. When I leaned over her, she turned her head. With one hand, I took her by the cheeks and made her face me.

She wasn't close enough. She was physically drained, but her guard was still up emotionally. I had to break her. We had no map for this. No list to check off.

I had to trust myself to know what she needed.

I had to trust she'd tell me if it was going wrong.

"So we're clear," I said. "I want this to hurt. Every time you cry, my dick gets hard."

I put my fingers in her mouth, down deep with my clean hand until she made gurgling sounds. I removed them, and I slapped her cheek. Not hard. Just enough to hurt her feelings.

Her eyes got wide with shock.

"You like that? It's what you wanted."

Before she could answer, I slapped the other cheek a little harder.

Her eyes welled up with tears. Her chin shuddered. I did it again, and tears flowed.

That was it. The train pulled out of the station and we were on it, speeding toward her breaking point. I got off her thighs and turned her onto her stomach. She didn't have a hell of a lot of fight in her. I slapped her bottom so hard my hand hurt.

I didn't need to torment her with cruel words. I didn't need to make her tell me to go fuck myself again, but I needed to finish this with her.

I put my fingers in her ass and stretched it. She was still lubricated enough. It would hurt for a minute, but if I took it slow, she'd be fine.

The head of my dick stretched her. She screamed into the pillow and resisted. I held her still and slowly, inch by inch, took her ass.

The extension cord slid down the vertical bed railing. I pulled her hair back but fucked her gently.

"Up on your knees," I said, slapping her ass.

She did as she was told because she was breaking and she knew it. I could feel her falling apart. Falling into me. Opening like a flower. After the second stroke, she was released from pain and she pushed her hips back into me.

Turning her on her side, I bent her leg on my shoulder. Her face was so puffy and tear-streaked, I didn't recognize it. I reached between her legs and rubbed her clit. She made a vowel sound that was half surrender and half battle-cry.

"I can't! I can't come like this."

"You can." I leaned into her face. "You can, and you will."

It wasn't long before she bucked and stiffened under me. When she came, her ass clenched around my cock over and over until I exploded inside her.

When I pulled out, she cried harder than I thought possible.

I needed to get us into a bath. I needed to clean up. I needed to feed her. I needed to check every inch of her body to make sure she was unharmed. But once I untied her and she put her arms and legs around me, she wouldn't let go. She wept long and loud from the floor of her heart to the ceiling of her soul. Not one ounce of sadness was left unpacked.

When I tried to let go of her, she clung harder.

I gave up and held her as tightly as I could, rocking back and forth. The scene finished and I had nothing to add to what I'd done. I was all right. I'd kept it under control and given her what she needed. I knew her. I loved her. Through the entire thing, I'd loved her, and it was the love that kept me from breaking along with her.

I was safe and sane, giving her a gentle, guided ride back to the reality of her power.

Chapter 46

When she was too tired to cry another tear, I took her to her little bathroom and managed to hold her off the floor while I drew her a bath. It was a hilarious comedy of errors she only had the energy to smile about.

"I just want to go to sleep," she said as I put her in the hot water.

"I know."

"This feels really nice."

I washed her legs from toe to thigh, then I got in the tub, sitting behind her so her shoulder blades were to my chest. I had more cleaning to do, but it could wait a minute while I wrapped my arms around her.

"I'm going to miss my father." Her voice was husky. "Knowing he doesn't exist anymore. Not even anywhere. Gone. I can't visit. Can't say hello. Can't play cards anymore. I don't know what to do with all the things we did together." She leaned her head on the bend in my arm. "I'm not his daughter anymore. I'm... I don't know who I am."

I kissed her behind her ear. "You're mine."

"I'm still sad."

"I'll break you again when you can't stand it."

"Before," she said sleepily. "Did you mean what you said before?"

"That I was going to rip you apart?"

"No. I know you meant that. The other thing. In the kitchen."

"What thing?"

She didn't answer. The sound of dripping water echoed off the tiles, and I felt her breaths on my arm.

"That I love you?" I asked.

"Yes."

"I meant it."

"Really?"

"It's probably the only thing I've said all day that I really meant. It might be the truest thing I've ever said. Even more true now today than all the other times I've said it."

She turned as much as she could to face me. She was cried out, empty of her grief for now, but somehow fresh and new. "I love you too."

"Good."

"All of you. And you don't have to love the submissive me."

"Diana—"

"It's okay." She turned, getting on her knees to face me, clouds of suds dripping off her breasts. "But if you just love the regular me—"

"I love the regular Diana, and I love the submissive Diana. I love all the Dianas yet to be discovered. If you just stay with me long enough to show me all the parts of you I don't know yet, I'll prove it to you. I can love you more than you even thought possible. I'll love you until it annoys the hell out of you."

"I dare you to try."

"Challenge accepted."

We kissed. She tasted like rosewater. She tasted like freedom and captivity. She tasted like the rest of my life.

Chapter 47

Thirty-five days.

They'd sped by so slowly, I barely had time to digest them, and yet, they'd filled me completely. I didn't know so much change could be packed into such a short time, yet when I held her the morning after I took her body completely, I was a different man than I'd been on day one. Every fiber of my being had been torn down and rebuilt. I'd gone bankrupt because of her, and I'd reorganized into a functioning human for her.

A bird chirped outside the window as the sun came up. The window of her childhood room looked across a narrow alley, into the building next door. We'd crawled into her old bed the night before, leaning into each other to keep from falling off the smaller space. Her neck was bruised from my belt, and her eyes were puffy with tears. I still had to check her anus for damage. I had to care for it if I was going to use it again.

Her lashes fluttered on my arm, letting me know she was awake. Even after that, she didn't move and I didn't rouse her. The world could wait.

A phone rang from the other room.

"That's you," I said.

"Let it go to voice." She took a deep breath, her body expanding and contracting against mine. "The freeze is over and we have to get the business going again. Fill the slate. Find new writers. There's so much. So much."

Her face took on a distant look, as if she was reading the to-do list inside her head.

"We should go so you can get started."

"One more hour."

So we stayed there. I stroked her hair. She stroked my arm. I touched where she was sore, and she groaned. She touched where I was hard, and I pinned her wrists together behind her back.

"Straddle me," I said. "Face the other way."

She rode me. Her ass was sore, but it clenched when she was close. I pulled her hair and made her wait to come. I made her beg. I made it impossible for her to wait, then I let her release, touching her so gently her orgasm went on and on in waves.

"You're so good," I said when she was back in my arms. "So perfect."

"I wish I could unsay all the things I said about not loving you."

"No. I don't. I'm glad you did it."

"I was a bitch."

"I was an asshole."

"You still are."

I rolled on top of her. "Really?"

"Master Asshole, sir."

I laughed, but the words, even in jest, made me hard. So I fucked her again, good and slow. Plain old missionary vanilla style. Because I could.

Her phone rang again.

She groaned. "Can you get it and tell them I'm indisposed?"

"You have to get up to go to the bathroom anyway."

"How do you know?"

"You're human. Come on, I have to look you over. This is dereliction of duty."

I slapped her ass. The sound of it made me want to fuck her again, but we'd never leave the apartment if I started fucking her as much as I wanted to.

The ringing stopped and started as we got into the bathroom. I heard it while I checked her throat, the bruising on her arm, and her anus, which didn't look half bad. I'd been more gentle than I thought.

By the time we were dressed in the previous day's clothes, my phone joined the chorus.

"I'm afraid to answer this now," Diana said, holding up her ringing phone. The name *Kayti* was on the screen.

"How bad could it be?" I said.

"Don't tempt fate." She slid her finger across the glass. "Hello," she said into the phone.

I pretended to read my email while I watched her reaction. A sigh. Resigned. She rubbed her temples. Sat down. Got her little pad out of her bag and scribbled, mostly saying, *yes, all right,* and *I don't know.*

"Is the building burning down?" I asked when she hung up.

"Not quite. What are you doing today?"

"Besides saving the world?"

"I can't... I can't deal with this myself. Can you come to SoHo with me?"

I took her by the shoulders and made eye contact. She looked lost, panicked, and determined at the same time.

"I'd fall off the edge of Manhattan with you."

We got in the Jag and headed downtown.

Chapter 48

The entire staff of McNeill-Barnes had gathered on the sidewalk, clutching coffee cups in the fresh spring air. The entrance to the building itself was behind police tape, and traffic was diverted to the other side of the street.

The sidewalk was littered with broken glass from the front window, opening Ticky-Taqui—the high-end shoe store on the first floor—to thieves, who had taken their pick. Kayti ran up to us, folder tucked under her arm.

"Hey," she said with laser focus on Diana, ignoring me and rattling a string of words without punctuation. "Okay, so they confiscated the security video and I'm sorry if you didn't want us to but the lawyers said—"

"It's fine," she said.

"—we should and Ticky's saying they're going to sue us those shoes are—"

"Have you spoken to the police?"

"—two grand a pair yeah I talked to Officer Gareth right over there he's super hot so I have no idea what I said." She let out a little giggle and turned fire-engine red when Officer Super Hot approached.

"Hi," Diana said. "I'm Diana McNeill-Barnes. This is my building."

He shook her hand. I kept mine in my pockets.

"Let's go inside," he said. "I have something to show you."

She followed him under the tape, but turned as she got to the entrance. "Adam? Are you coming?"

"You have this."

She swallowed then stomped toward me, heels crunching broken glass, knuckles a tight white on her shoulder bag. "Okay, look," she said when she was close enough to speak softly, "I know you're not part of the company anymore. I get it. But I need you, okay?"

How could I deny her? I'd tried and failed so many times.

I got under the police tape and went with Diana to meet Officer Gareth by the front door.

"Are you an owner, sir?" he asked.

Diana and I exchanged glances. The deed was in the company name, and the company was in the process of moving back to her family trust. So technically, yes. But actually, no. Lying or fudging with law enforcement was probably the stupidest thing a person could do, even if they hadn't done anything wrong.

"No."

"Yes," Diana interjected. "He is."

"Can I wait for her in the office? I have the key."

"Go ahead." Officer Gareth held his arm out so I could get in.

"It's fine," I whispered to her as I passed.

She nodded. I kissed my ex-wife on the cheek and went upstairs.

Chapter 49

Her desk was too clean. That was the first indication that something was wrong. My Lego tower was exactly where I'd left it. I pushed an errant brick onto the blanket.

Lloyd's desk was organized but busy with piles of paper, as befitted a man whose career had started before fax machines. It would have to be sorted and cleaned out and it would hurt Diana to do it. I didn't want her to hurt. I texted Kayti.

—Who's cleaning out Lloyd's desk?—

—The office has been closed since he got sick. So. No one?—

—See if they'll let you up here—

—They won't—

How did Diana deal with this level of daily obstruction? I thought Kayti resented me because she didn't report to me and I still asked her to do things when "things" equaled her fucking job. She'd move mountains for Diana, but everyone else? They could fuck a duck.

—Ask again—

I went to the freight elevator and grabbed some discarded boxes, stopped at the supply closet for packing tape, reset the thermostat, and went back to Diana's office.

Diana was already there, leaning against the back of the couch with her arms crossed.

"Where were you?" she asked, spinning like a lawyer intimidating a hostile witness.

I dropped the boxes by Lloyd's desk and put the tape on the chair. "Back hall. How did it go?"

"They asked me if Dad owed anyone money. If he had gambling debts. If he had a girlfriend. I mean, really? As if they shouldn't be interrogating Jason Taqui."

"I'm sure they are."

"My father was a fucking pillar of the community."

"Yes. He was."

"He didn't have any enemies. Not one. No one would come here and break a window because they were pissed he what? Died without paying a debt? What. The. Fuck?" She was pinched and raw, buzzing with emotions she couldn't hold in check.

I closed the office door. "Huntress."

"How dare they. How dare they try to soil his reputation over a stupid broken window."

I held her face. When she tried to jerk away, I held her tighter.

"You're all right," I said in my dominant voice. Then more softly but with just as much conviction, "You're all right."

"How? You don't see it. I haven't told you. This whole thing is falling apart. I can't think of new projects. There are bills on top of ledgers and I don't know what to pay unless accounting points at a dotted line. I can't handle it. I can't. And now? I was keeping it together for him. Why am I here now?"

"You've been training to run this company since you were sixteen. You've run it the past five years. You have this."

"With you," she said, then her face lit up. "Are you coming back? Will you? Please."

I didn't know how to answer her. I hadn't even considered it. The publishing business wasn't interesting to me. I'd saved the company for her and only her. Without her in the picture, the entire building would have been turned into third-party-managed condos and the backlist would have been sold in bulk to an aggregator who couldn't give a shit. I'd walked away from what was profitable and walked into what was satisfying. I'd done everything I could to rebuild a failing publishing house; and I never failed in business. Never. Not for myself and especially not for her.

No matter what she said, McNeil-Barnes Publishing was in good shape.

Its owner and president? Less so.

"You don't need me." I didn't think she'd believe me, but it was the truth.

"How can you say that?"

"Listen to me. Breathe and listen. You have this."

"I don't finish things."

"Yes." My hands slid to her shoulders. "Yes, you do. I won't let you fall. But I won't let you undermine yourself either." I pointed at her seat. "You're going to move that desk so the window is at your back. You're going to sit framed in the city like the queen you are. You're going to take Lloyd's stuff and go through it. You're going to respectfully pack what you have to keep and throw away what you don't. Then you're going to run the shit out of this place. By yourself. You were born for this. And me. You were born for me."

She bit her lip. Consternation or arousal? Both? It didn't matter, because I'd broken through the fear for the moment. We slid our arms around each other.

"I don't need a pep talk, Steinbeck."

"What do you need?" I grabbed her ass so hard she let out a sharp *ah* of pain.

"That."

She was so hungry for it. In the past month, she'd been willing, but I'd been too wrapped up in my own doubts. I hadn't seen how right she was for what I had to offer. Sex tangled with violence and I fisted her hair, settling her into my cock as it hardened.

"I was too easy on you yesterday," I said in her ear.

"Yes, sir."

"Take off my belt."

I held her head so she couldn't see it, leaving her fumbling for the buckle. Having her so uncomfortable, trying to please me despite what I was doing to her, excited and calmed me at the same time.

She got the leather belt through the loops.

"Very good." I took it and let her hair go. It stayed knotted in the back, a reminder that I'd controlled her. "Are you wet?"

"Yes."

"Prove it. Touch yourself and show me."

She made short work of her fly, unbuttoning and unzipping in seconds, getting her hand down in there as if it was her job.

She held up her slick hand, trying to staunch a smile. I brought her fingers to my lips and tasted her juice. Then, because I suddenly had no self-control at all, I kissed her so I could christen her mouth with it. I tasted every corner, touching her deepest crevices with my tongue. I wanted to make sure every soft surface she had knew I owned her.

Taking the belt, I pushed her against the window, pressing my body against hers.

"I liked working with you," she said when we separated to catch a breath.

"You made me crazy." I pushed my erection against her until her lids fluttered.

"You loved it."

"Regardless. I'm punishing you for it." I stepped back and pointed at the window. "Face New York."

She turned to face the window. The people walking up, down, across, around the street looked like boats on a currentless grey sea. Across the way, the windows of the office building sat in silent witness.

"Let me see your ass."

She hooked her thumbs in her waistband. I made a plan for the perfect ovals of her bottom if last night's marks were gone. Another plan for a series of light pink welts, and yet another if it turned out she was still bruised and red. All involved pain and pleasure. All were meant to satisfy her need to forget herself.

I slapped the belt against my palm when her pants were halfway down, and in response, a sharp knock came from the door.

Her head whipped around to look at me even as her bottom remained in my direction.

"Who is it?" I called.

"Hi. Hey. It's me? Kayti. Have you seen Diana?"

"Yes. Why?"

"Officer... um... the hot one wants to see her? They got the security tapes."

I looked at her, still bent but without the look of anticipation. I knew the moment had been stolen from us.

"I better take this," she said. When I nodded, she stood straight and called to the door, "One minute, Kayti."

"We'll reconvene tonight." I put my belt back in the loops.

"My place or yours?" She pulled her pants up and fastened them.

"Ours."

She smiled for a second then looked at her father's desk. The sadness wasn't there, but something more businesslike. I didn't know exactly what she was thinking, but I had a clear sense of what she was feeling, and it wasn't fear or hopelessness. They'd be back while she grieved for Lloyd, but she had a handle on it.

"You're not getting the condo for free." She went for the door. "I earned it fair and square. Now you have to earn it back."

"Oh, really?"

"Yes. I demand one hour. Tonight. If you can make me pinochle out in one hour, you get your half of the loft back."

I'd missed her. I didn't realize how much. "If I do, I'm moving back in."

"Yes, sir."

"And the car," I added.

"Forget it. Go get the Mustang off blocks."

She opened the door wide enough for me to see Kayti, who smiled like a schoolgirl. She practically jumpy-clapped when she saw me, then she fell into line behind her boss, who walked to meet Officer Gareth like the world's only badass.

How was I going to get a woman like that to safe out?

Chapter 50

It took me fifteen minutes to get back to the R+D office. I spent fourteen of them devising ways to push Diana's limits while staying within my own. I had a few ideas, but they'd take more than an hour. My wife was stubborn. If she knew she only had to last an hour, she'd last an hour. Then she'd demand more and more opportunities to sign over the loft. Each time, her limits would expand and the game would get harder to win.

I didn't care about the deed to the loft. I had plenty of property.

I cared about winning the game for our mutual benefit. I wanted to live with her.

"You look chipper today," Eva said, all in red as I came through the back entrance.

"First day of the rest of my life, et cetera."

"Does that have anything to do with the long-stemmed rose in reception?"

Odd. Why would Diana send me a flower? I could use it later on her body, certainly, but it wasn't her place to make suggestions.

"Have Britt leave it on my desk."

"Not a real flower." Eva's words stopped me as I tried to walk off. "Don't be so literal."

I knew who she was talking about before she'd even finished the second sentence. "Thanks, Eva. And no."

We walked toward my office together.

"No?"

"I'm not chipper because of her."

"That's almost an answer to a personal question."

I texted the receptionist on our messenger service.

—Send her in—

"I'll give you one more question," I said without thinking. And fuck it, because I loved making her smile that wide.

"Can I save it?"

"Save it and you get interest." I held up two fingers as I got behind my desk.

"Two questions? Please. No more. I'll die of happiness before I can make a list."

"Don't die. I need you."

"Now you're getting mushy. I'm leaving before you embarrass yourself."

"Thank you."

She passed the long-stemmed rose on her way out. I'd been right. It was Serena in black slacks and sage-green polo shirt. Even Eva turned to look at her when they passed. My ex-sub usually walked around as if she was well aware of that fact that she was the most beautiful woman in the room. She moved with precision when she walked down a runway and when she kneeled and opened her mouth for a cock. She spent her life striving for aesthetic perfection and came close to achieving it.

It was boring as hell, but that wasn't my problem. I didn't have to live with her.

"You can close the door," I said.

When she did, I held my hand out to the chair on the other side of my desk. I had a perfectly serviceable couch, but I didn't want her to get the wrong idea. By checking on her so often, I'd already given her enough reasons to think I wanted her.

She sat in the chair and crossed her legs so that one of her feet hit the floor, resting sideways in her stiletto, and the other stretched to the side of the chair. Her crossed legs were not decorous and demure. She was tense and engaged. Purposeful, yet somehow fragile.

"What brings you?" I asked.

"I know something." She played coy, adding a sheen of seduction to her expression, running her finger along the crease of her pants. "I thought you'd like to know too."

"Maybe. Depends on what it is."

She broke into a self-conscious smile. "This seems silly. I didn't ask how you were. Didn't tell you what a nice office this is."

"It's just an office. It's for business."

She cleared her throat and turned back into a sophisticated supermodel in the blink of an eye. "Of course."

My hands were folded on the desk. I tapped my thumbs together. "You said you had something to tell me?"

She uncrossed her knees, letting the cross fall to her ankles. "I had an experience the other night. When you were kneeling in front of your ex-wife?" More than the knowledge that she'd seen me kneel, I bristled at ex-wife. "Stefan saw it. It inspired him."

"To what?"

"Kneel."

"I'm sorry?"

"Yeah. The exact same thing. After you left."

I didn't believe what I was hearing. I'd gotten on my knees for Diana in a moment of unbearable pain. I knew Stefan loved Serena, but apparently I hadn't known how much. "What did you do?"

She cleared her throat and lifted her chin, making eye contact. "I was shocked. I was anxious. It turned everything upside down, but he wouldn't get up. He's a very stubborn man."

"Apparently."

"Then something changed. I felt kind of... gratified... from the inside out, instead of the outside in. And that... well, there's no other way to put it. I got turned on. Very turned on. I couldn't keep my eyes open."

"Ah." The pieces clicked together in my mind.

"It's not like he was there for twenty minutes. The whole thing took seconds."

People evolve. Sexual urges and needs can be unlocked at different life stages. Stefan and I hadn't seen Serena's inner Domme because she wasn't ready, or the Dominant side didn't exist. Had this side of her been conceived in Montauk? Or before? Or had she been gestating for years? And did it matter?

"I don't know, but subbing hasn't been working for a long time. It doesn't feel right anymore. When I heard you were back and you'd been vanilla all those years, I thought I could try it. You wanted to try it with me and I rejected you. But when Stefan kneeled, I knew vanilla wasn't what I needed."

She was all balls. I was proud of her on the one hand. On the other, I couldn't leave the door open half an inch for her, or she'd burst through and insist I train her as a Domme.

"I can't help you explore this, Serena."

"I know, I know. But I've had three masters, three real ones I care about, in my life. You're one of them. I want your blessing."

"That's very submissive of you."

"Do you want me to kneel for it?" She raised an eyebrow, as if the prospect had appeal despite everything she'd said. But the expression also had a tinge of a dare, as if she was the one in control.

"No." I stood. "You have my blessing and my encouragement."

Her grin was worth ten thousand dollars. Literally. "Thank you!"

"Now you can top from the top."

We shook hands as equals. I didn't realize we hadn't been equal in my mind, but until I showed her out, she'd been a pest or a toy. That guilt was on my shoulders, not hers. Not the community's. I knew in my head that the sub was an equal partner, even though they gave up power.

I'd been operating under some kind of delusional fog.

Had Diana cured me of it? Only the fear of her being beneath me had driven me away. I could never see her as anything less than an equal. Had Serena just been the proof of the truth as I came to know it? How many more years of loneliness and upside-down thinking did Diana save me from?

Thank God for her. Thank God for her a million times.

Chapter 51

How do you break a masochist? If receiving pain is part of their identity, how do you cause so much pain they forget who they are? Reveal their secrets? Bare themselves to you?

One hour.

I didn't want the loft anymore. I did. I wanted a life with her inside that loft or outside of it, but the loft was ours. It was *us*. And there was no *us* without the truth.

Once I decided to trust her with submission and then trust myself with her self-determination, the resistance washed away like years of caked-on dirt because I loved her. I'd give her anything she wanted, but not without letting her enjoy the fight.

She kept a mug of pens on the bar, next to stacks of paper and business cards she'd never get to. I picked out a pen, made sure it worked, and put it in my pocket. She was mine, and her body was going to announce it.

I was snapping the last of the blackout drapes closed when I heard her keys jingling outside the door. I shut off the last lamp. The loft went black.

The darkness was cut by an arrow of light from the hall. I grabbed her wrist before she could flip on the hall lamp.

"Close the door," I said.

She did, and I clicked the deadbolt.

"Hello to you too," she said to the sound of her bag falling on the floor.

My watch glowed when I touched it and beeped when I set it. "One hour."

"Yes, sir."

I was in the same darkness she was, but I'd been in the loft for a couple of hours. The darkness was mine. I knew where everything was. So when I stepped away from her, I knew where to go.

"Strip down. Quickly. Then put your hands behind your back and stand with your feet apart. Close your eyes."

Her clothes rustled and her boots *clonked* on the hardwood. When the rustling stopped, I flicked on a very small, very powerful flashlight and pointed it in her eyes. She put her hand up to block it, a porcelain statue in a dark room.

"Ow, hey."

"Close your eyes or you're going to be punished in a way you don't like."

She scrunched them tight. I shut off the flashlight, took her by the wrist, and put her hand behind her back. She gasped with arousal.

"Your safe word?"

"Pinochle. But forget it. I'm not saying it."

A silver cuff set that looked like two intertwined rings sat by the coats. I crisscrossed her wrists behind her back and snapped it closed around them. "The Jag says you're wet already."

"I'm not taking that bet."

I put a black velvet hood over her head and tied it around her neck to keep her eyes from adjusting. "Do you know where the credenza is?"

"Yes."

I smacked her ass hard. The darkness seemed to echo the sound more than the light ever did. "Yes, what?"

"Yes, sir."

"That was for forgetting." I smacked her ass again. "That's for not closing your eyes." Again and again, I felt her ass give under my hand and the sharp clap of pain. "For not keeping your hand behind your back. For trying to make deals, and three more just because you love it."

Smack, smack, smack. She was already panting. I held her up so her knees wouldn't buckle under her.

"The credenza," I said. "There's a window to the left of it. Can you walk to it?"

"Yes, sir." She took a step.

I stopped her and push one shoulder toward me and one away until her feet twisted and turned. I spun her again and again, leaving her facing the kitchen.

"Go then."

She stepped toward the kitchen, which was nowhere near the credenza, and yelped in pain. "What...?"

"You said you wanted children. I'm giving you a taste of it. Keep walking."

"I don't... ow!"

I put the flashlight at her feet. The black Lego brick was stuck to the bottom of her foot. She rubbed it against her knee, and it clacked and bounced on the floor.

Letting the flashlight run up and down her body, I soaked in her submission. Hands behind her back, off balance, fighting every painful step as she tried to avoid the bricks I'd covered the floor with. She was the picture of ungainly, awkward, unsexy obedience. It was the most arousing thing I'd ever seen.

She bumped into the back of the couch and growled in frustration. "Which direction am I facing?"

I smacked her ass.

"Sir. What direction?"

I put the flashlight on her face. I couldn't see her expression past the hood, just the bottom of the fabric going concave, convex, concave with her heavy breaths. Her chest heaved, nipples like pebbles. I put my hand between her legs, and she opened them for me, squeaking when she stepped on a Lego. Soaked. Her arousal was dripping inside her thigh.

"I'll tell you on one condition."

She groaned. I pinched her clit. A long N sound came from beneath the mask. That was new.

"Okay," she gasped, rotating with my finger, "what's the condition?"

"You get there on your knees." I slid two fingers inside her, hooking the fingers until I found the bundle of nerves just inside. She cried out. Back to vowels.

"There're these things on the floor all the way there?"

"Yes."

"You're a sadist."

I touched her nose through the hood. "Correct."

"Or you won't tell me which way I'm walking?"

"Nope."

She turned her head right, where she'd bumped into the couch, then left, where she'd started. She was calculating where she was, and if she managed to do that, she'd find her way too easily and we'd have no fun.

"Also, I moved the furniture," I said, still rubbing between her legs.

"Jesus."

I didn't know if she was praying for relief from my cruelty or for release from my fingers. I took them away from her sex, and she jerked toward them as if on a string.

"If we spend the whole hour with me knocking around here, you're not going to get your pinochle."

"You underestimate how much these things hurt the twenty-fifth time."

She didn't answer. Without seeing her face, I was only guessing at what she was thinking, and my guess was she was thinking she could kill an hour.

I was right. She stepped forward, right onto a nasty two-by-two brick.

"Ow! Shit!" She lost her balance trying to shake it off, but without her hands, her foot landed hard on another brick. She screamed.

"I'll tell you what," I said as she rubbed it off, letting it bounce. She put that foot on top of the other. I allowed it. I wanted her safe word, but I didn't want to be a brute. "They're brutal on the knees. But if you crawl, I'll clear the way under your knees." I let my pause hang. "On one condition."

"I thought this would be easier."

"You want to stop?"

"Hell, no."

"Do you want to hear the condition?"

"Yes." She caught herself just in time. "Sir."

"You tell me the truth when I ask you a question."

She barely let me finish my sentence. "Yes."

I turned her ninety degrees. She was a straight line to the blackout drapes on the center window, which started a foot above the floor and ended higher than either of us could reach. I removed the cuffs, and I used my foot to clear a space in front of her.

"On your knees."

She fell to her knees. She didn't land one at a time, nor did she drop cautiously. She trusted me, and I was filled with satisfaction. There in the dark with her naked and unsure, I felt a contentment that everything inside the space was under control. My control. She was my partner, giving me everything she had so we could trade pleasures.

She put her hands down. Squeaked at the sharp edges I'd never promised to move.

"Straight."

Standing behind her, I put the flashlight on her back, watching her go two paces and stop when she got a brick in her knee.

"You're supposed to wait for me to ask a question." I took the brick out of her skin.

"Right. Okay."

"When you went to the Greens to meet with Insolent, did you intend to let him touch you?"

"I knew you were the only one. I kept trying to think of myself taking an order from another man. I let Insolent boss me on text, but I pretended it was you. And the thought of someone else breaking me... being vulnerable in front of them. It's not supposed to be creepy. Right?"

"Creepy isn't your kink."

"I told myself I'd let you go after thirty days but I knew I wouldn't. I'd fight for you to the end. I'd put off the fight until later, but never, ever give up."

I reached under her and cleaned the space in front of her knees. She took two paces, using her fingertips to avoid the sharp bricks, and stopped before she got her knee on one.

"Go."

She took one step on her hands and knees then stopped.

"Will you do whatever I ask?"

"Yes."

Another painless crawl forward. I had about four left before she reached the window, and she wasn't getting to the window without safeing out.

"Serena came to my office today," I said. "Do you want to know what she said?"

She tensed.

"You all right?" I asked.

"That's not even a question."

"Do you?"

"I trust you."

"I know." I crouched beside her and ran my fingers along her spine. "That's not what I asked you."

"You're asking me if I'm curious?"

"Yes." I caressed her bottom then thwacked it. "Now answer."

"Fine. Tell me."

"Is that how we ask?"

"That's another question."

She was particularly on the ball so she'd make it the hour. I was going to have to go outside her comfort zone very quickly.

I swooped some bricks away, and she moved forward a pace.

"No," she said. "That's not how we ask."

Good thing she couldn't see my face, because I had to bite back a laugh. She was a formidable and worthy opponent. She was going to make me earn my Dominance over her for the rest of my life.

I put my hands between her shoulder blades and leaned close to her ear. "Do you want to know what she proposed?"

"You're scaring me."

I took my hands off her, kneeling back on the balls of my feet, waiting. I had fifty-five minutes, and I'd take all of them if I had to.

"Okay. Tell me."

"She's changing sides and wants a try at you. What do you think?"

She tilted her head, making the tie of the hood drop between her shoulder blades. "What?"

"She can tie you down and fuck you. I'll watch."

She got up on her knees and grappled with the hood's tie. "Fuck you. Get this off me." She made the knot worse, and I didn't move. "Stop it now, all of it. Let me out."

"You're breaking the scene."

"Fuck the scene."

"Fuck the scene?"

I put the flashlight on the floor, facing the ceiling, then undid the string on the hood and lifted it off her. She was sweaty and beautiful, panting. Her eyes were crystal-clear blue, the lenses refracting the hard, limited light from the flashlight.

"You're considering—?"

"Nah."

"What?"

"She's flipping, but she didn't bring you up. Or me either," I said.

"You made it up?"

"Yes."

"Why?"

"I only had an hour, Diana."

Her eyes went wide and her mouth opened enough to reveal the little crease in her bottom lip. I tried not to smile and succeeded.

"You..." She drifted into silence where all the worst insults lived.

"Yeah, well. I want to live with you. I want to share a bed and a couch. I want to use that blue pot to make us a dinner just because you put a hole in the wall with it. I want to share your air again. Your space. Everything. So yeah, I played a trick on you, but Serena gave me the idea—"

"Serena what?" She'd gone utterly white. Her face practically glowed in the dark.

"Don't freak out."

"You really spoke to her?"

"She came to the office. I'm not pursuing her."

"Were you ever?"

"No. And she's not pursuing me. She needed my approval to feel right about becoming a Domme."

"You think you're so indispensable."

I laid my hands on her arms until they unfolded. I caught her fingers and laced them in mine. "I am indispensable."

"To me."

"Goddess of the hunt." I kissed her fingers one by one, leaving the left ring finger for last.

I hadn't intended to make any big gestures during our hour together. I only intended to win the game. But being with her in the darkness and talking of mundane things reminded me of what I'd longed for from the minute I met her. Before the lies. Before the games. When I met her and the sky opened above me, I wanted to possess her in a way that ached so badly, I had to deny it for five years. All I'd wanted to do was share her life, please her, care for her, mark her as mine.

"I am going to spend the rest of my life with you," I said. "That's non-negotiable."

Her smile was magical, unintentional, a reflection of her body and heart. Not all of her smiles had that glow of truth. She was undeniable when her expression so matched her true desires. "Thank you."

Her gratitude took my breath away. Never had she been so beautiful. Never had I needed to own her so badly. Not even in the deepest colors of my blind infatuation. Not even when I thought I'd saved her company and her family and done everything I'd set out to do with her. Not even the first time she opened her heart in submission and I tried to deny that I loved her.

I placed her left hand on mine and spread the fingers, isolating the fourth. I kissed the pad of it, ran my tongue along it, took the whole thing in my mouth and sucked it. She groaned until I bit down on the base. Then she gasped and tried to pull away, but my teeth held. I sucked hard, and I saw from the twist of her hips that she was moving inside the space between arousal and pain, pushing her finger in my mouth and yanking to the side at the same time, as if she wanted both and neither sensation. Or as if she understood that from now on, she'd associate one with the other.

I let go and held her hand to the flashlight. A layer of spit and the indents of my teeth were on her ring finger. "The bruises will last until you put your ring back on."

"That really hurt." She observed it closely in the beam of light, like a curious nude painted by Caravaggio in layers of glaze.

"I have forty minutes to get your mind off it." I got on my feet and stood over her.

Looking up at me, her eyes clear and open and ready for anything, she placed her hands behind her back and looked down.

"I'm going to push a limit," I said. "Can I trust you to safe out if it's too much?"

"I'm not going to safe out twice in one scene. Even if you cheated the first time."

"We have a lifetime of pushing boundaries together."

She sighed. "You're right, sir. We do."

"The flashlight. There's a hinge on the bottom panel. There's a strap inside for your wrist."

She picked up the flashlight and poked at the bottom, more curious than obedient. She opened the bottom, took out the four-inch plastic loop, and closed the compartment. Opening the loop, she started putting her hand through it.

"No," I said. "It goes in your teeth. The strap."

She bit it, letting the light swing below her chin, illuminating her breasts in a kinetic glow.

"Now you can see." I stepped out of the way. "Crawl to the window and open the drapes."

Between her and the window stretched a path of black bricks. It was worth the extra cost to get the single color. They looked painful, and anticipation of pain was where the sex was.

Behind her, watching her crawl with her ass up as the light swung, stopping when sharp edges went into soft skin. The way she kept going because I wanted her to, without complaint, not out of fear. She endured the pain because she wanted it, and she wanted it from me.

The power was laced with adrenaline and gratitude. I wanted more. I wanted to take her places only I could guide her to, because I'd own them. Open her in ways she'd never imagined, because she'd let me. Care for her because she'd given me a gift no one else had. She'd given me the gift of my true self.

I was bursting out of my skin for her violation, her degradation, and her honor.

She raised herself on her knees, shook off sharp little bricks, and opened the blackout drapes. The loft was flooded with the nighttime light of New York. We were above the streetlights. Their illumination was soft and shadowless. The lights from the department store across the street had a warm bite that slit Crosby sixteen hours a day, casting long shadows in the evening, and dimmed down to romantic-dinner levels after closing. Before the neighborhood changed, the building across the street had had the same use as our loft —a factory with big casement windows for free lighting and ventilation.

"Stand," I said, pushing her gently onto the six-inch-high ledge under the window.

She stepped up, and I stepped back. Her body was silhouetted by right angles. The black grid of the window panes. The yellow glow of the department store windows. The uneven colors of the bricks across the street. She was a goddess on the hill, staring down at the field of battle. She took my breath away.

I put my hands on her hips, ran them along her ribs and down again, trying to locate the source of her supremacy. She shuddered under my touch, transferring her power through my arms to my heart.

Why couldn't I love a sub before? Because they made me no better than a Dominant. Diana, the goddess of the hunt, loaned me her power and made me her equal.

"Turn around." My voice was pitted as a broken stone. Her existence pushed my limits, challenging my ability to dominate her, and in that moment of awe, I was surprised and honored that she obeyed.

On the ledge, she was almost my height, but she kept her gaze down and let the flashlight display the glorious velvet of her skin.

I needed to lift myself to her level. I needed to mark the moment. Put myself on her, in her, with her. Degradation had its moments, but as I pulled the pen from my pocket, I felt only the reverence of a supplicant writing their name on a piece of paper and putting it at the feet of a sponsoring saint.

Brushing my hand across her left bicep to her right and back again, I took stock of the room I had to say what needed saying.

"I'm not a poet," I said, taking the flashlight out of her mouth. "But I want you to indulge me. Repeat after me, but only if what I'm telling you to say is true. Do you understand?"

"Yes, sir."

I clicked the flashlight off and put it away. "This isn't a game. I'm taking you at your word."

She glanced up as if checking my sincerity. She nodded and put her eyes back on her feet.

"I belong to Adam." Third person sounded comedic coming out of my mouth, but I needed to hear the words exactly that way from her.

"I belong to Adam."

I bit the cap off the pen and spit it to the side. I started at one of her shoulders and wrote across it.

I BELONG TO ADAM

"He belongs to me," I said.

She looked at me, eyes dark in the night, and bit her lip. "He belongs to me."

I wrote under the last line.

HE BELONGS TO ME.

I thought I had a unifying line for the bottom, which would fall just above her breasts and over her heart. But as I drew out the last E, the sense of the words left me, and I tented my fingers on her sternum as if I could draw the intersections of our feelings through them. "I want to say, 'When I write it here, it's real.'"

We stood still with it for a minute, then she said gently, "On this body and in the book of life, it is written."

"It's perfect, but it may take two lines."

She shrugged, and a smile curved her mouth. "Take all the time and space you need."

ON THIS BODY AND IN THE BOOK OF LIFE, IT IS WRIT-TEN.

I stepped back to look at my work, placing the pen on a side table and crossing my arms. "Too dark in here. Turn around. Let the city see."

When she faced outside, I got up on the ledge and put my back to the window. I could see how she was marked, her hard nipples, the glow of the street on her skin.

"Do you know what I'm feeling?" I asked.

"Sexy and dominant?"

I brushed my fingers along the letters and across her breasts. "Proud and honored."

Her eyelashes fluttered when she looked down, and she pressed her lips together to keep from smiling. I enjoyed humiliating and hurting her. I was who I was, but those acts made her moments of fulfillment all the sweeter.

"Thank you," she said, pausing before the last word. "Sir."

"Put your hands on the glass and show me my options."

Her breasts hung as she bent to get her hands on the cold window. I got the flashlight from my pocket and tucked the strap away, facing the window with her.

Sometimes, after closing, people milled around the floor across from us. Designers, store buyers, renegades from a cocktail party on the third floor.

That night, with Diana no more than a body in a window, a young couple had split from what looked like a meeting on five and were chatting in the empty store with a row of white and silver mannequins behind them.

"They'll see you if they look," I said, clicking the flashlight on.

She sucked air through her teeth. "Can I say something?"

"Speak."

"You're so fucking filthy." She said it as if she had bacon fat and brown sugar rolling around her tongue. "If I'd known that when we met, I never would have married you."

"I know. Now open your mouth." I put the back end of the flashlight as far down her throat as I thought she could take. "They won't see your face with the light here. But your body's lit by the street. Be their inspiration. Their north star."

I took my cock out, fisting it for her. I needed her to see it, accept it, before I tore her apart with it. She acknowledged it with a low *mmm* in her throat, and I got off the ledge.

Grabbing the place where her ass met her thighs, I opened her to me.

The couple across the street faced us, but they weren't paying attention to anything besides each other.

"Watch them," I said, putting my dick where she was wet, sliding along her slick line. She bucked. "Watch for when they see your light."

I rammed inside her, and a split scream and growl came from her as I buried my cock as deep as I could. As if he heard the pressures of the mass and volume of the universe shift, the man across the way looked at his reflection in the window and straightened his tie. I dug my fingers into Diana's hips and thrust twice. The second time was so hard, the flashlight tapped against the window, and though he likely couldn't hear it, the young man across the street had definitely noticed the light.

Diana went *hmp* around the shaft of the flashlight, her head turned slightly toward the couple. She saw him looking.

"North star," I said. "Are you ready?"

She made a bouillabaisse of sounds around the flashlight. A sentence.

"Are you safeing out?"

She shook her head.

I took a handful of hair and bent over her to whisper in her ear. "Then just take it."

I rammed her, driving so hard and so fast I had to hold her hip to keep her steady. With every move, I aimed for her heart, to go deep enough to touch it, own it, crawl into it and expand it. My life was written there. I wanted to enter her and explode, covering the world in all-consuming fire. Inside. Deep. So deep we became linked at the soul.

"*Ook!*" she grunted, spit dribbling off her chin.

So sexy, the depths of her debasement. How far down she had to crawl to love me. I followed her stare to the couple across the street. They were watching. Her fingers were at her throat. His were in her hair as he said something in her ear.

"They're going to worship you." I reached around her, getting four fingers on her hard clit.

He was behind her now, rubbing his dick on her ass. Saying dirty things. One hand on her breast and the other reaching for the hem of her skirt. An R-rated version of the goings on in heaven.

"Look what you're doing to them. God, Diana, you're that sexy. That powerful."

The woman pulled her skirt up as he dug his fingers down her underwear. She buckled at the same time as Diana. My wife's voice came in a stream of long sounds. Her fingers curled against the glass.

"You want to come?"

She nodded.

"Wait for her."

It didn't take long for the woman's back to arch. Her mouth opened, and he had to hold her up. Diana let loose, pulsing around me, knees stiffening, her legs going out from under her. She trusted me to hold her up, and I did, lightening the pressure of my fingers so her orgasm sat on the edge of pain without crossing into it.

She fell against me, limp and boneless, folding to her knees like a map.

I did that. I gave her so much pleasure she couldn't stand, and she gave me the control to do it. I felt wrapped and right with the world.

"Beautifully done." I took the flashlight out of her mouth.

"Oh, God. Thank you." Her words were molded around her breaths. "For that. Sir."

I looked in her face. She was high on endorphins, pliable and pleasured.

I was bigger on the inside than the outside. My dick was going to explode.

Taking her cheeks in one hand, I forced her mouth open and guided myself into it. She took it. All of it. Marked with ownership of her heart. Sweat-streaked. Mascara running black. Spit dripping, messy-haired, she opened her throat for me. I got two strokes in then pulled out.

"Look up." I jerked myself with her body's juice.

When she exposed her chest, I came on it, marking those words true.

I BELONG TO ADAM

HE BELONGS TO ME

ON THIS BODY AND IN THE BOOK OF LIFE, IT IS WRIT-TEN.

Chapter 52

"Last night, you tried to tell me something. While I was fucking you."

The morning sun cracked the skyline at a little after seven. The days were getting longer, pushing out the nights of the longest, most miserable winter of my life.

"Which time?" Diana replied with sleep in her voice.

"In front of the window. With the flashlight in your mouth."

"Mmm." She didn't say anything after that. I thought she'd forgotten the question. "Oh yeah. The north star."

"What about it?"

"It's steady in the sky. So if you were going to make me move around, you missed the point."

"Thank God for the flashlight." I kissed her shoulder and got out of bed. "I'm making breakfast. What you do you want?"

"You're cooking?"

"I'm ordering in." I got into last night's pants

"Coffee. And scrambled eggs."

"Okay, fifteen minutes."

"And bacon."

I kissed her. "Anything else?"

"Two pancakes. No. Three." She held up three fingers. The bite mark on her ring finger was gone, and the bruising wasn't more than a pale yellow. I was going to have to do something about that.

"Are you sure you're not pregnant?"

"I'm not. Just hungry. I've been too sad about Dad to eat."

Laying my lips on her shoulder, I closed my eyes and told myself how much I loved her. More than the day I met her. More than the day she left me a note that hurt more than any other betrayal. More than I deserved.

"I'm going to knock you up or die trying."

"Challenge accepted."

When I was almost to the bedroom door, she stopped me. "I never filed the deed transfer, by the way. So half the loft is still yours."

"A win for me."

"The gospel according to Adam."

"Amen."

I left it there and called for breakfast. Serena was going to have to be dealt with. And Stefan. Their gossip could only be destroyed face-to-face. Probably with Diana present. I didn't want her involved in that crowd. It had been a hard limit. I'd told myself it was because I didn't trust the culture, but that wasn't true. I hadn't trusted *her*. I hadn't trusted her stamina as a sub. My instincts had told me her submission wasn't real.

The doorman buzzed as I set out the plates. Diana appeared out of the bedroom, hair still wet, wrestling her sweater on over jeans as she walked. She hit the button on the intercom with a flat slap.

"Is it food?"

"Yes," the doorman squawked.

"Send him up." She let the button go. "Hide the furniture. I'm going to eat anything that doesn't move."

"Sit." I held the chair out for her.

She sat. I put the cloth napkin on her lap, but just as I was pushing her in, the doorbell rang. She was up like a shot, slapping the door open to a delivery guy holding a huge thermal bag with a receipt on top.

"Ah. Yes! Mine!"

"Sign, please," the man said from behind the bag.

Diana slapped her pockets, looked around. "Pen."

"I can't get it," said the delivery guy. "If you reach into my pocket—"

"I have it." I got the pen I'd used to mark her the night before and signed on the dotted line. When he took the paper back, I noticed a tattoo on his hand and was inspired.

I wasn't going to put a ring on her finger. I was going to do better.

She dug into her eggs and toast first. Watching her eat food I'd provided gave me a flood of satisfaction. She moved to the pancakes before I'd even finished my toast.

"Oh," she said around a mouthful. "I found out about the window. So sad."

"Really."

"Yes. Are you going to drink your coffee?"

I popped the top off my cup and poured my coffee into hers.

"Remember Nadine?" She jammed a bite into the corner of her mouth while she spoke and sopped up maple syrup with a triangle of her next bite of pancake. "The kid with the blanket and Lego... hey. Wait a minute. You didn't steal that child's Legos?"

"I did not. Those were all new."

"That would be truly sick."

"The window, huntress. Stay with me."

"Nadine's soon-to-be ex-husband. So sad. It's just getting uglier and uglier." Her pace slowed. She poked at her next bite instead of shoving it in her mouth like a hostage.

"Do you think we could have become that?" I asked.

Her head cocked at a slight angle. One eyelid dropped a few degrees. She was trying to read me. "I don't know. Except that you broke a window."

I laughed. "I forgot about that."

"Are you serious?"

I nodded and she laughed, dropping her fork as if she'd jut heard the craziest thing she'd ever hear in her life.

I tapped my finger on the edge of my coffee cup, bent the plastic edge then let it find its shape again.

"Insolent," I said.

"Can you drop it? How long are you going to—"

"I lied." I interrupted her because she was upset at me for the wrong thing. She'd be plenty upset at the right thing in a minute. "Not technically. He did live in his mother's co-op, but he inherited it and it was really very nice."

"Okay? So?"

"I let you think he was a threat so you'd be scared of other Dominants, but he wasn't. At least not to your safety."

"What kind of threat was he then?"

She wasn't going to cut me any slack. She was going to drill down until I scraped the bottom of my worst behavior.

"I gave you the impression that he was a slob who never left the house."

"And he's not?" She squeezed more syrup onto her pancakes.

"He was...no. He's not."

"He was what, Adam? Come on. Don't hold out on me. Was he tall? Handsome?"

Insolent had been sharply dressed, handsome if you're into that kind of thing, calm and well-spoken. He was Dominant without being a dick and he'd had a good sense of humor about the entire thing. But I'd walked away from him with a nagging fear.

"I was pretty sure you could fall in love with him," I said. "So I made him sound unattractive. It was petty, and I'm sorry."

"If we see him at the Cellar I want you to point him out. I'll be the judge of who I can fall in love with, thank you." She took a stack of pancake slices in her mouth and let the fork scrape her teeth on the way out.

"I'm letting my membership to the Cellar lapse," I said, changing the subject.

"Why?"

"I have you. I don't need the scene."

She flipped open a Styrofoam container with the edge of her fork, revealing a stack of bacon in a napkin. The move wasn't motivated by curiosity or hunger. It was too contemplative for that. It replaced words she wasn't ready for.

"What?" I asked. "Nothing you say is going to turn me off."

She smirked and speared a strip of bacon. "When we met, I didn't think people needed to talk about sex. Then, five years in, I felt like I *couldn't* talk about sex and I wanted to. And now, well, I guess I'm surprised by what I'm about to say."

I let her bite the bacon and put the rest on her plate. I didn't need to encourage her to finish her thought.

"Whether it's the Cellar or not, it doesn't matter. But..." She took a deep breath and looked down at her lap. "When people watch, it really turns me on. They can see you dominate me, and it's like... that makes it valid and real. Three-dimensional. But because it's you, it's safe and I can get lost in it. Being your toy in front of people is like a drug. I see myself through their eyes and through yours. And I go out of myself..." She shuddered. Her eyes met mine, their blue as clear and intentional as the tide. "If you don't want that, I can live without it, but I really like it. The Cellar seems like the best place to get it."

I didn't want to smile. I didn't want to tell her what letting people watch did for me. The way it multiplied the effects of my domination exponentially.

"Can I think about it?" I asked.

"I'm not going anywhere."

She wasn't. I'd claimed her. Earned her back. She'd been mine to accept or reject for weeks, but I hadn't believed she'd stay until she did what she'd been too afraid to do when we were married. She told me what she wanted from our games.

Chapter 53

ONE WEEK LATER

I'd left Diana at the loft with instructions to finger herself for five minutes every hour, but not come. No matter where she was—the store, the street, the office—she had to find a private place and think of me while she touched herself.

The Greens was packed for a weekday. I nodded at the maître d and walked right up to Charlie's table. He was sitting with a sub I didn't recognize. She was in her twenties with wavy brown hair spilling over her shoulders. Her posture was off, and she looked nervous with her skirt around her waist and her hands flat on the table.

I sat across from her.

"Hello to you too, mate," Charlie said.

"I have to talk to you."

"Of course you do." He didn't take his eyes off the sub. "Scarlett, open your legs and say hello to Adam. You'll address him as 'sir.'"

She shifted. I couldn't see under the table, but I assumed she was spreading her knees.

"Good afternoon, sir."

"You staying for lunch?" Charlie asked.

"Nah. I came to thank you."

"For?"

"Giving her that card. Insolent."

"I thought you'd try to kill me."

"I almost did, but I've heard about that cane."

He smiled and yanked the handle off the cane halfway, until the silver blade was visible. "That cane?"

"Yeah. I'd have to disarm you then kill you. It's way too much trouble."

"You drove all the way from Montauk to tell me she loved you. You looked like a man who'd found a seam of gold. Then you turned into a massive twat. I should have put the knife on you."

He had been happy. He'd practically handed me a cigar. When I told him I thought we could do it without being part of the community, that I could keep her safe from others seeing her submission, he'd agreed it was possible. Doable. Others had done it, so could we. I'd sped back to Montauk like a man on fire, only to find the kinky community had already infiltrated our relationship.

"Scarlett, sweetheart," Charlie addressed the sub, "pick up your shirt. Show me those lovely tits. Let everyone see how hard your nipples are."

Scarlett's sharp breath rolled with arousal and shame.

"Then put both your hands back on the table for sixty seconds. Then use your right hand to touch yourself and be very quiet about it. Understood?"

"Yes, sir." She grabbed the edge of her shirt.

I didn't watch her finish. I didn't want to see her tits. My exposure to other women was going to have to be dealt with.

"Good girl." His last word drifted into the glass ceiling and a smile crossed his face.

I followed his gaze to the door. Serena was walking through the tables where people could only fit single file. This was where subs trailed Doms by three paces. She was only one step ahead of Stefan, who held her hand behind her.

Stefan saw us and tugged on Serena's hand, then he whispered in her ear when she stopped. They both looked our way.

There was something different about her. She was dressed the same, in a spring-yellow polo and black slacks. Her heels were sensible and didn't trip her up. Her hair was up in a twist and the bangs were pushed back. When she smiled and waved at us, the nature of the change became obvious.

"She did it," I said.

"Apparently topping from the top is better than topping from the bottom."

"What about Stefan?"

"He's not going to change." Charlie waved them over. "They're going to try sharing subs. Scarlett's about to try it. Aren't you, Scarlett?"

Scarlett nodded, though her face was scrunched in pre-orgasm tension.

"Hold that thought," Charlie said to her. "Until you're told to let go."

Serena walked as if marking territory. Surveyed the room as if it were her property. Took stock of Scarlett as if she could own her any time. Stefan looked like a proud parent. We greeted each other with kisses and handshakes. Serena kissed me quickly on each cheek.

"Hello," she said, trying Dominant confidence on for size. She was about to sit at a table with her three Masters, as a Mistress. The difficulty only showed for a second.

"Nice to see you, Mistress."

Stefan held the chair out for Serena. "So," he said, "you've come to meet Scarlett?"

"No," I replied, pushing in my chair. "I'm leaving. It's been fun. Nice to meet you, Scarlett. Don't boss these two around too much."

Scarlett's face twisted in strain. "Okay. Yes. Sir."

"Will I see you in the club?" Serena asked, posture straight and commanding. Had that always been there? No, I was sure it hadn't been. People could change. They did it all the time.

"I don't know."

We said another quick good-bye, and I walked to the door. Turning for a second, I saw Serena whispering in Scarlett's ear while Stefan and Charlie conducted business as usual.

I was about to get in the car when Serena caught me outside.

"Adam, are you... back there, you looked unsure."

"I'm not."

"Really? This doesn't bother you?"

My approval was important to her. It was no more than that, and no less.

I hadn't realized the extent of her hurt. She'd been nineteen, new to the scene, sheltered, a virgin, and as defenseless a sub as I'd ever handled. I'd been reckless. I knew enough about her to know what would make her vulnerable, and I'd exploited her need for acceptance and her desire to please the way I'd exploited those desires in any sub. For pleasure, pain, dominance. But she was new. She'd needed more care. She'd chosen me. She'd chased me. She'd topped from under Charlie and under me, and we'd let her hurt herself through us.

"Yes. Diana's waiting. I have to go."

She seemed relieved for a second, then she straightened up to a Dominant posture that would eventually become a habit. "Say hi for me."

"I will."

She went back inside, and I hurried to Diana. She was my chance to right old wrongs and turn mistakes into successes. She was my chance to win in a way that was real and permanent. Every minute without her was empty. Every minute wondering if I could spend eternity by her side was meaningless. A life without her was a life wasted.

Chapter 54

SIX WEEKS LATER

That morning, I'd tied Diana up before she was fully awake and fucked her while she sang "Happy Birthday to Me." She couldn't come until she finished the song, but I made her start over and over until she was in tears and I was ready to explode inside her.

We went our separate ways. She went to McNeill-Barnes to publish books. I went to R+D to buy and sell property. A month after we wrote our names in the book of life by christening her body in sex and felt tip pen, we went about our daily business as partners, and our nightly business as master and servant.

I never looked back unless I wanted to remember the how stupid I'd been. She was everything I'd ever wanted in a woman. She was smart, bold, intrepid, principled. Everything I could admire in another human being, I admired in her, and she was all I desired. Warm, yielding, open-minded, honest, submissive, and perfectly masochistic.

Sometimes, when she fell asleep in my arms or when we went to the

Cellar and some well-meaning cocksucker of a Dom asked if I'd share her, I thought I was kidding myself. She couldn't possibly want to deal with my shit. Couldn't be letting me fuck her face while who-even-knew watched from behind the glass. But she did. Time and again, she let me break her and rebuild her. She gave and gave. I struggled to keep up, taking better care of her, giving her more of what she needed inside and outside the game. The score was never even. I was always down, owing her more than I could ever repay.

But, goddammit, I wasn't going to stop playing.

"Rings?" she said when I told her what she was getting for her birthday. "Are we having a ceremony?"

It was six thirty on the Thursday before a long weekend, and half her office was gone already. The air felt thin with electricity as the days got longer and the temperature invited bare throats and open toes.

"This is even better." I pulled out her chair, and she let it roll back. "Come. It's something new."

"Really?" She seemed intrigued.

"Stand here. Arms on your head. Legs apart. Come on."

She did as she was told, eyes cast down as she'd been taught. I could do whatever I wanted to her and she'd let me. She'd beg me. That knowledge alone was enough to send a rush of rousing chemicals through my blood.

I opened her fly. "Look at me, birthday girl."

Her tempered-glass eyes flicked up. I felt around my pocket for the little silicone toy. It was the size and shape of a flattened walnut.

"We're going to see someone I trust. That's all you need to know."

"Yes, sir."

I ran my finger along her folds until she was wet, then I laid the toy between her underwear and her pussy. I snapped her underwear in place and closed her pants.

"What was that?"

"Surprise." I kissed her. "Let's go."

Once we were in the elevator, I fingered the remote control in my pocket with one hand and held her hand with the other.

"Stay calm," I said as the doors whooshed open to let in half the accounting staff.

"Why?"

She barely got the word out before I pressed a button. She gasped, even at the lowest setting. Everyone turned around to look at her. She was bright red, smiling, the owner and visionary of the company with a vibrating egg kissing her clit.

I shut it off when everyone was out of the elevator.

"Oh my god," she said as I led her across the lobby. "What are you doing?"

"Giving you a birthday present. Remember what I said about trusting me?"

I let her go through the revolving doors in front of me, and she held her question until we were spit into the street where a black car waited. Thierry opened the back door.

"Why?"

"It's not fun if you don't trust me. That's why."

"Hi, Thierry," she said.

I helped her into the car. She looked both intrigued and worried, just the way I liked her.

"What is this thing?" she asked after I slid in across from her and Thierry closed the door. "Some kind of vibrator?"

"How does it feel?"

"Good, but—"

I flicked the button to buzz her, and she jolted.

"Open your mouth."

I took an envelope from my inside pocket and put it between her teeth. She bit down.

"Happy birthday."

Her expression was precious. Curiosity plus incredulity plus struggle. I had to laugh.

"Open it. Go ahead."

She plucked it from her mouth and ripped it open, making a mess out of the envelope.

"I'm so intrigued," she said, sliding out the card. She opened it, and a smile crept across her face. "This is my present?"

"Part of it."

"You're filthy."

"I'm sick of signing you in."

She held on to the invitation to membership at the Cellar when she hugged me. "Thank you. It's what I always wanted."

"If always equals a month?"

"What else? Is there more? I love birthdays. Dad always made them feel like national holidays."

Her face crinkled. She blinked hard. She was working through her father's death one tear at a time.

"That's my job now. Slide to the edge of the seat and open your knees. Keep your feet on the floor, but I want a hundred-twenty degrees between your legs." The car lurched to a start, and we headed downtown. "Hands behind you on the seat. No talking."

She complied beautifully, and a calm settled over me.

"I'm not giving you something you can unwrap. We're past that. This will be the first birthday where I get to give you what you truly need. I'm going to give you what I should have given you in the first place."

She ground her hips into thin air.

"Did you hear me?"

"Yes, sir."

"What did I say?"

"Birthday. Something. Can't wrap it. Something. *Mmmm*."

"Do you want me to tell you?"

"Sure."

She was fully pliant, in the drunken space just past manageable arousal where my patience and violence found their outlet. But she was also complacent.

I fisted her hair and pulled her to the floor at my feet.

"Take it out," I said as she got her knees under her. "Take it out and suck on it."

She fumbled with my belt, hook, zipper, cock. She'd been at this long enough to know I didn't want her to suck like a hooker. She opened her mouth and her throat.

"Don't come," I said. "Or the punishment's going to fit the crime."

I pushed her head onto my lap, rubbing my head on the back of her throat. I hadn't felt guilt about my cruelty in weeks, even as I remembered the sound of remorse in the back of my head. She wanted my cruelty as much as my kindness. Needed both as much as I did.

I pulled her head off me, and she gulped air.

"I should have had you alone in Montauk. This weekend, I will."

Before she had a chance to react, I pushed her face on my dick and she took every inch like a fucking champion.

"You and me alone." I pushed her down, let her breathe, pushed her down again. I pulled her off me so I could look in her eyes. "That's the first half. Are you ready?"

"Yes," she whispered with spit dripping from the bottom half of her face. "If you think so."

"I do."

She was in heaven. With her clit vibrating and my fist in her hair, she snapped deep into a sexualized high. I was responsible for keeping her safe while she was like this, and I always would. Her protection was my pleasure.

"Swallow." I put my cock back in her mouth. "All of it. Good girl."

I came in her mouth just in time for Thierry to turn onto Ludlow Street.

• • •

We'd cleaned up before letting Thierry open the door. He knew damn well what was going on in the backseat, but I paid him to not care.

"Wait," Diana said. "We're going in here?"

She pointed at the religious artifact storefront. I'd turned off the egg. She seemed more awake and aware.

"In the back."

We were ignored as we walked through the cluttered room, past the seven-day candles, incense, and Holy Books. Figurines carved in wood with bone skulls on top, wreathes of money, dancing skeletons with red bulbs in the eyes. A stone fountain tinkled as a stream of water came from the mouth of the monstrous death mask carved into the top. The water fell into a bowl shaped like a rib cage. A stone heart sat in the center. Diana stopped in front of it and dug into her pockets.

"I want to make a wish." She came out with a quarter.

I held her hand back and drew out my own coin. "Switch."

I gave her my quarter, and she gave me hers. We both made a wish. I didn't know what she wished for, but I hoped it was the same thing I did.

I wished for her to be happy.

"You're the Steinbecks?"

A guy with a long beard and plaid collared shirt stood in the doorway to the back room. He wore a leather collar with a silver ring in the front.

"Steve?" We shook hands.

"Missus," he said to Diana. "I'm your artist."

Before she could ask, he snapped open the black velvet curtain to reveal a barber's chair and a table with instruments of torture. The walls were covered with snakes, crests, lions, knives, dragons, and skulls.

"A tattoo?" she asked. "I'm getting a tattoo for my birthday?"

Steve went into the room to work on preparations, which was good. I was suddenly nervous. I didn't think she'd refuse me. I wasn't nervous about her. I was nervous about me. That I'd make the moment less than perfect. That I'd misread her and that gentleness would be a liability.

Facing her, I ran my hands down her arms and back up again. "We did everything right the first time, you and I." I cleared my throat. "We had a wedding. We had a reception. We wore rings. We didn't work. It was our fault. I'd love to blame it on the tired traditions, but it was us. We broke what we built and then we blew it to dust. We have something now. We're unbreakable. We're non-negotiable. Do you feel it? I know it's not just me."

"It's not just you. I thought I trusted you before, but this is different. You're different. And the same."

"Both."

"Neither."

"I want everything to be different."

"I love this already."

"Are you ready for it? I have plans. I don't think you're ready."

She looked into the tattoo room, where Steve waited, then back at me. "Challenge accepted."

I took her by the chin and made her look at me. "If you pinochle out, you'll safe out of the scene, but you'll never safe me out of your life."

She pressed her lips between her teeth, then smiled as if she couldn't hold it back another second. "Will it be fun?"

"I think so."

"So what's the tattoo thing?"

I surprised her and myself by picking her up under her arms and knees, carrying her to the chair, and setting her on it.

Steve put his phone down and sat straight. "So!" He slapped his hands on his jeans. "Here's what I have so far."

He opened a folder in front of Diana. I sat next to her. I felt her excitement and the tug of her curiosity. I wanted her to know she was safe.

"We're tattooing big red targets on your butt," I said. "One on each cheek."

I slapped the back of one hand into the palm of the other. Steve laughed, and she let herself smile a little.

"I'm going to assume you're joking," she said.

"Maybe I'm not."

"You are. You'd never cover the pink it turns." She smirked coyly at Steve. She was safe with him. His collar told her everything she needed to know.

I relaxed when she did.

Steve opened the folder. "All right. I worked on these based on your names."

He handed her a page with the outline of two left hands, one smaller than the other. On the ring finger of each were our names. The smaller hand said ADAM'S and the bigger hand said DIANA'S.

"Oh. These are... Adam. They're perfect."

"I'll get you another diamond ring, but under it—"

"No, this is it. This is what I want. We can't ever take it off."

"I worked up other designs." Steve pulled other papers from under the folder.

"I want to see all of them."

Had I wished for her happiness five minutes before? Had I put a time limit on it? Because I wanted her to stay exactly like this, reacting to my silly gift. It wasn't expensive or flashy, but she understood it because she understood me. She knew I wasn't after a big gesture but a solid signal of permanence. We would die with each other's names on our bodies, wrinkled, grizzled, papery, and old, our marriage couldn't be taken off. It couldn't be hidden. We couldn't walk away ever again.

I'd meant to use the egg while she was getting inked, to pair pleasure and pain with shame and safety, but she was so childlike when she talked to Steve about the design, showing him her hand, that I couldn't disrupt her. I didn't even know what they were talking about. I didn't even care. She was happy with me. Because of me.

"Which one?" She held up her favorite two designs.

"Whatever you like." I couldn't work through an opinion. They were both good enough. What mattered was the way her eyes sparkled.

"Boss me," she said with her mouth behind the paper. "Sir."

Every time she looked at the tattoo, she'd remember this day. She'd remember what I demanded and what I acquiesced. Keeping her happy meant not always letting her get her way. It meant making sure she knew she was safe in the world because I was in charge of a corner of it.

I pulled a third option from the pile. I didn't even look at it. For all I knew, it was the ugliest one in the bunch. It didn't matter *what* I chose, it mattered *that* I chose. "This one."

"That was my favorite," Steve said.

Diana's eyes stayed with mine as she let Steve take her choices away. "Yes, sir. Who goes first?"

"Me."

I held my hand out for Steve. He swabbed it, and Diana and I began our journey for the hundredth time.

Every day we'd start all over. A journey to oneness and independence. Stability and uncertainty. Happiness and melancholy. Pleasure and pain. Shame and confidence. Opposites locked in permanent tension. We would hold our worlds together with the ribbon of love.

Epilogue

SIX MONTHS LATER

"It has to be hot all the way through," she said, not for the first time. I held the phone between my shoulder and ear while struggling to free a five from a roll of twenties. "If it's not hot, I'm going to go down there and shove it up someone's ass."

"I'll do the shoving." I redirected my words to the round guy with the doughy skin and sweat-stained hat who plucked the five from my hand. "They hot?"

"Hot. Yes." He slapped open the metal door. Steam escaped the silver compartment, gathering under the umbrella. The humidity by the little pushcart was as thick as taffy. "Since this morning. I put them in." He wrapped two knishes in wax paper.

"Mustard," I said.

"Brown mustard!" Diana said from the phone. "If it's that yellow shit, I'm gonna—"

"I know, I know. Give someone a mustard enema."

The doughy guy raised an eyebrow.

"Mustard. Not French's," I said to him. "You got Gulden's?"

"This New York or what?" He pulled a rod out of a silver container. It was coated in brown mustard. He rubbed it on the knishes, wrapping them in a practiced motion.

"Are they hot?" Diana asked.

"Yes."

"Did you check?"

Doughy Man handed me a brown paper bag already soaked with grease. I took it and headed back into the building as fast as I could without making a scene.

"No. I did not check."

"How could you not check?"

"He said it was hot." The elevator was already open, and I squeezed in just as the doors were closing.

"He lies. You have to check yourself."

"I'm not sticking my finger in a strange knish."

The businesswoman next to me smirked.

"If it's cold—"

"I know, huntress. I know."

The signal cut out.

• • •

As infuriating as she was when she demanded I manhandle food, when I burst into the pink-and-blue waiting room, dodging out of the path of a woman in a lab coat, I was reminded why I'd run all over Manhattan to soothe her.

Diana sat alone, hands woven together in her lap, hair half in-half out of the ponytail, skin blotchy from the hormone stew in her blood.

She was beautiful. Everything about her. From her ever-rounding belly to the way she dropped into bed after dinner. Perfect. The only thing marring a perfect pregnancy was her anxiety about the baby.

Today, we were getting rid of that. She was going to start enjoying this.

I sat next to her, put a napkin on her lap, and opened the bag.

"I'm not hungry," she said, wringing her hands and staring into the middle distance.

"Yes, you are."

"It's not hot. I know it isn't. Cold potatoes are gross."

"They're delicious. Can a million Irish mothers be wrong?"

"Our appointment was fifteen minutes ago. They don't want to see me because of last time."

I put the bag to the side and took her hands, prying the fingers open. She was strung tight enough to break. "Would you like me to set the building on fire?"

"Stop."

"I can shove a clock up someone's ass." I rubbed the tattoo on her left ring finger. ADAM'S. Always mine. Her hand relaxed into my palm.

"I need this to be over with."

"Tell you what. I can do that thing Superman did in the movie. The old one."

"Pick up a car?"

"That. But also, he flew around the earth to make time go backward. But I can go the other way. Make it go forward. Any time between the sonogram and when he graduates from college."

"That sounds great. Skip right through."

"If you say so." I leaned back. "We'd miss a lot of sex."

"Oh. Yeah."

"And the actual parenting part."

She pointed at a dark-skinned technician in pink scrubs sharing a clipboard with a guy in scrubs. "Can we skip to Dolores coming here and saying we're next?"

"Yes."

The technician nodded, took the clipboard, and approached us. "Are you ready?"

...

This wasn't our first rodeo, though every time felt like it. Diana didn't want to hear the heartbeat. She didn't want to see anything, so she clamped her eyes shut so she wouldn't see the screen. She didn't want to fall in love. She'd wept with joy when she heard the first *whoosh whoosh* of the baby we lost, and she didn't want to cry again over something she couldn't have.

So though this was her third sonogram for this pregnancy, only the tech had heard the heartbeat. I'd seen the grey blobs on the screen, but Diana acted as if she was just gaining weight. Dolores knew our history and knew how shut down Diana was. She handled us personally, making sure the gel was warm and her earphones were plugged in before the sound of the heartbeat came through the speakers.

"You understand today is it," she said, rubbing the gel around with the sonogram wand. "The issue you're worried about, if it doesn't show today, it's not going show up at all."

"I understand," Diana said.

I sat next to my huntress, holding her hand. Actually, she was holding mine in a death grip. I didn't complain. That's what I was there for. Death grips were my specialty.

"There could always be something," Dolores continued as she adjusted knobs, sliding across the linoleum on a round stool.

"I understand." Diana had done a lot of robotic understanding in the past months.

"Even during the birth, things can go wrong."

"I understand."

"Child could also be a brat. Not our fault."

"She understands. Brattiness is her fault," I said.

Diana's eyes were still squeezed shut, but she faced me. "You love my brattiness."

"I do."

"Right," Dolores continued. "Do you want to know the sex?"

"No," I answered half a millisecond before Diana said, "Yes."

"I see you guys decided." She flicked a switch, and the screen lit up. There was our baby in glorious lo-fi black and white, swimming in static. "All right. Let's see." She leaned into her screen, moving the wand. "Well, knock me over with a feather. Happy to report Baby Steinbeck is as right as rain."

"Diana," I whispered, "did you hear that?"

She nodded but her eyes were shut so tight her upper lashes dovetailed with her lower.

Dolores marked numbers down, shifted the wand, clicked buttons and switches while Baby Steinbeck hovered behind me.

"You can look," I said.

"I'm scared."

"You don't have to be." I put my body between her and the screen. "Here. I'm between you and the screen. Open your eyes."

She took a deep breath and did it, hanging her gaze on mine as if my attention was a six-inch-ledge over a hundred-story drop.

"Good girl. Are you ready to meet your... Dolores? Boy or girl?"

"Congratulations. You're carrying a boy."

All of my wife's anxiety rushed out of her in the form of tears. "A boy?"

she choked out.

"Are you ready to see your son?"

She nodded.

I moved out of the way, letting the light of the screen shine on her. She looked full and round, swollen with a joy she'd been holding so tightly she couldn't let it go until it got too big for her fist. Her face twisted into sobs and spit, becoming more beautiful in relief and release.

"Do you want to hear the heartbeat?"

"Yes," Diana answered before Dolores finished the question.

The whooshing came through the speakers, loud, strong, and steady.

"Heartbeat's just about perfect." Dolores continued, showing us where the spine was (exactly where it should be), where his penis was (same), and his placement in the placenta (just fine).

But we weren't listening. I was watching my wife let go of months of taut apprehension, and she was staring at the screen through sheets of tears.

Dolores said something about leaving us alone. She froze the image and left, clicking the door behind her.

"It's over," Diana sobbed.

"It's over." I wiped her face with a handkerchief.

She turned away from the screen to make eye contact with me. "I finished."

"Not quite, huntress."

Every tear the handkerchief wiped away was replaced with two new ones. I kissed her cheeks, tasting brine and perfume. I couldn't help it. They were the stuff life was made of. Salt of clarity. Water of growth. The elixir of change.

She put her arms around me, and I held her. I didn't comfort her with pats or hushes. I didn't tell her it was going to be all right, because it wasn't. Life was messy, and God was an irresponsible parent. None of it mattered. I held her to keep her company. I was her companion, her complement, and her protector. The celebration of her light and the consummation of her darkness.

We were no more than bound, no less than gods, creating life from the love between us.

The End

Also by CD Reiss

About the Author

CD Reiss is a *New York Times* bestseller. She still has to chop wood and carry water, which was buried in the fine print. Her lawyer is working it out with God but in the meantime, if you call and she doesn't pick up, she's at the well, hauling buckets.

Born in New York City, she moved to Hollywood, California to get her master's degree in screenwriting from USC. In case you want to know, that went nowhere, but it gave her a big enough ego to try her hand at novels. She'll tell you all about it out back, where a cord of wood awaits.

If you meet her in person, you should call her Christine.

CPSIA information can be obtained
at www.ICGtesting.com
Printed in the USA
LVOW07s1702140217
524243LV00003B/717/P